Something old, something new,
something borrowed, something…

wrong!

For Isabel, Caroline and Delaine, first true love
turned false. But not forgotten.

Now Dan, Reese and Max want another chance.

This time, they won't give up.
This time, they won't give in.

three ardent tales of couples reuniting

ABOUT THE AUTHORS

Susan Wiggs—With more than a dozen novels, several novellas and a children's book to her credit, award-winning author Susan Wiggs loves the challenge of a new project. Schooled in Brussels and Paris, she has traveled extensively in Europe, North Africa, the former Soviet Union, the United Kingdom and Mexico. She holds a master's degree from Harvard University, and taught mathematics for several years before devoting herself full-time to writing. She, her husband and a daughter have recently moved to the Pacific Northwest, where she continues her avocations as a gardener of topiary and a sculptress of butter!

Janice Kaiser—A former lawyer and college instructor, prolific author Janice Kaiser now has to her credit over forty novels—translated into twenty languages—and a worldwide following. She turned to writing in 1985 after marrying her husband, Ronn, also a writer. She and Ronn collaborate on women's fiction for MIRA Books, and make their home in Northern California, although Janice's fascination with exotic locales has taken her to over forty different countries.

Muriel Jensen—*Romantic Times* Career Achievement Award winner Muriel Jensen began writing poems in the sixth grade. By high school she had switched to short stories about boys and romance, and her friends would gather at her desk to read the newest installment before classes began. Thirty-five books later, she still finds the subject fascinating. The mother of three grown children, Muriel lives in Oregon with her husband, two calico cats and a malamute named Deadline.

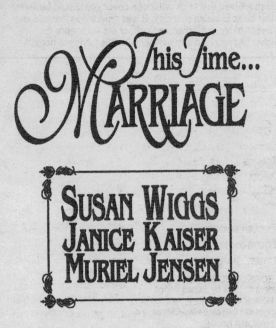

This Time...
Marriage

Susan Wiggs
Janice Kaiser
Muriel Jensen

Harlequin Books

TORONTO • NEW YORK • LONDON
AMSTERDAM • PARIS • SYDNEY • HAMBURG
STOCKHOLM • ATHENS • TOKYO • MILAN
MADRID • WARSAW • BUDAPEST • AUCKLAND

HARLEQUIN BOOKS

ISBN 0-373-83314-8

THIS TIME...MARRIAGE

THE BORROWED BRIDE
Copyright © 1996 by Susan Wiggs
THE FORGOTTEN BRIDE
Copyright © 1996 by Belles-Lettres, Inc.
THE BYGONE BRIDE
Copyright © 1996 by Muriel Jensen

CONTENTS

Dear Reader,

The Borrowed Bride is the first book I wrote after moving from a big city in Texas to a tiny island in Puget Sound, Washington. Packing up my family and relocating deep in the woods on a Christmas tree farm was more than just a physical move for us—it was a giant and thrilling leap in terms of life-style. Not coincidentally, this story takes place in the wilds of western Washington, my newly adopted state. I wanted to share my love of the pristine beauty of the islands rising up out of the Sound, and the distant white mountains shimmering on every horizon.

Still, the essence of this story is not a place on the map, but a place in the heart. Dan and Isabel, the main characters, grew out of my absolute conviction that everyone deserves a second chance, because not everyone gets it right the first time. Reunions always seem to have a bittersweet flavor to them, don't they?

On a personal note, I'll have to admit that my marriage to Jay is the result of a second chance only in the most literal sense: I fell for him the "second" I met him, and fifteen years later our feelings haven't changed a bit!

I hope you enjoy *The Borrowed Bride*. It's one from the heart.

Warmly,

Susan Wiggs

I'd love to hear from you!
Susan Wiggs
P.O. Box 4469
Rolling Bay WA 98061-0469

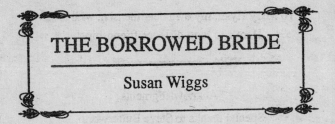

THE BORROWED BRIDE

Susan Wiggs

To Mary Hyatt, my own dear mensch, with love.
Here's to long-distance friendships!

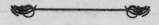

Acknowledgments

Special thanks to Steve Butterworth,
a real-life wild man.

Thanks to the usual suspects:
Barbara Dawson Smith, Betty Gyenes
and Joyce Bell; and to Barbara Samuel,
Anne Stuart and Brenna Todd.

Thanks to Marsha Zinberg, for a new opportunity.

Dance. Everywhere, keep on dancing.

—Native American prophecy

Chapter One

ISABEL WHARTON'S DREAMS were finally coming true—or so she thought. Surrounded by a burst of springtime and eleven chattering women, she prepared to join their intimate circle, to become their daughter, sister, niece, cousin when she married Anthony Cossa.

The bridal shower, held in the garden of a cottage café on Bainbridge Island, was winding down. Isabel tore open the second-to-last package and peered at the gift, then beamed at her future sister-in-law.

"It's lovely, Lucia. Simply lovely." *What is it?* The thing resembled something she had seen in her ob/gyn's office. She bit the inside of her cheek to stop herself from asking. Lucia and Connie and Marcia would be the sisters she'd never had.

"A silver pasta server." Connie, Lucia's younger sister, set aside the package. "Leave it to Lucia to assume you want to cook pasta."

Ah, but Isabel *did* want to cook pasta. And cannoli and *tiramisu* and *gnocci*, all for Anthony. She wanted to do everything for Anthony. He would make the perfect husband, and better still, he came with a family that was so large, so boisterous and so loving that she was engulfed by a feeling of belonging.

They would warm the cold, empty places inside her. At least she hoped so.

"I saved the best for last." Connie perched on the edge of her white wicker garden chair.

Isabel caught Mama Cossa's eye and winked. "I'm not sure I trust your daughter."

"I haven't trusted Connie since she tried out for the seventh-grade wrestling team."

Isabel laughed and removed the slick, metallic gold wrapping paper. Female hoots filled the garden as she lifted a wispy silk garment from the box.

"Now *that*," Connie said with great pride, "is hot."

Isabel stood, holding the lacy red teddy against her. The silk felt as cool and insubstantial as mist. The lace plunged to her navel; the legs were cut sinfully high. Even held against her India-cotton skirt, the teddy felt wicked and wild.

"I figure Tony will have a heart attack when he sees you in it," Connie said. "But at least he'll die happy."

The women's laughter chimed like music in the garden. Isabel felt a wave of affection and gratitude, along with a feeling of contentment so sharp and sweet that her chest hurt. These women—Anthony's sisters and aunts and nieces, his beautiful mother—were to be her family. Her *family*.

Ever since she'd moved to Bainbridge Island and established her plant nursery, she'd begun to feel as though she really belonged somewhere. All that had been missing was a family, and now she was about to get that, too.

They began to drift homeward then; most of the guests were staying on the island, where the wedding would take place in just one week. Mama Cossa, good-humored but limping from bursitis, gave Isabel's hand a squeeze. "See you at the rehearsal dinner, dear."

Only a few women remained when a faint hum sounded in Isabel's ears. She gazed down the length of the garden. The flower beds and trees were drenched in the glory of April sunshine. Just past the tops of the towering fir trees, she could see the sparkling waters of Puget Sound.

The island, she decided, was paradise on earth. She had built her life on a foundation of shattered dreams, but finally everything was falling into place.

The roaring grew louder. It was the sound of a boat motor or a car without a muffler—urgent, industrial, a faintly animalistic low grumble.

Connie and the others, who had been bagging up torn paper and ribbons, paused and turned. Isabel frowned. And then, right where the gravel driveway turned off from the road, he appeared.

He was an image out of her worst nightmare. Clad in black leather. A bandanna around his head. Inky, flowing hair. Mirror-lens sunglasses. The Harley beneath him bucking and spitting gravel like a wild animal.

"I smell testosterone," Connie murmured as the machine roared up a terraced garden path.

Isabel stood frozen, immobile as a block of ice. The apparition skidded to a halt, jerked the 750 onto its kickstand and walked toward her. Long, loose strides. Tall boots crunching on the path. Tiny gold earring winking in one ear. Long brown hands hanging at his sides.

"Somebody call 911," Lucia whispered.

He yanked off the mirror glasses and stared at Isabel. Dark brown eyes dragged down the length of her. Then he reached into the lingerie box on the table and plucked out the red silk teddy.

"Very nice," he said in a rich drawl, inspecting the garment. "You were always a great dresser, Isabel."

She snatched it away and thrust it into the box. "What are you doing here?"

He gave her the old cocky grin, the expression that used to make her go weak in the knees.

It still worked.

His looks had attracted her in the first place. She had been drawn to his aura of seductive danger, the faint sulkiness of his full lips, the powerful body as well tuned as his Harley. The long hair so thick and gleaming that she yearned to run her fingers through it.

The direction her thoughts had taken ignited a blush in her cheeks. "This really isn't a good time."

"There never was a good time for saying the things we should have said to each other," he said with that lazy, Sunday-morning, stay-in-bed-all-day drawl. "But I figure it's now or never."

Her blush intensified. "Maybe you could come back later, after..." She let her voice trail off. Her mouth was dry, her thoughts scattered.

"Nope, Isabel, won't work. We've got some unfinished business." He hooked a thumb into the top of his black jeans and shifted his weight to one leg. "I figure you'd rather settle things in private, so you'd better come with me."

With a force of will, she was able to drag her gaze from him. "Connie, this is Dan Black Horse."

"Perfect," Connie whispered helpfully. "Just perfect." She sent Dan an adoring look. "I have all of your albums. I've been a fan for years. Too bad you've quit."

"Pleasure to meet you," Dan said with effortless gallantry.

Connie gave Isabel's shoulder a nudge. "Go ahead," she said with sisterly wisdom. "If you've got something to settle with this guy, take care of it now, because next week it'll be too late." She lowered her voice and said, "If you weren't my friend, I'd kill you for not telling me you knew Dan Black Horse."

Isabel stooped to pick up her woven straw purse. "I won't be long." She forced her lips into a smile. "I'll be all right, really."

Dan Black Horse pivoted on a boot heel and led the way down the garden path. When they reached his bike, he eased it off the kickstand and held out a black, slightly battered helmet.

"No way," she said, stiffening her spine. "I'll follow you in my car."

"Nope." He plunked the helmet on her head and fastened the strap. "Where we're going, you don't want a car."

She clenched her jaw to keep from screaming. *Priorities, Isabel,* she reminded herself. *Keep the priorities straight.* The most important thing was to avoid making a scene.

She heaved a sigh, hitched back her cotton skirt, and got on the bike.

"Way to go, girl," Connie murmured, not far behind her.

"We'll go to the Streamliner Diner," she told Dan tautly. "And I mean to be back by—"

The thunder of the large engine swallowed her words. He rolled forward, then opened the throttle. The bike jerked into motion.

Instinctively, her hands clutched low on his hips. A feeling of the forbidden seized her. She gritted her teeth, moved her hands to the cargo bar behind her, and held on for dear life.

He wasn't wearing a helmet, she observed as they turned onto the narrow wooded highway that bisected Bainbridge Island. Maybe a cop would pull them over.

Officer, I've been kidnapped by a man I swore I'd never see again.

But as they roared southward toward the quaint little township of Winslow, even the two stoplights turned green, conspiring against her.

Craning her neck around his bulky shoulder, she saw the diner up ahead, looming closer... and then farther away as they veered past it, down the hill toward the ferry terminal.

"Hey," she shouted in his ear. "You said we'd have our little talk at the diner."

"*You* said that, sweetheart." He tossed the words carelessly over his shoulder and passed the tollbooth.

The last straggling cars were pulling onto the ferry. A female attendant wearing a bright orange smock was about to cordon off the loading platform.

Dan thumbed the horn. It emitted a chirpy beep. The attendant grinned and waved him through. He drove up the ramp and parked. Immediately, a horn blew. Too late to get off.

As the ferry eased away from the terminal, he turned around to face her. "Damn, Isabel," he said, "you're one hard woman to find."

THE SECOND HE KILLED the engine, Isabel struggled off the bike. "You're crazy," she said, "but I suppose you know that."

"Maybe." He favored her with a look she remembered well, the one of sleepy arousal that used to make her happy to dive back into bed with him for long, languid weekend mornings.

"This is ridiculous," she said in exasperation—both at him and at her wayward memory. She braced her hand on the iron wall to steady herself as the ferry headed for downtown Seattle.

When Dan didn't reply, she turned and stomped up the stairs to the lounge. The spacious waiting room, flooded with April sunshine, was crowded with islanders heading to the city for shopping or an evening on the town. She spotted a familiar face here and there and managed to nod a greeting.

Great, she thought. All she needed was for the bank clerk or the hardware store owner to see her going to Seattle with a sinfully good-looking man.

She went out on deck, where the wind caught at her skirt and hair. Gulls wheeled and sailed along beside the ferry. In the distance, a sea lion splashed in Puget Sound.

It didn't take Dan long to find her. Within minutes, he joined her on the open-air deck. "Here." He pushed a paper cup of *café latte* into her hand. "Skim milk, one sugar packet, right?"

She took the cup and sank to a bolted-down bench. "I hope you know you've ruined the afternoon for me."

He sat beside her, resting his lanky wrists on his knees. A dark fire smoldered in his eyes, and she sensed a tension about him, a coiled heat that disturbed and fascinated her. "Couldn't be helped. Besides, it's better than ruining the rest of your life."

She almost choked on a mouthful of hot coffee. "What's that supposed to mean?"

He reached forward and caught a drop of *latte* with a napkin before it stained her India-print skirt. "You can't marry him, Isabel." His voice, with the unforgettable low rumble of masculine passion that had filled the airwaves for two years, was harsh. "You can't marry Anthony Cossa."

"Since when do I need your permission?" she retorted. The breeze plucked at her hair. Her permed curls were now a deep chestnut color, thanks to an expensive salon job. She pushed a thick lock behind her ear and glared at him. "How did you find me, anyway?"

He sent her a hard-edged grin. "Through Anthony."

"Oh, God." She set down her cup and folded her arms across her middle. "What did you do to Anthony?"

Dan stretched out his long legs and crossed them at the ankles. He leaned his head back against the wall. The movement and pose were graceful, vaguely feline, subtly dangerous. "I don't remember you being this suspicious."

"I'm generally suspicious of men who kidnap me from my own wedding shower."

"Fair enough. I had business with Anthony. And what do I see when I get to his office? Your smiling face in a silver frame on his desk."

She tried to picture it. Dan, all in rebel black, with his long hair and earring, facing Anthony, immaculate and trying hard to look laid-back in his Banana Republic chinos.

"He's a good guy, Isabel," Dan said expansively. "He's real proud to be marrying a gorgeous, successful woman."

"He's no slouch in the looks and success departments," she argued. "Maybe I'm real proud to be marrying him."

"Maybe," Dan said, jamming a thumb into his belt and drumming his fingers on his jeans.

Isabel jerked her attention from the insinuating pose and glared out at the Sound.

"That's what I thought at first," Dan went on. "I was going to blow the whole thing off, wish you a happy life with your upright, square-jawed bachelor-of-the-month, and bow out."

"I wish you had." She took a gulp of coffee. She probably shouldn't ingest caffeine. Being with Dan made her jumpy enough. "Why didn't you?"

"There are things I've always wondered about, Isabel." He sat forward, gripping the edge of the bench. It was there again, the pulsing rhythm in his voice, the mesmerizing glitter in his dark eyes. "Five years ago, you walked out on me and never looked back."

I couldn't look back, Dan. If I had, I would have gone running into your arms.

She gave up on the *latte* and rose from the bench to drop her cup into a waste barrel. "What do you want from me?"

"Just a little of your time."

Her eyes narrowed. "How much?"

He sent her the same lazily sexual smile that had cast a spell on her five years earlier. She had been twenty-one, a terrible driver, and while backing out of a parking space in front of an ominous-looking nightclub, she had knocked over a large black motorcycle.

Terrified but determined to do the honorable thing, she went into the club to find the owner of the bike.

He was performing that evening, playing to a small, grungy but clearly appreciative crowd. The lead singer of a local band, he strummed a wild, primeval tune on a battered Stratocaster guitar. To Isabel, he looked like eternal hell and damnation in the flesh. He was gorgeous. She was spellbound.

He forgave her for the damages, took her out for a *latte* that had stretched into an all-night conversation, and stole her heart.

She backed warily away from the memory, for it was still as dark and seductive as that moonlit night had been.

"How much time, Dan?" she asked again, telling herself she was older, wiser, immune to his devilish smile.

"That depends," he said, "on how long it takes for you to realize you're marrying Anthony for all the wrong reasons."

"Oh, please." She turned away and gripped the rail of the ferry. "I'm a big girl now. And I'm not stupid. I don't want you back in my life."

The boat was nearing the downtown pier. Good. The minute they got to the terminal, she would call Anthony at his office. The situation was bound to be awkward. Best to explain this to him before Connie got started.

A flash of electric awareness came over her. She felt Dan behind her, although he wasn't touching her. Despite her anger, a vital tension tugged at her.

"Turn around, Isabel," he whispered in her ear. "Look me in the eye when you say you don't want me."

Her entire body felt slow and hot, as if she were swimming through warm honey. She forced herself to turn to him, pressing the small of her back against the iron rail.

He clamped one hand on the bar on each side of her so that she was trapped. She looked at him, really looked at him, and her throat went dry.

He had hardly changed at all. Still the same magnificent face that made women stop and stare. Same velvet brown eyes with gold glinting in their depths. Same lean, unyielding body, filled with a hard strength that made his tender touch all the more astonishing. Same perfectly shaped lips . . .

His mouth was very close. She could feel his heat, could feel the clamor and clash of panic and desire inside her.

"You were saying?" he whispered. His lips hovered over hers, and she felt a fleeting reminder of the wildness that had once gripped her whenever he was near. "Isabel?" His intimate gaze wandered over her throat now, no doubt seeing her racing pulse.

"I was saying," she forced out, "that I don't . . ."

"Don't what?" His thumbs brushed at her wrists, lightly, gently.

". . . want you . . ." she tried to continue.

"Go on," he whispered. His tongue came out and subtly moistened his lower lip.

". . . in my life again."

His hands stayed on the railing. Yet he moved closer, his hard thighs brushing hers, searing her through the wispy fabric of her skirt. She felt every nerve ending jolt to life. By the time he grinned insolently and pushed back from the railing, she was dazed and furious, and the ferry was unloading.

"Just checking," he said.

"You bastard," she whispered.

A pair of women with straw shopping bags passed by, sending Isabel looks of rueful envy.

Dan stepped back, smiling his I'm-a-rebel smile.

"I need a phone," Isabel said. "And then I'm taking the next ferry back to Bainbridge."

"We haven't settled a damned thing."

"We settled everything five years ago. It didn't work then, and it won't work now."

"Five years ago was only the beginning."

"No." The word sounded strangled as she headed for the stairs. "It was the end."

He caught her wrist, and she froze. There was not a trace of a smile on his face when he brought her around to look at him.

"Don't you think you owe me one more chance?" His voice was a low rasp that reminded her of the smoky, yearning love ballads he used to sing to her. "After all, you almost had my baby, Isabel."

Chapter Two

DAN BLACK HORSE couldn't believe Isabel had agreed to come with him. But then, he couldn't believe he had said such a blatantly manipulative thing to her.

She had even called the clean-cut Anthony and told him not to worry; she'd be in touch.

And so here they were—a couple of hours southeast of the city, at his guest lodge in a wilderness so deep and untouched that there weren't even roads leading to the property.

He looked across the timber-ceilinged lounge at her and could not for the life of him think of a damned word to say.

She stood at a window, one slim hand braced on the casement, gazing out at the dense old-growth forest that rose like a sanctuary around the lodge. In the green-filtered glow of the afternoon sun, she looked fragile and lovely, the shape of her legs visible through the thin, full skirt, her back straight and proud, her hair flashing with burnished light.

A wave of tenderness washed over him. Always, she managed to look isolated and alone, even when she was in a crowd of people. It was one of the first things he had noticed about her.

"You changed your hair," he said at last, then grimaced at his own inanity. Bootheels ringing on the floor, he crossed to the bar and took out a can of beer for himself and a soda for her.

She turned around to face him. Her full breasts strained against her cotton jersey top. "You changed your life."

Her face was more striking than he remembered. Large doe eyes. High, delicate cheekbones. A full mouth that drove him crazy just thinking about it. An air of winsome uncertainty that made him want to take her in his arms and never let her go.

Ah, but he had let go. Five years earlier, he had not been brave enough, smart enough, to hold her.

He handed her the soda and gave her a lopsided grin. "Yeah, I guess you could say I made some changes."

"A few, it would appear." She strolled around the rambling room. "Where's the phone? I had no idea you were taking me *this* far away. I should check in with—"

"No phone," he told her quietly.

"What?" Liquid sloshed out of the can, but she didn't seem to notice.

"There's a radio for emergencies, but the phone lines don't come up this far, and it's too remote for cellular."

She sagged against the back of an armchair. "Whatever happened to the city boy? Didn't you find fame and fortune with the Urban Natives?"

"Depends on your standards for fame and fortune. The band did okay. The last album went gold, and it got me into this place."

"I noticed the name of this place on the door—The Tomunwethla Lodge." She brushed her hand over a woven wicker bean jar on a side table. "What does that mean?"

Ah, she had trained herself well. He had always hoped she would acknowledge the past, maybe even come to cherish it as he did. But given Isabel's background, that wasn't likely.

"Cloud Dancer Lodge," he said. " 'Cloud Dancer' is a song I once wrote. A really bad, crying-in-your-beer song. Probably the most popular thing I ever did."

Isabel rose and stood on a braided oval rug in front of the massive hearth. "So what's the point?"

"Of the song?"

"Of everything."

He set down his beer and took her hand, leading her to the huge sofa facing the fireplace. A moose head with baleful glass eyes stared down at them.

"The point of everything," he echoed, blowing out his breath. He tried another grin on her, but she remained solemn. "Lady, you asked a mouthful." He half turned, hooking a booted foot over his knee. God, he wanted to touch her, *really* touch her, to wake up the passion he knew was only sleeping inside her. But the way she was looking at the moment, he was afraid she might shatter.

Just as she had five years ago.

"First, my granddad got sick," Dan said after a moment. "I moved to the town of Thelma to help look after him. And damned if I didn't start to like it out here again." He linked his hands behind his head and stretched out his legs. "Used to be, I couldn't wait to get away from the rez, from the country." Through half-lidded eyes, he watched her for a reaction. There was none. If anything, she seemed even more subdued. More withdrawn.

Well, what did you expect, Black Horse?

"My granddad died."

"Dan, I'm sorry."

"He was eighty-three. He left me a grant of land that's tied to a treaty with the government dating back to the 1880s. Right around the time of his death, a timber company approached the tribal council, wanting to make a deal on clear-cutting."

"But this area is sacred ground," she blurted out. Then she looked surprised at herself and fell silent.

"Exactly," he said. "But the deal was real tempting. When you don't know where your next meal's coming from, lunch with a grizzly bear looks pretty appetizing."

That coaxed an extremely small smile from her.

"So I did some research. The lands are protected, but the council was leaning toward the timber company. I made a counteroffer. Got a special grant to develop a recreational area, sank everything I had into it and built this place. Just put the finishing touches on it a week ago."

"It looks as if it's been here forever," she said. "The lodge is really beautiful, Dan."

"It's supposed to have that rustic flavor." Flipping his wrist outward, he did a perfect imitation of Andy, the band's former keyboard player, who had switched careers to interior design. "Without skimping on creature comforts."

Isabel laughed softly. The sound gripped Dan where he felt it the most—in his heart.

"So that's the short version," he said. "If this is a success, I could open lodges in Alaska, maybe Belize or Tahiti in the winter—"

"Why?" Her question was sharp and humorless.

"Because I know what I'm doing." *Sort of.* "Somebody else would come in and build a theme park. Probably stick totem poles up everywhere and sell shaman baskets for yard ornaments. I wanted something better. I wanted to do it right."

She stood and crossed the room, inspecting a cloth wall hanging and the tuber mask beside it. "This is just right. Really." Even as his chest filled with pride, she paused. Maybe she was beginning to unbend a little. "I take that back. The snowshoes hanging on the wall are marginal. And the antler ottoman has got to go."

"It's my favorite piece of furniture."

She sat back down on the sofa. "So now I know why you're here. Why am I here?"

He paused. "A picture's worth a thousand words?" he offered.

"Fine. I came. I saw. I'm impressed. Now take me back to the city."

"I can't exactly do that," he said in a soft, slow voice.

"What do you mean?"

"We have a lot to talk about. I need time."

She shot up again. "I don't *have* time. I'm getting married exactly one week from today. I have to meet with a caterer. A florist. A dressmaker. Photographer, videographer—" She counted them off on her fingers and turned on him in frustration. The pale skirt floated around her slim legs, and for a moment, she looked as exotic as a gypsy dancer. "Sorry, Dan. I just didn't schedule in being abducted by an ex-boyfriend."

He'd had no idea she was so bitter. This was going to be harder than he had thought. A lot harder.

"In other words," he said, "you want me to say what I have to say and then get the hell out of your life."

She blew out an exasperated breath. "That's putting it a little bluntly." Then she looked defiant. "I don't have time to play games with you."

He crossed the room in two strides and clamped his hands around her upper arms. She felt delicate and breakable. He used to marvel at her softness, her femininity, the way it contrasted with his own hard edges and roughness. But when she flinched at his touch, he grew angry.

"Is that what you think this is, lady? A game?"

"Tell me different." She glared up at him.

"I brought you here because you ran away, and I was fool enough to let you go. Well, not this time."

"What?"

He stared into her eyes, seeing his reflection in their depths and, in his mind, seeing the dreams and desires that used to consume them both, feeling the ache of an unfulfilled promise.

"I can't let you go, Isabel. I can't let you just walk out of my life again. You're making a big mistake, marrying that guy, and I can prove it."

"How?" she challenged, lifting her chin.

"Like this." He lowered his mouth to hers and cupped his hand around the back of her head. This was not how he had treated her aboard the ferry. He was not teasing her or, in some mean-spirited way, trying to assert his masculine power over her. This was a kiss designed to bring back the wildness and passion they

had once shared. To remind her—remind them both—
of all they had lost and all they could be once again if
they tried.

She held herself rigid. At first, she made a resentful
sound in the back of her throat. He softened his mouth
on hers and skimmed his thumb down her temple to
her jaw, lightly caressing. A small sigh gusted from her,
and her clenched fists, which she had put up between
them, relaxed. Her palms flattened lightly against his
chest.

Ah, he remembered this, the thin, keen edge of desire he felt only with her, and the way she swayed and
fit against him. Her mouth was soft, and the taste of
her—one that had lingered for years after she left—was
as familiar and welcome as the springtime.

His tongue traced the seam of her lips, and she
opened for him, almost shyly, her trembling hands over
his heart.

Finally, when it was all he could do to keep from
making love to her right then and there, he lifted his
mouth from hers. She looked up at him, and he down
at her, at the sheen of moistness on her lips.

The sheen of tears in her eyes.

"Isabel?" His voice was low and rough.

"I can't believe you'd do something so cruel."

He dropped his arms to his sides. "What the hell is
that supposed to mean?"

She drew an unsteady breath. "You're just trying to manipulate me. To make me feel unfaithful to Anthony."

"What about being faithful to yourself?" He pivoted away, furious at her, furious at himself for wanting her. "I guess you never learned that, did you?"

She caught her breath as the dart struck home. Though Dan knew it wasn't her fault, she had turned away from the part of her that was like Dan—the Native American part.

"I moved on, Dan," she said. "I moved past that. It's known as growing up."

"I'm sorry. I didn't find you again to hurt you. I did it to ask you for a second chance."

She brushed at her cheeks with the back of her hand. "It's no good. I can't. You—you bring up a darkness in me. I get all twisted around inside when I'm with you. I can't live like that."

"There are those who say you should seek out your darkest places. Explore them. Find the sunshine that will burn the shadows away."

"Don't you see? That's what I'm trying to do."

"You're running away, Isabel."

She crossed to the door and went out onto the porch to stand, glaring at a magnificent view of Mount Adams. "It's my choice."

He came out and stood behind her, placing his hands lightly on her shoulders. She didn't pull away.

At length, she said, "Take me back to the city, Dan."

"I'll take you back this instant," he said, "if you can say you really mean it when you tell me it's all over between us."

He turned her in his arms. He saw the truth written all over her face. She had been just as aroused by the kiss as he had.

But he could see that she was close to breaking. It was time to back off, to give her space, to let it all sink in.

"I have to feed the horses," he said. "They've got internal clocks that tell them exactly when five o'clock rolls around."

"I can't believe you have horses. You wouldn't even keep a goldfish in your apartment in Seattle."

He grinned and spread his arms. "Hey, I'm a responsible citizen now."

She eyed his earring, his black ponytail, his T-shirt with the slogan Question Authority. "Yeah, right."

Whistling, Dan jumped down the porch steps and headed for the stables. "Believe what you like. You're stuck with me for one more night."

Chapter Three

ISABEL WATCHED his long, lanky frame disappear down a wooded path. He strode gracefully, showing the same ease with which he used to walk onto a stage in front of a crowd of fans. He didn't *look* like a crazy man.

But she knew better. And he made *her* crazy when she was with him.

She touched her lips and closed her eyes while warm pulsations of remembrance passed through her. Why did he have to kiss her? Why did he have to bring back all the glory and pain and messy, magical moments that used to make each day with him an adventure?

Why did he have to remind her that she felt none of this savage, dangerous passion with Anthony?

The thought of her fiancé jolted her into action. She pushed open the screen door and grabbed her purse from the bar. Slipping the strap onto her shoulder, she marched down the steps.

If Dan wouldn't take her off this mountain and back to the city, she would do it herself. Rope-soled espadrilles notwithstanding, she would walk to the nearest phone, wherever that was.

Why hadn't Anthony just said no when she had called him from the ferry terminal? As in, *I think it's a lousy idea to spend the day with your old boyfriend. Get the hell back here right now.*

But no, not Anthony. "Sure, babe," he'd said in his breezy way. "If it's something you think you need to do, go for it."

Part of her wished he had just enough of the caveman left in him to stake his claim. To sling her bodily over his shoulder and take her off to his lair.

As Dan Black Horse just had.

But Isabel had to remind herself that Dan's methods had been worse than primitive; they'd been downright manipulative. Mentioning their lost baby had really hurt.

She tossed her hair back and continued down the path—if this faint indentation was indeed a path. The cleared area around the lodge gave way to old-growth forest so dense and primitive that she felt like Eve in the Garden of Eden.

She tried to get her bearings. They had arrived on Dan's Harley. She still had the grass stains on her hem from the bouncing cross-country ride. But there had to be a path to follow, maybe a logging track or the road the builders had used to haul materials to the lodge.

Dan had explained that lodge guests would typically arrive by helicopter, landing on the helipad a short hike uphill. That had a lesser environmental impact than clearing the woods for a road.

Muttering under her breath, she continued down the hill, thinking that if she just kept going down, eventually she would reach the dirt road and then the highway.

Within half an hour, she had decided that bridal-shower clothes were not appropriate for treks through trackless wilderness.

In another half hour, she paused to note that the sun was to her left. That was west. Seattle was to the northwest. But another hour after that, she realized the sun was setting, and if anything, she had wandered into even denser woods.

Finally, to top off a really good day, it began to drizzle.

The foul word that came out of Isabel surprised even her. The hem of her skirt trailed over a spray of thick fern fronds.

That is the nokosa *plant,* said an almost forgotten voice in her mind. *Our people use it to heal wounds.*

"Sure thing," Isabel muttered. "So what do you use to keep from getting lost in the wilderness?"

Not that she would heed any advice from that voice. It was the voice of the first man who had betrayed Isabel: her father.

She clenched her teeth. This was outrageous. She saw the headlines now: Prominent Businessman's

Bride Found Dead. *She just wasn't herself that day,* Connie would helpfully recall for the press.

Isabel plodded on, keeping despair at bay with sheer stubbornness. The shadows grew longer, the forest floor wetter. With every step she took, she devised a new torture for Dan.

The light rain misted her hair, then plastered strands of it to her forehead and neck. Her skirt and cotton jersey top were soaked through. Her espadrilles absorbed moisture like a pair of sponges.

Miserable, wet, lost, and furious, she shook her fist at the cloudy twilight sky. "Damn you, Dan Black Horse!" she shouted.

A few minutes later, she spied a movement in the distance. Low branches of Sitka spruce nodded and bobbed as something huge and menacing stirred beneath them.

Another choice headline popped into her mind: Bainbridge Bride-To-Be Butchered By Bear.

Isabel screamed.

WHEN DAN CAME BACK from feeding the horses, he assumed Isabel had gone to look around the place.

Good, he thought. He had worked hard to build the lodge. Harder than he had ever worked at anything. Making it in the music business had been a cakewalk compared to this—to wresting a working enterprise out of a virgin forest without disturbing the very essence of that wilderness. The property consisted of the lodge and outbuildings, a central yard with a spectacular view of Mount Adams, the stables, garage and helipad. It would have been quicker to bring in bulldozers and cement mixers, but he had done everything the hard way. By hand, with local labor. Native American labor.

He hoped Isabel liked it, hoped she realized what it meant to him. Maybe she would open her mind to the past, and her heart to the tribe she'd been made to leave so long ago.

He sat on the cedar porch swing, waiting for her to return and planning what he would say to her tonight.

First, dinner. Grilled salmon from the river, some greens and herbs from Juanita's garden and a nice Washington State wine. Then he'd tell her everything. Almost.

He figured it was a little too soon to tell her he was on the verge of bankruptcy. And maybe too late to tell her that he loved her.

After a while, he grew restless. He got up and paced the porch. He called to Isabel. He walked the length and breadth and circumference of the entire property.

Finally, the sick realization sank into his brain.

Isabel was gone.

"LADY, YOU LOOK like you seen a ghost," said the stranger.

"A bear." Isabel's legs felt wobbly. She leaned back against a large rock. The surface was soaking wet, but no wetter than she already was.

"A bear?" He looked around, his long hair whipping to and fro. "Where?"

"You," she said, fully aware that hours of exposure had probably addled her brain. "I thought you were a bear."

"Cool." He pushed back a low-hanging branch. In every respect but one, he appeared a typical American teenager—oversize hiking boots, baggy, low-slung jeans, a plaid shirt with a hood trailing down his back, the sides of his head shaved, the hair long on top. Yet one more element stated clearly who he was.

He stood high and dry beneath a broad fiber mat supported by three straight sticks. The design woven into the mat was a tribal bear crest.

"I'm Isabel Wharton," she said, "and I guess you could say I'm lost."

He grinned—the half shy, half cocky smile of a teenage boy. "Gary Sohappy," he said, "and I figured you were."

"You..." Her pulse was finally returning to its normal rate. "How did you know to come looking for me?"

"Dan radioed down." He held out the woven shelter so that it protected her. "He said to keep my eyes peeled for a real good-looking woman with a chip on her shoulder." Gary took her elbow and started down the slope. "Watch your step here." He glanced at her, still bashful, still full of mischief. "I don't see no chip."

"I left it with Dan Black Horse," she said through gritted teeth. "I take it he's a friend of yours."

"Yep." He continued to lead her down the slope. It was almost dark now, and she could see no discernible path, but the boy seemed to know where he was going. "My uncle and I and a lot of guys from the rez helped him build the lodge. He said you were his first guest."

A tiny dart of guilt stung her. She had not paused to look at it that way. Dan had built a virtual woodland paradise, and she had shown little appreciation for his hard work.

"He caught me at a really bad time," she said with wry understatement.

The woods seemed to be thinning. Rain pattered down almost musically on the mat umbrella.

"Guess so," Gary said. "I hope the Seahawks like it better than you did."

She frowned. "The Seahawks? As in Seattle Seahawks?"

"Yep. He's been trying to get a contract to bring the whole team up for R&R. Like a wild-man weekend or something."

Realization clicked in Isabel's mind. Anthony was a promoter for the Seahawks. *That* was how Dan had come into contact with him and figured out how to find her.

But if Dan needed the contract, then why would he jeopardize it by dragging her back into his life at this critical moment? Anthony was a tolerant man, but maybe not *that* tolerant.

Darkness had fallen by the time they reached a level clearing. Isabel saw a cluster of buildings hunched against the side of a hill. She made out the shapes of an antique tractor and a battered pickup truck.

"How far are we from the nearest town?" she asked Gary.

He stopped beneath an awning at the back door of the main house and shook off the umbrella. "Probably ten miles to Thelma. Maybe Dan'll take you there Monday night. There's a dance at the fire hall."

"Dan's not taking me anywhere," she muttered. They entered the house, and the world seemed to tilt on its axis.

She had never been here, had never seen this place, but she knew it. There was a place like this in her heart. She had been running from it for years.

She stood on a fiber mat in a small kitchen. The linoleum floor was cracked but swept clean. The yellow countertops had a boomerang design in the Formica, circa 1960. A butane-gas stove held a battered teapot and a large cast-iron dutch oven. A curl of steam, redolent with the fragrance of herbs, seeped from beneath the lid of the pot.

On the wall was a gas-station calendar with a photo of Mount Rainier. The picture was fading, and the calendar had not been turned since February. In the doorway stood a small, slim woman whose smile showed no surprise, only welcome.

"Hi, Gram." Gary parked his hiking boots on a rubber mat just inside the door. "Found her."

"That's good. Supper'll be ready in a minute."

Gary left the room, and the woman inclined her graying head. "Juanita Sohappy."

"I'm Isabel Wharton. I guess Dan told you about me."

Juanita nodded, then lifted the lid of a basket. "Here. Take off your shoes and wrap up in that. Sit down at the table. I'll get you some stew."

"I'm not hungry, thank you." Isabel pulled the blanket, worn soft with age, around her shoulders.

Juanita's black eyes glinted with warning. "Everybody eats when they come to my house."

Isabel sat down, instantly obedient and secretly delighted by Juanita's aggressive hospitality. In the kitchen, she observed a poignant collection of poverty and pride. Four dishes stacked just so in the cupboard. A collection of World's Fair 1962 tumblers. Juanita's apron had been made from a flour sack with intricate, beautiful embroidery at the edges.

Isabel took it all in with a lump in her throat, and a stark truth hit her.

She had built her life in Bainbridge. But she had left her soul in a place like this.

Chapter Four

PETUNIA SWUNG her head to the side and cast a baleful glare at her rider. She was the best horse in Dan's stables, but he knew she deeply resented getting wet and wasn't too fond of the dark, either.

Dan made a sound of sympathy in his throat and urged her down the hill. Horseback was the best way to find Isabel. Elevated, he had a broader range of vision—at least until it grew dark. Unlike the bike, the horse was quiet, and he could hear Isabel if she answered his calls.

The rain hissed through the woods, spattering onto the broad, lush tongues of primeval ferns and drumming dully on the hood of his poncho. He ought to check with Theo and Juanita. If Isabel wasn't with the Sohappys, he would radio the forest search service.

In the meantime, he yelled until his throat ached.

Damn it, where *was* she?

In one way or other, he thought, heading north toward the Sohappys' settlement, he had been searching for Isabel Wharton for the past five years.

Only now he knew what it took to hold her—if he could get her to sit still long enough to listen. If he could get past that wall she had built around her heart.

If he could find the words he had never bothered to say to her.

He remembered the first time he had ever seen her. The scene was branded on his memory. He had been twenty-three, cocky as hell, driven by a need to escape and rebel and shock people. The ponytail, the leather, the earring, the attitude—all were donned with calculated purpose, and he wore them like a second skin. His appearance tended to scare nice people.

He liked that.

When Isabel came into his life, Dan was playing his guitar and singing to a crowd as dark and ominous looking as he. His music had already gained him some startled praise from area critics—not that he cared. He just sank into the sharp, rough rhythm, letting it surge around him like the constant, broken pulse of the sea. Through his music, he expressed the wildness and mystery inside him, expressed it with an insistence and a precision that was profitable, but ultimately destructive.

He spotted her through the heated, angry glare of stage lights. Only a vague impression at first, but totally mind-blowing given the usual crowds at the Bad Attitude. She was dressed all in white with a burnished halo of sable hair framing a troubled face and the largest, saddest eyes Dan had ever seen.

He stepped back from the mike, doing idle riffs while he watched her. She bent to speak to Leon Garza, the sound man. Her hair fell forward, obscuring her face. She tucked a lock behind her ear then, with a quick, nervous motion of her hand.

Leon lifted his eyebrows, skimmed her with a hungry expression Dan suddenly wanted to pound from his face and then nodded toward the stage.

Dan let his riffs trail off and signaled for Andy to take over on the keyboard. She looked up as Dan approached. The expression on her face would live in his heart forever. She showed the usual nice girl's shock and fear. Her slim hand clutched tighter around her purse strap. But it was her determination that caught his attention.

That, and the quick, unmistakable signal flare of sexual interest. She probably wasn't even aware that her breath caught. That the tip of her tongue briefly touched her lips. That her eyelids dropped to half-mast.

Yeah, she was a nice girl, but her soul was wild.

"My name is Isabel Wharton." She handed him a business card. "I think I just wrecked your motorcycle."

That was the beginning. He felt it then, and so did she—the heart-catching awareness and a wanting that tore at his gut.

It was so powerful it should have—could have—lasted forever.

"I won't lose you again, Isabel," he said under his breath as he rode on.

THE SITTING ROOM was small, tidy and shabby. Gary was in the next room playing the air guitar with the headphones on. Isabel could hear the tinny rhythm even from a distance. It was one of Dan's songs.

Juanita sat in a fading armchair, knitting a muffler of red wool. On the sofa sat her son, a soft-spoken man called Theo, who had come in shortly after Isabel. His booted feet were propped on a stack of farming and forestry journals.

"I figure Dan'll be here pretty soon," Theo said. "It only takes about twenty minutes on foot."

Isabel sent him a rueful smile. She was warm and dry, and her curls were now a thing of the past. *It's that Indian blood,* her foster mother used to say. *Makes your hair straight as a board.* Isabel had spent three weeks' allowance on a permanent that very day, and had worn her hair curly ever since.

"Twenty minutes?" she said. "I was out walking for at least two hours."

Theo kept his face solemn and impassive, but his eyes twinkled. "Guess you took the long way. You must've been plenty mad."

She blew out her breath. "Not mad. Just impatient."

Juanita made a light, noncommittal sound in her throat.

Isabel winked. "Well, maybe a little mad." She felt unexpectedly—almost reluctantly—comfortable with this family. And there it was. The operative word. *Family.*

She had never really had one. She remembered a few happy times on the reservation back before her daredevil father had gotten himself killed. After that, she recalled only a murky haze of formless months. Although she'd still had her mother, an Anglo, the woman had only been there in a physical sense. After her husband's death, she had severed all emotional connections with Isabel.

Eventually, with a sort of dazed resignation, she had surrendered her daughter to foster parents.

The O'Dells had been older, excruciatingly kind and absolutely convinced that Isabel's dark moods were caused by her ambivalence about being half Native American. They hadn't meant to make her reject her heritage, but their subtle emphasis on Anglo ways had changed her. With the very best of intentions, they had scoured her soul, emptied her mind of the ways of her father's people.

When Isabel graduated high school, the O'Dells had retired to Arizona. They still exchanged Christmas cards and the occasional letter.

Family. Without consciously knowing it, she had gone off in search of one.

With Dan, she had almost found what she was looking for. She remembered staring in awe and cautious joy at the results of the home pregnancy test. She remembered rushing off to the club where he was playing that night, practically bursting as she waited for him to finish the set, then leaping into his arms to tell him the news.

His reaction was the beginning of the end. He looked panicked, muttered a choice swear word, then gave her a fake smile and false words of hope. They would marry, of course. Get a little house in West Seattle. Shop for furniture and dishes. Build a life together.

Two weeks later she lost the baby. Two weeks after that, she lost Dan. He was away on a gig when the bleeding started. By the time he made it to the clinic, it was too late.

He held her and wept with her, but even through a fog of painkillers she saw it. The look of guilty, sad relief in his eyes.

"You're a million miles away," Juanita said. She had a wonderful smile, her creased face a relief map of a long, well-savored life.

Isabel smiled back. "I guess I was."

Juanita set aside her knitting and wrung a steaming, fragrant cloth into a basin next to her chair. She wrapped the cloth around her right elbow. "Arthritis," she explained.

"Ma, the doc at the clinic said to take the pills and use the heating pad," Theo said.

"My way's better." She looked directly at Isabel. "I use an old Indian salve. Bethroot and wormwood steeped in hot water."

"It smells wonderful," Isabel said. But it was more than that. Just being in this house caused a deep fluctuation inside her. These people didn't question or accuse, but just accepted who she was, what she had done. As Juanita had bustled around the kitchen, getting supper and then steeping her herbs, the old folkways seemed to seep back into Isabel's bones. And to her surprise, it didn't hurt.

The rain stopped as softly as it had begun. Isabel excused herself and walked out onto the rickety front porch. Stars of searing brightness shone over the dark hulks of the mountains. The air smelled of evergreen and fresh water. It was cool at this elevation, and she wrapped the warm shawl tighter around her.

She heard Dan before she saw him. Or rather, she heard the horse. The damp thud of hooves, the occasional ripple and snort, the creak of saddle leather.

It wasn't every day a man came for her on horseback.

He appeared in the darkened yard, a slick, hooded poncho enshrouding him. "And I thought," he said in his rich, silky voice, "that going to Bainbridge to get you was a pain in the ass."

Theo came out on the porch. "You okay, Dan?"

"Yeah. Petunia's good and mad at me, though."

"Petunia?" Isabel asked.

"She came with the name. Won't answer to anything else."

"You can put her up in the barn for the night," Theo said. "Gary'll ride her to your place in the morning. You want to stay here?"

"I'll borrow your truck if you don't mind."

Isabel opened her mouth to protest. Then she thought about the small house, the meager supplies. It wasn't fair to impose on the Sohappys.

But the prospect of spending the night alone in a luxurious wilderness lodge with Dan Black Horse didn't thrill her, either.

Or maybe it thrilled her too much.

Chapter Five

"YOU MEAN THERE'S a road leading to your place?"

Dan smiled into the dark and ground the pickup's gears a notch higher. "It's an old logging trail. Real old. You have to know where to look for it."

She clutched at the edge of the seat as they bounced over a rut. "Good," she said. "Then you'll have a way to get me home tomorrow."

He said nothing. He didn't want her to go home tomorrow. More than that, he didn't want her to insist on going home tomorrow.

Finally, he asked, "Did you like the Sohappys?"

"Very much."

"They're my nearest neighbors."

"I was lucky Gary found me."

"He's a good kid. Wasn't always, but he is now."

"He told me you hope to get the Seahawks up here. Why didn't you tell me?"

He drove to the front of the lodge and parked. "Because now it might not happen."

"Why not?"

Dan killed the engine and draped his forearms over the steering wheel, turning his head to look at her. The rain had ruined her fancy hairstyle and made it glossy and straight. He liked it better that way.

"'Cause I stole their promoter's girlfriend," he said.

"Oh, please." She jerked the door open and jumped out, climbing the porch steps to the front door.

"Go on in," Dan said. "It's not locked."

She hurried in. He'd built a fire in the hearth of the main lounge, and the leaping flames seemed to draw her. He stood behind her, watching her tense movements and feeling such a surge of tenderness and passion that his chest hurt.

"Look," she said, staring as if mesmerized by the fire. "Number one, I wish you'd been straight with me and told me about your business with Anthony. And second, you didn't 'steal' his girlfriend."

"Borrowed, then?" Dan suggested.

"I don't belong to either of you. He was amazingly understanding when I called him today."

"Then he's a fool." Dan took her by the shoulders and turned her to face him. "Like I was a long time ago. I never should have let you go, Isabel."

Just for a moment, she swayed toward him.

An unbearable tension seized him; he wanted to cover her mouth with his, to taste her and plunge his hands into her hair.

Then she seemed to catch herself and pulled back. "There was never a question of you 'letting' me go. I left. That's all there is to it."

"Then why are you crying, Isabel?" he whispered.

She lifted her hand to her cheek and seemed surprised to feel tears. "It's been a long day," she said in an unsteady voice.

He took her hand, the one that was wet with her tears. "Come on. Your room's ready."

She seemed a little dazed as she followed him upstairs. He gave her his favorite room, the one Juanita had done in timber green, with a wall hanging depicting a dogwood blossom.

A man's flannel pajama top lay folded on the bed. Isabel looked at him questioningly.

He grinned. "It's one of mine."

"But you never—" Her face flushed as she broke off.

"Nope, not when I lived in the city. It gets cold up here. I didn't get the heaters up and running until a few months ago." He handed her the nightshirt and pointed her toward the massive bath and dressing room done in gleaming green tile and chrome-and-glass brick. "I'll go make you a pot of tea. Okay?"

Her brief smile was weary and resigned. She disappeared into the bathroom, and he went to make the tea.

When he returned with a tray a short time later, he stopped in the doorway, propped his shoulder on the doorjamb and grinned. She was already in bed, fast asleep.

ISABEL AWOKE amid snowdrifts of eiderdown com-
forters. This was, she decided with an indulgent
stretch, the most decadent bed she had ever slept in.
It was also the most restful night she'd had since she
could remember.

Then, peevishly, she figured that walking for miles
in the rain was bound to make anyone sleepy.

She bathed in the sunken oval tub with the massage
jets turned on full blast. She left it only when she realized how hungry she was. Wrapping herself in a thick
terry-cloth robe that had been draped over a towel
warmer, she finger combed her hair and helped herself to a new toothbrush that lay on the counter.

Then she went in search of her clothes, not relishing
the thought of putting on the damp, muddied skirt and
top. She was amazed to find the clothes, along with her
espadrilles and a cable-knit cardigan sweater, on a luggage bench just inside the door. Everything had been
cleaned for her.

She found Dan in the kitchen, locked in a stare-
down with a can of biscuits.

Unable to stifle a laugh, she said, "You just have to
press a spoon on the seam, and it'll pop open."

He glanced up and grinned at her. She blinked, and
for a moment her legs felt wobbly. Dan had always had
a dazzling smile, one that caught at her heart and made
her fiercely proud to be the object of it.

He handed her a spoon and the can of biscuits. "I've never been big on breakfast."

"I remember."

His gigs had kept him out late every night. The next day, he usually staggered down to the espresso stand on the corner for *latte* and *biscotti*.

As she popped open the can, he watched with amazement and asked, "Is that legal?"

Laughing again, she peeled apart the biscuits and put them on a baking tray. He slid it into the oven and poured them each a mug of coffee. "It's good to hear you laugh, Isabel."

"I slept well last night."

"Pretty quiet up here, isn't it?"

She added cream and sugar to her coffee. "I can't believe you washed my clothes."

"As survival skills go, laundry isn't too much of a challenge."

"I remember a time when you couldn't toast bread."

"I've figured a few things out." His voice dropped, and his strong brown hand closed over hers. "Isabel."

She knew she should take her hand away. She knew she should insist on going back to the city immediately. She knew she should not be feeling this overwhelming attraction to a man who had broken her heart.

Yet she simply sat there in the bright, sunlit kitchen alcove, sipping coffee and holding hands with Dan Black Horse.

It was wrong. So why didn't it feel wrong?

She felt warm and dreamy and relaxed. She loved the way he looked in the sunlight through the window, his long hair gleaming, his denim shirt parted at the throat to reveal his tanned chest, his dangerous smile and his deep brown-black eyes.

I've missed you.

She almost said it. Then the oven timer went off, and they jumped simultaneously. Dan retrieved the biscuits and brought them to the table with butter and honey.

While they ate, he talked. "I always thought I'd have no trouble handling the band's success," he said. "But when it started happening for us, it never quite felt right. I guess you could say it messed with my internal chemistry or something." He ran a hand through his loose hair. "I didn't fit into my own life anymore. The tours, the schmoozing, the politics, putting up with Jack and Andy and all their problems..." He shook his head. "I kept waiting to feel like myself again. To do something real."

A faint smile curved his mouth. "'The great mother calls home her own.' That's how my grandfather explained it. Once I found this place again, there was no way I could ever go back to what I had before."

"I read about your departure from the band," she said. It had been all over the local arts journals.

He waved his hand. "We hung together for as long as we could. Had a few laughs, made some good money. I pick up the guitar now and then when I'm in the mood. That's enough for me now."

She looked out the window and saw a bird land on a tangled marionberry bush at the edge of the yard. "What time is it? I really need to be getting back."

His eyes hardened almost imperceptibly. He had never been big on clocks and schedules. It was one of the things she had found so charming about him at first, so exasperating later.

He squinted at the clock on the stove. "Looks like around noon."

"Noon!" She almost choked on her biscuit as she shot to her feet. "I can't believe I overslept."

"No such thing as oversleeping at this lodge. That's a house rule."

"But—"

He stood and pressed a finger lightly to her lips. She tried to ignore the frankly sensual feeling that simmered inside her.

"Listen," he said, slowly taking his hand away. "I remember what you said about your busy week. But you can't get any of that done on Sunday. At least take a look around, Isabel. See what I've done with the place."

She remembered how petty she had felt yesterday for ignoring his accomplishments. After he took her home, she would never see him again. The least she could do was admire what he had built.

The rain had washed the forest clean. Everything was a rich, glistening green. A light breeze shivered through the trees. Isabel felt a piercing sense of connection with this place, and she understood Dan's affinity for it.

They walked along a path to the stables. The long, low building, surrounded by a fenced yard, housed four horses, three of whom put out their heads to see who had come. Isabel patted one hesitantly on the nose.

"You never did care for horses, did you?" Dan asked.

"You know why. My father died—killed himself— in the Yakima Suicide Race." She winced at the memory. She had been ten years old. With a gang of other men from the reservation, he had joined the dangerous cross-country race on horseback, hurtling down almost vertical ravines, leaping streams and fallen trees. Her father had plunged off a ninety-foot cliff to his death.

The next year, an animal-rights group had outlawed the use of horses in the race, and it was presently run on motorcycles. Of course, that was too late for her father—and also for her mother and Isabel.

She stared at the big bay horse. "It wasn't the horse's fault any more than a car wreck is the car's fault."

"The race is different now," Dan said.

"And how would you know?"

"I know," he said simply. "The local wineries are really big on sponsoring the race. It's—" He broke off, as if he thought better of what he was going to say. "Come on." He took her hand and continued the tour, showing her the best places to fish for salmon and trout, a shed where the white-water kayaks and rafts were stored, an equipment barn crammed with a tractor, an off-road motorcycle, a mower, a snowmobile, cross-country skis, fishing and rain gear.

She studied him, leaning against the rough-cedar building, surrounded by soaring trees, and she couldn't suppress a smile.

"What?" he asked.

"How does the saying go? 'The difference between men and boys is the price of their toys.' You have every toy."

He laughed. "No golf clubs yet."

"This all must have cost you a fortune."

He pushed away from the wall. "Everything I had. People are supposed to want to come here and play."

"So you're counting on getting this contract with the team."

"It'd keep me out of debtors' prison." He sent her a devilish grin. "Do they still have debtors' prison?"

As they started back up toward the lodge, she thought, what an adventure this was. It made her plant nursery on Bainbridge seem dull.

But safe. Very safe.

DAN SHOWED ISABEL the beginnings of the garden Juanita had started for him. Tiny herb, flower and vegetable seedlings sprang from rows of damp black soil. Isabel surveyed the area, cordoned off from deer and rabbits with electrified wire. Here was something she knew, something quiet and orderly like the life she had made for herself.

She walked along stepping stones between the rows, enchanted by the old-fashioned homeyness of the garden. The foxglove were the sort raised a century ago, antique strains she rarely saw these days.

She stooped to pinch off a sprig of fragrant Yakima tea, used for brewing or making potpourri. "This is a little more familiar territory."

Dan leaned back against the garden gate. "How did you get into selling plants anyway?"

"The temp agency I was working for sent me to Bainbridge to set up work files for a nursery. I ended up staying on, eventually taking over the management of the whole business."

He moved toward her, plucking the tender cutting from her fingers and dropping it to the ground. "And you're happy growing plants, selling them?"

"Well, of course," she said. His proximity raised a tingling awareness in her. She stepped back, feeling a little defensive. "I guess it doesn't compare with grunge-rock tours and wild-man adventures, but it's perfectly fine and I'm good at it."

"And your plans to marry?" A dangerous edge crept into Dan's voice. "Also perfectly fine?"

"Yes," she said too quickly.

"So you're not looking for anything better than 'fine.'"

Somehow, without her realizing it, Dan had backed her against the garden gate. He was so close that she could see him in sharp detail—the regal sweep of his cheekbones, his coal black lashes like individual spears around bottomless dark eyes.

Isabel had always known Dan Black Horse possessed a special magic. The critics and music fans knew it, too; in a matter of a few short months, they had boosted him from obscurity to stardom. And then the rest of the country discovered him—on the covers of trade and fan magazines, on CD and concert posters.

Even those who had never heard his music were drawn to him. It was that aura he had, a subtle yet wrenching wounded look that made people stare and wonder and ache for him.

"I can't do this," she said in a choked whisper.

His hands rested easily on the top of the gate on either side of her. He wasn't touching her, but he was like the electric fence—falsely benign, waiting, ready to administer a hot shock if she dared to touch.

"Can't do what?" he asked.

"This . . . Be with you, damn it! Be near you."

"Why not?"

"I can't think straight," she blurted out. "You're playing games with me, and it's not fair."

He didn't move a muscle, but his eyes and mouth hardened almost imperceptibly. "I wish you'd listen to yourself, Isabel. You're standing there admitting you still have feelings for me."

The words hit her like a punch in the stomach. For a moment, she couldn't breathe, and her eyes watered as a tearing pain swept through her. His image blurred and softened, and she felt as if she were drifting toward him, closer, her hands already anticipating the rough denim, hard-muscled texture of him.

But before she could move or speak or make sense of what was happening, Dan shoved back from the gate and stalked away. Stricken, she stared at his long, slim, retreating form. Then she saw that Gary Sohappy was riding into the yard on the horse called Petunia. He and Dan spoke for a moment. Gary held a parcel wrapped in a hooded sweatshirt under his arm. He handed it to Dan and dismounted.

Isabel left the garden to say hello to Gary and to thank him again for finding her last night. When she reached them, she stopped short and gasped, spying the bundle in Dan's hands.

"What happened?"

"Not sure," Gary said. "I found her on the way up here."

She was a bald eagle. Only her head was visible, sharply defined in line and color. The great hooked beak was vivid yellow, the eyes bright obsidian, the distinctive head sleek and white.

Gary's hands were covered in scratches. "She was pretty hard to catch," he said with a grin.

Dan held the bird under his arm. "Get inside and wash up, Gary. Use the disinfectant soap. We'll be in the barn."

Isabel picked up the trailing reins of the horse and followed Dan.

He stared at the bundle. "Ever seen a bald eagle close up before?"

"No." She was riveted. The bird was watchful, almost brooding. "I had no idea they were so large. How did Gary know it was a female?"

The bird pecked at Dan's arm. He winced. "Her temperament?"

"Sexist," Isabel muttered.

In the barn, she tethered the mare in cross ties and went with Dan into a small tack room. Barrels of feed stood along one wall beneath an array of reins. Dan set the bird carefully in a dry sink. The eagle struggled, fighting the makeshift bandage. There was something heartbreaking about seeing such a majestic creature floundering and helpless in an alien environment.

But apparently Dan's voice worked on the bird, too. "Shh," he said, and spoke a patois of English and Yakima in a mesmerizing singsong. He used his hands with a light, knowing touch, stroking the smooth feathers and even the sharp beak with one hand, while the other hand unwrapped the bird. She still acted edgy, as if ready to explode into flight at any moment.

Except that she couldn't fly, and as soon as Dan set aside the sweatshirt, they saw why. One wing hung limp. Isabel could see a little blood.

"Must've been wounded in the storm," Dan said. "I don't think the wing's broken, so that's something." He kept up his singsong patter as he opened a metal wall chest to reveal a selection of horse liniments, containers with handwritten labels, jars with rusting lids, a few giant syringes. Dan selected a plastic bottle of antibiotic powder and dusted the wound with it.

The bird erupted into a panic. Dan gathered it awkwardly to his chest and held it there, grimacing as a set of talons sank into his forearm.

Isabel bit her lip. "What can I do?"

He shrugged. "Hell, I don't know. We should probably immobilize this wing."

"Let's try that."

Even with Gary helping them, it took over an hour to bind the wing. The bird had the temper of a pit bull, with razor talons and a can-opener beak to back it up. By the time they had fashioned a bandage of gauze, all three of them bore a few nicks.

Gary lined a crate with straw and positioned it under a single light bulb for warmth. He placed the bird inside, and they stood back, watching. The bird still had fire in her eye and a haughty air, and her chest rose and fell rapidly. Gary went to put up the horse.

"I guess we should feed it something," Dan said.

She shuddered. "Don't eagles eat raw meat?"

"I think so," he said.

"Couldn't we try a can of tuna fish or something?"

As they walked up to the house, Dan draped an arm across her shoulders. The movement was so natural and felt so right that before Isabel even thought about it, she leaned her head into his shoulder. His knuckles grazed her cheek, and she shivered.

"I should get my purse," she said, wondering why her voice sounded so lifeless and flat. "I guess we'd better get started for Seattle."

"Nope." His stride didn't falter as they mounted the steps.

Isabel stopped and looked at him. "What do you mean?"

He gave her a smile that raised a hollow ache in her chest. "Too late, Isabel."

"Anthony said to take all the time I needed. I'll never be too late for—"

"I mean too late in the day. It's dark out."

She blinked, then looked around. Through the black-leafed trees, the sky was deep purple with twilight.

"You're stuck with me for one more night, Isabel," he said unapologetically, then turned and went inside.

Chapter Six

THE NEXT MORNING, Dan caught his breath when Isabel walked into the kitchen. He had probably, at some point, seen a more beautiful sight, but for the life of him, he couldn't remember when.

Her face was scrubbed clean, her hair slightly damp from the shower. She wore a gray sweat suit with the University of Washington seal on the front. The soft folds of fabric enveloped her small frame.

She helped herself to coffee. "I found the sweat suit in the closet in my room. I hope you don't mind."

"'Course not, Isabel. It's chilly this morning." He rose and handed her the sugar bowl.

She smelled like every warm, fragrant dream that haunted a man in the dead of winter. When she didn't fuss with her hair, it relaxed into a long waterfall of silk he wanted to bury his fingers in.

"Did you check on the bird?" she asked.

"A couple of times in the night, and then at the crack of dawn."

What he didn't tell her was that he had also stood in her room in the dark, watching her sleep while wave after wave of tenderness and regret rolled over him.

Five years ago, she had slipped into his heart through a side entrance when he thought he had barred all the doors. He set his jaw and clenched his eyes shut, remembering.

The day she had told him about the baby was branded on his memory. She was so thrilled and so scared. So was he. No, he was terrified.

His feelings for her suffered from some sort of paralysis. Too young and too thickheaded to understand that the first bloom of love needed to deepen and ripen and mature, too stupid to see that responsibility wouldn't stifle him, he panicked.

Her grief and rage over the miscarriage provided him with the opportunity to escape. Like a fool, he took it.

"Dan?" Her voice intruded on his thoughts.

He opened his eyes and blinked at her.

"Is the bird okay?"

"Yeah." He couldn't stop staring at her.

She took a sip of her coffee, regarding him over the rim of her mug. "Are *you* okay?"

His grip on the edge of the tile counter tightened. He had to anchor himself somewhere, to something, or he would explode. "Yeah. Only—"

"Only what?"

"I always thought you were the one who left five years ago, Isabel."

"And now what do you think?" She seemed to have no trouble switching into his train of thought. He could almost believe the past was on her mind, too.

"Physically, you left, you walked out. But I didn't give you many options. Stay in hell with me or save yourself. Not much choice there."

She started to move away. "We were young—"

"*Were* young," he echoed harshly, grasping her wrist. "We're different now, and you know it."

She was breathing hard with some inner struggle. Dan made himself let go of her hand. "Sorry." He carried her cup to the table for her.

Both of them were edgy and emotional this morning. Dan's nerve endings felt raw with desperation. All he knew for certain was that he could not stand the thought of her getting married to someone else. He had no idea what alternative he could offer her, but he had to make her see that what they had shared was not over. It would never be over.

"Did the eagle eat the tuna fish?" she asked, shifting gears again.

"Some. It didn't seem to be to her taste." Dan forced himself to release his need for her at the moment. There was an intensity to his feelings that she would probably find frightening. He had to back off, get a grip. "I tried canned salmon this morning. She picked at that. I was thinking we could try to get her some fresh fish today. It'd probably be better for her."

"We should," Isabel said quickly.

He grinned. "Any excuse to go fishing."

She grinned back. "Any excuse."

DAN FELT as if a time bomb were ticking somewhere at the back of his mind. If he mentioned it to Isabel, it might go off. If he didn't mention it, it might go off anyway.

Armed with rods, a creel, and a picnic lunch, they plodded in hip boots down to the lake. Isabel looked vibrant, as beautiful and understated as a doe in a forest grove—and as fragile.

All right, he thought. *Say it.*

He stopped walking and touched her shoulder. "I meant to ask you earlier. If you need to make a call, I can radio someone in town—"

"It's okay." Color stained her cheekbones. "Anthony said I should take all the time I need."

"Anthony is a first-class fool," Dan said, "and I thank God for that."

She started walking again, so he couldn't see her reaction to his words. "He's always been very understanding. And I've always been moody. So it's a perfect match."

"Yeah, right."

At the lakeshore, they waded in, flailing their arms to keep from falling as the mud sucked at their boots. After they tired of standing, they slogged ashore and took off their boots. Dan rolled out a thick fiber mat so they could recline. Isabel baited her own hook, arguing volubly about the merits of canned corn versus salmon eggs. She looked gorgeous, fitting the scene like an emerald in a perfect setting. Before Dan's eyes, she seemed to relax, the inner tightness he sensed in her uncoiling.

Mother Earth doing her sacred duty, he decided whimsically. As he lay back on the mat and let the warmth of the sun bathe him, he imagined he could feel the slow, steady heartbeat of the earth beneath him, a subtle, comforting rhythm that he had ignored for too long. He had been deaf to it until his grandfather, filled with a dying man's reflective wisdom, had awakened him to it once again.

Perhaps that was what Isabel was feeling now, that sense of homecoming.

She glanced at him. "What are you thinking?"

He sent her a lazy smile. "That it's a perfect fishing day." He touched her slim thigh with one finger and traced it gently, teasingly. "Enough nibbles to keep things interesting, but not so many that it starts . . . to feel . . . like work."

She laughed—a little nervously, he thought—and shifted away from him. "You're a bad influence, Dan. I don't think I've spent so many hours doing nothing and—" She bit her lip.

"And loving every minute of it?" he asked in a low voice. "To an outside observer, it might look like not much is going on." He touched a lock of hair at her temple. "But there's plenty happening here, Isabel. We'd both be lying if we said otherwise."

ISABEL HAD NO IDEA how long she had been sleeping. The excitement of fishing again—something she hadn't done since her father had taught her—must have worn her out. But she hadn't realized a nap in the fresh air could give her such a sense of renewal. She awoke to blink at the late-afternoon sun, squinting through breeze-blown leaves, listening to the soft lapping of the lake on the shores and to the quiet cadence of Dan's breathing.

He had fallen asleep, too. In his faded jeans and plaid shirt and hiking boots, a John Deere cap pulled down over his eyes, he was the consummate woodsman— wholly masculine, with a rugged splendor that made him a part of the forest and mountains.

Something still existed between them, some magnetic attraction. She could no longer deny that. But for now, she refused to shape the idea into words. She was simply taking the time she needed—

Needed for *what?* asked the wary cynic inside her. To rediscover that, yes, Dan Black Horse was still the sexiest, most fascinating man she could ever hope to meet? And to rediscover that he still had the power to break her heart?

Helping herself to a long drink of lemonade from the thermos, she scowled at him. "You're not doing me any favors, Dan Black Horse."

He awoke with a luxurious, long-bodied stretch that made her hormones jolt into overdrive. "What's that?" he asked in a sleepy voice, taking the thermos from her.

"Nothing," she snapped. "You—" A buzzing sound interrupted her. With reflexes tuned perfectly by instinct, she pounced on her rod and set the hook. Moments later, she reeled in a plump, silvery trout, by far the best catch of the day. Laughing, she said, "I *told* you I was right about the corn."

He laughed with her, and the tension dissolved. They packed up their gear and hiked back to the lodge.

The eagle snapped up a small fish in her big yellow beak. She scarfed another, then cocked her head, waiting for more.

"She likes sushi," Dan said.

Isabel clutched his arm and nodded. "I think we're spoiling her. She won't know how to survive in the wild after this."

"She's a grown bird. I don't think a few days with us will make her lose her taste for the wild." His finger traced a shivery line down the side of Isabel's throat. "Right?"

Stung, she lurched away. "I need a bath," she said hastily. "It's been a long day."

He winked at her. "It's not over yet."

SHE LUXURIATED in the tub, letting the massage jets pummel her muscles. She loved the sense of unreality that enveloped her here at Dan's lodge. She was remote, detached from the rest of the world.

Free.

But *freedom* was just a nice word people used instead of *lonely,* or maybe *desperate.*

What Isabel had wanted—had *always* wanted—was a sense of connectedness. To know that she belonged.

Anthony was perfect for her. He came fully equipped, a package deal with a large, loving family that surrounded and enveloped her like a hand-stitched quilt. *He* was what she needed.

Not Dan Black Horse with the heartbreak in his eyes and a body that promised enough forbidden pleasure to make her legally insane.

She realized she had been in the tub brooding for far too long. Feeling sheepish, she got out and dressed in her skirt and top and the cardigan sweater Dan had loaned her yesterday.

She stood in front of the mirror wishing for mousse and a curling iron until she realized what she was doing, what she was thinking.

It shouldn't matter how she looked for Dan.

But oh, God. It did.

"THAT SMELLS HEAVENLY," she said, a soft smile curving her mouth. "When did you learn to cook?"

"It's not cooking, it's grilling." Dan grinned at her as he set down a platter of trout and vegetables. His long, glossy hair was still damp from the shower, and he smelled of soap and wood smoke. "I know more recipes than Robert James Waller."

He served a chilled local wine and even lit candles on the dining-hall table. They sat across from each other and lifted their glasses.

For Isabel, the moment froze in time. In the blink of an eye, she was hurled back to the night she had told him about the baby. After she'd told him the news, she'd had ginger ale and he'd had beer, but they had laughed and clinked their glasses and made promises with no idea how to keep them.

The soft *chink* of his glass against hers brought her back to the present. "Isabel?" he said in his low, rough voice. "What'll we drink to?"

"The eagle's health?" she suggested, pleased that her voice did not sound as wobbly as she felt.

He chuckled and made the toast. Isabel grew warm and flushed with the good food and the chilled wine, and the moments slipped past.

She glanced out the big bay window to see violet shadows streaking the mountains. "I suppose," she said, "you'll tell me it's too late in the day to start for Seattle."

"Isabel?" His large hand covered hers.

"Yes?" The wine and his nearness gave her a pleasant, floating sensation.

"It's too late to start for Seattle."

"What a surprise to hear you say that." She forced herself to stop smiling. "Tomorrow, then," she said decisively. "First thing."

"Seeing as how you've been getting up at the crack of noon, that shouldn't be a problem."

"It's easy to sleep here," she blurted out.

His hand lifted to her face, knuckles grazing the curve of her cheek. "I'm glad you like the lodge."

"I didn't say I—"

"You didn't have to." His finger made a tender exploration, finding the shape of her chin and then tracing her lips until she almost cried out for mercy.

"Dan—"

"We could go somewhere," he said lightly.

"Where?"

He didn't answer, but got up and took her hand. He held out a leather jacket, and when she slid her arms into the slick lining and felt its comforting weight on her shoulders, she nearly wept with the poignancy of her memories.

He had owned the leather jacket for as long as she had known him. Its shape was his shape. Its scent was his scent. It seemed to carry the very essence of him, to envelop her with the intimacy of a lover's embrace.

He seemed not to notice the effect it had on her as he took her hand and led her out to the shed where he kept his Harley.

She asked no questions, and he offered no explanations. She simply got on, wrapped her arms around him, closed her eyes, and leaned her cheek against his back. She felt protected and alive as never before.

The bike roared down the mountain, headlights sweeping the wooded slopes. She had complete faith in his driving. Even at night, he knew the wilderness like an old song memorized in his youth.

After a while, they came to a dirt road, and a few miles beyond that, the paved one. Isabel was startled and intrigued when they rolled into the town of Thelma.

Chapter Seven

"I CAN'T BELIEVE you brought me to a dance," Isabel said, standing in the foyer of the fire hall.

Dan grinned and slid his leather jacket off her shoulders. "We used to go dancing a lot."

She turned her head and sent him a wry look. "Getting crushed in the cramped space of some seedy concert hall was never quite my idea of a good time."

"You should have said something. Shouldn't have let me drag you along." He exchanged greetings with Sarah Looking, who was in charge of the coat check, and handed her the jacket.

Isabel gave a little laugh, though he noticed the strained sound of it. "I wanted to be where you were, Dan."

Do you now? he wanted to ask her. *Do you want to be where I am now?*

"I guess I didn't really know where I wanted to be," he said, leading her into the dance hall. "But I never meant to force you to do anything that made you uncomfortable."

"You never did, not really."

He drew her against him for a dance. The ersatz country swing music was whiny and slow, but somehow satisfying. It was, he conceded, more than likely the fact that he was dancing with Isabel. She felt like heaven in his arms, her frame supple and willowy, her soft hand cradled in his, her face shy and shadowy in the dim light.

"Care to ditch that no-'count Indian for a cowboy, ma'am?" someone asked.

Isabel gasped in outrage, but Dan stepped back, laughing.

Clyde Looking, head of the tribal council, lifted his ten-gallon hat in greeting, and Dan made the introductions. Within moments, Clyde danced away with Isabel, and Dan eased back to the refreshment table to help himself to a drink.

Lucy Raintree served him. Theo Sohappy stopped by. People were easy with one another, chatting and joking, some just smiling and tapping their feet to the overdone percussion from the cheap keyboard. The music should have made Dan cringe, but instead it was as comforting as a greeting from an old friend. Later, he would perform a song or two; he always did.

Dan felt—had felt from the start—an unexpected sense of community with these people. The feeling had always eluded him in the city. He'd had friends, sure, but with them he had never found this level of comfort, this quiet settling of the soul.

Dan had never known he was missing it, but maybe it was part of the reason he had been so savage inside, had made mistakes on important matters. Like Isabel.

Had he ever told her he loved her?

"So she's still here." Theo watched Isabel dance with Clyde Looking. "And you didn't even have to tie her up to make her stay."

Dan laughed, his eyes following the dancers. Clyde was the perfect host, pausing in his two-step now and then to introduce Isabel to someone new. She looked flushed and bright-eyed. Dan had feared she would feel awkward here, that her laughter and conversation would seem forced, but he could tell her enjoyment was genuine.

"Nope," he said, "I didn't tie her up, not that the thought didn't cross my mind."

"Don't blame you. God, she's a looker. Part Indian?"

"Yeah, but she was raised in an Anglo foster home."

"Ma told her she had to step out of the shadows, be herself. You know how Ma is."

"If anybody can thaw out Isabel, Juanita can," Dan said.

Theo clapped him on the shoulder. "Looks like you did a pretty good job of that yourself. Is she going to stay for the race?"

Dan felt a twinge of apprehension. He was signed up to ride his motorcycle in the Yakima Suicide Race. He owed it to Isabel to tell her, but he just hadn't found the right time. She'd try to talk him out of it. And he already knew he wouldn't listen.

"I don't know, Theo," he said. "I guess that's up to her." His gaze was riveted to Isabel. The song ended, and she excused herself from Clyde and made a beeline for the pay phone in the corner of the hall by the drinking fountain.

Dan's gut sank like a stone. Quite obviously, nothing had changed, and she couldn't wait to call her boyfriend and tell him so.

EVERYTHING HAD CHANGED, and Isabel knew she could no longer put off calling Anthony. Her fingers felt cold as she lifted the receiver and dialed his number, punching in her credit-card code and then waiting with growing impatience through six rings.

The answering machine kicked on. She listened to the bland, cheery message, then said, "Anthony, it's me, Isabel. If you're there, pick up. We need to talk. You see—"

"Sure, babe." Anthony Cossa's real voice interrupted her. "What's up? Are you ready to return to civilization yet?"

"The lodge up here doesn't have a phone. I'm in a town called Thelma."

"Listening to lousy country music, if I'm hearing the background noise right." He laughed easily.

"I was planning to come back sooner, but something came up. A couple of things." She had no idea where to begin, what to tell him, what was fair. An injured eagle? An unresolved past? A sudden need to look into a part of herself she had kept in the dark for years?

"Having second thoughts, babe?" Anthony asked.

She could discern no inflection in his voice. She tried to picture him—he was probably wearing khakis or jeans, in his pristine Santa Fe-style condo on Western Avenue, drinking a beer from a microbrewery and being paged every sixty seconds while channel surfing on his forty-eight-inch TV.

She tried to remember the last time they had shared a bottle of wine and just listened to music for a few uninterrupted hours. She tried to remember the last time they had gone dancing.

"Isabel?" he prompted.

"Anthony, I just don't know. Saturday, I saw our whole lives rolling out ahead of us like a giant red carpet. But now—"

"Now what?" Still she heard no sharpness in his voice, just curiosity.

"Maybe the red carpet took a left turn somewhere. I'm having to take a good look at myself, Anthony, and—"

"Just a sec. I have another call coming in." He clicked off.

She stood staring at the telephone keypad, wondering whether or not she had a right to be irritated.

"Okay." Anthony was back. "I've got someone on hold. Long-distance."

She was leaning heavily toward being irritated now.

"So what do you want to do?" he asked. "Postpone the wedding? Call it off?"

She felt the burn of tears in her eyes. "Your family has everything all planned—"

"My family," he said. "That's really what all this is about, isn't it? That's what it's always been about."

"I adore your family, Anthony. I'd hate myself if I disappointed them."

"Yeah, well, look. You do whatever it is you have to do to get your head straight, and call me tomorrow, okay, babe?"

"Yes, but—"

"I better take this other call. Talk to you soon." He was gone with a gentle click.

Isabel stood with the receiver still held to her ear and leaned her forehead against the cold, shiny metal of the pay phone. She'd believed she belonged with Anthony. She had thrived on the fast pace of his life-style, and he had seemed eager to move to Bainbridge Island, although he had joked about not being able to use his cellular phone there. At least she *thought* he'd been joking.

But his abruptness and bland reaction had seemed exaggerated in their phone conversation. Perhaps it was the odd juxtaposition of hearing Anthony's voice in a fire hall in Thelma. Or perhaps it was the things Clyde had said about Dan still echoing in her ears.

According to Clyde, Dan had saved the tribal council—the whole town, for that matter—from financial collapse. The lodge enterprise had employed people who hadn't had jobs in years.

Of course, Clyde had said cautiously, Dan had run through a lot of his own money getting started. A *lot* of money.

The rapid-fire beep of the off-the-hook signal startled her. She quickly replaced the receiver in the cradle and turned.

Dan stood a few feet back, watching her.

The sight of him made the breath catch in her throat. He had always been easy in his tall, broad-shouldered frame, and he seemed so now, with his weight shifted to one leg and a thumb stuck into his belt. He was backlit by the muted lamps in the hall so that she could not see his face, only the inky waves of his long hair.

He was too far away to have heard her conversation; yet she felt a heated blush rise in her cheeks as if she had been caught doing something wrong.

Ridiculous. *He* was the whole reason she was in this dilemma. If it had not been for him, she would still be in the bosom of the Cossa family, getting ready for her wedding.

Moments passed. They both stood unmoving. Some part of Isabel yearned for him so fiercely that she nearly wept. Then, before she could decide whether or not to go to him, he turned on his heel and strode away.

She felt a deep, invisible agony rip through her, but she stood there mute and helpless. She wanted to be angry, wanted to blame him for her doubts, but he was ignoring her, stalking past dancing couples and groups of people chatting together.

She should not have been surprised when he stepped onto the low platform and picked up an acoustic guitar. But she was. Somehow, she had managed to forget that Dan was a musician, a performer. An artist.

The lights dropped even lower, and the other musicians tapered down the tune they were playing. The fiddler set a mike in front of Dan.

He was surrounded by shadow, alone in a pool of light as he had been when she had seen him for the first time. As perhaps he had always been. When he lifted an unseeing gaze to the listeners in the room, her heart lurched. How well she remembered that unfathomable look.

His long brown hands worked magic on the battered old guitar, drawing out chords of melancholic sweetness. It was the music of lonely places in the heart, of chances missed, of lost souls looking for a welcome somewhere.

Dan's gift with music had not diminished since his retirement. Instead, Isabel knew instantly that his talent had intensified and deepened. He had come back to the place where his soul had been made, and she heard a new awareness in his mesmerizing voice.

The words were simple, a refrain that rang true, that made women reach out and sidle closer to the men beside them, and made the men gently take the hands of their partners.

Through it all, Isabel stood alone, stricken, watching, knowing only one thing for certain.

She had never stopped loving Dan Black Horse.

There. She admitted it to herself. And it was the truest thought she'd had in years. She had let anger and fear eclipse her love and darken her heart, but the love had never gone away. It had just been obscured by a hundred other things. And she had allowed it. So had Dan.

But somehow, he had found a way to look back at what had happened and to learn from what he saw. That was what it was all about. His song, and his abduction of her, the whole crazy weekend.

The song ended with a smattering of applause. Dan grinned and chatted for a few minutes with the musicians. Then he walked straight to Isabel.

"Now what?" he asked, keeping his distance, watching her, waiting.

"Now—" Isabel's mouth felt dry as dust. If she followed her heart, there would be no turning back. Yet she had never felt more certain of anything in her life. "Now we go home."

Chapter Eight

DAN WASN'T SURE what she meant, but he knew what he wanted her to mean. He said, "I'll get your coat," and then nothing more as they rode back to the lodge.

After putting up the bike, he took her hand and started walking across the yard. The moon was up, and spidery shadows crept across the damp ground. The quiet was all pervasive, pierced only by the hollow hoot of an owl.

Dan stopped walking and looked down at her, at the fine, silvery light in her hair. Her breathing was quick and uncertain. He gently brushed a stray strand of hair back from her cheek. He wondered about that phone call she had made, but he didn't ask. He'd find out soon enough.

"Now what?" she asked, echoing his own question to her. She gazed up at him, looking as lost and lonely as she had the first time he'd seen her.

He felt a surge of tenderness as he slid his arms around her waist and pulled her close.

"Now this," he murmured, and settled his mouth on hers. He kissed her in a way that left no question as to his intent. The pressure of his lips urged her to open for him, and his tongue plunged inside, hungry, possessive. His body was so racked with desire that by the time he lifted his head, he could barely speak.

If she said no, he would back off. He had made that promise to her the first time he had kissed her, and he knew he would still honor it now.

When she spoke, it was a breathy whisper. "Yes." And nothing more.

But it was all he needed.

Hand in hand, they walked into the darkened lodge and up the stairs to her room. She had been here only two days, but already her presence was strong in the soft, soapy fragrance that hung in the air, in the overturned paperback book she had left on the bedside table, the shoes she immediately kicked off.

He knew there were things he should say to her, things he should ask her, but talking distracted him from the way he wanted to touch her. He stood behind her and took off the leather jacket she wore, letting it slither to the floor beside the bed. He bent and brushed aside her hair and kissed the tender flesh at the nape of her neck.

A soft sigh slipped from her, and she tilted her head to one side. His lips trailed across her heated skin, tongue flicking out to touch her earlobe, hands moving to her waist to release the front buttons of her knit top. He freed her of the shirt and slid his hands up over her breasts. He slid her skirt down and watched her step out of it. He ran his open-palmed hands up and down the length of her, feeling the contours of her body as if for the first time. She had not changed; she was still petite and slender and soft. So utterly feminine that she made him feel large and clumsy.

She gasped, reaching up and back with her arms and winding them around his neck to bring his mouth down. He turned her and kissed her then, and she brushed against him with an intimate, suggestive movement. She slipped out of her lacy under-things while he undressed, and neither felt awkward, for it was an inevitability that had been waiting for them for years, lying dormant and unacknowledged in their hearts until this searing instant.

They lay back on the bed, cool sheets and billowy eiderdown sighing beneath the weight of their bodies. Dan braced himself up on one elbow and let his caresses ripple down the length of her while he gazed into her face. She wore a slumberous look, moist lips slightly parted, eyes half-closed. Her hands reached for him; then her palms drifted down his sides to his hips. He had to set his jaw and squeeze his eyes shut to regain control.

Not until this moment did he realize the power she had over him. He bent his head and kissed her, drinking from her lips, his hands circling her breasts and then dipping lower, parting her thighs, finding her so ready for him that he could hold off no longer. He moved over her, their mouths still joined. Wanting her pleasure even more than he wanted his own, he lifted his head and waited, muscles straining, for some sign from her. She stared up at him, her shadowed expression unreadable.

"You're not..." he said through clenched teeth, "making this easy."

"Am I supposed to?" she whispered. But there was a smile in her voice, and her hands drifted down and clasped and guided him, and they were suddenly together as if they had never been apart.

He found a rhythm they both remembered, a dance of the heart that had endured despite the passage of time. She lifted and tilted herself, as giving as the earth in springtime, and her dulcet acceptance filled him and brought him such a shattering pleasure that he saw stars. When a soft cry slipped from her and she arched upward, he knew the reunion was complete, knew that neither of them would ever be the same.

Still their silence persisted, and it was a comfortable stillness, an abatement of worry. Neither spoke; they did not have to. Nor did they want to. That would mean entering the world again, entering reality, facing up to the unresolved matters that hung over them.

Dan gathered her close and made love to her again, slowly this time, lingering over every part of her as if getting reacquainted with an old friend. She gave herself to him with a sigh of surrender. He found all the little delights of her, the hollow of her throat and the tender inside of her wrist, the backs of her knees and inner thighs where the skin was softer, smoother than anything he could imagine. With hands and mouth, he brought her to ecstasy again—and again—until she was sweetly exhausted, snuggling against his chest and growing warm and heavy limbed until, just as dawn tinged the sky, she slept.

SHE AWOKE SLOWLY, hovering in a delicious realm somewhere between sleep and waking. Her mind was filled with memories of Dan—his voice, his touch, the taste of his mouth, the shattering power of the passion she had found with him.

Only him.

Willfully, she thrust aside the thought. Just for now, she would not worry about the future. Just for now, she would let herself be warm and lazy and slightly dazed by all that was happening to her.

"Dan." She whispered his name and opened her eyes, but he was gone. He must have gotten up to make coffee. She stretched, feeling interesting aches in certain parts of her body, then went to brush her teeth. Rather than pulling on the terry-cloth robe, she slipped into Dan's leather jacket. Wearing it, feeling its voluminous weight drop from shoulder to midthigh, she felt closer to him.

The jacket should have evoked bitter memories, for she had also worn it the afternoon she had come home from the hospital. Both she and Dan were so silent that day, neither knowing what to say. They both cried and held each other and looked at the doctor's pamphlet explaining how a high percentage of early pregnancies ended in miscarriage; it was generally a natural process and there was no reason they could not try again....

Somehow, they both knew they would not try again. The first time was an accident, but a second time would be deliberate, would force them to commit to permanence in their relationship, no more drifting through the days toward a hazy, shapeless future.

He had not been ready. And when Isabel finally realized that she could no longer wait for the full commitment of his love, she left.

Last night changed everything. Dan had never touched her so deeply, so intimately. He was different now. Settled. Responsible. Ready to love her. She was falling in love all over again. This time, it was for real. This time, it was for keeps.

As she walked bare legged and barefoot down the steps, she felt wicked and wanton. Dan had plucked her out of her controlled, rigid life and plunged her into a world of sensation and emotion. It was scary and sometimes it hurt, but she had never felt so alive.

Her hand encountered a folded piece of paper in the pocket of the jacket. She pulled it out—a flyer of some sort. As she read the words, she stopped on the second-to-last step. The blood froze in her veins. Her heart turned to a block of ice.

"No," she said in a low voice, forcing her legs to start moving again. Surely this was just something Dan had picked up and forgotten to discard. Surely... She forced herself to calm down and made her way to the back of the lodge.

The kitchen was warm and cheery with the scent of coffee. Dan was out on the back porch, leaning against the railing, holding a mug in one hand and an envelope in the other. He was looking out at the mountains.

He wore only jeans, no shirt or shoes. His muscular shoulders and chest gleamed in the muted morning sun, and his hair flowed down his back. The subtle shadow of whiskers softened the harsh line of his jaw.

There was such a stark beauty in him that for a moment Isabel felt completely inadequate. He could not possibly be hers. He was too perfect, too desirable.

Then she remembered her purpose and stepped out onto the porch. The screen door tapped shut behind her, and Dan turned.

His slow, easy smile held every memory of the splendor they had shared the previous night. "Damn, Isabel," he said, his eyes smoldering, "you always were a great dresser." He set down his mug and held out one arm. She went into his embrace, and he kissed her, his mouth tasting of sweet coffee.

"Did you sleep all right?" he asked her.

"Sleeping is about the only thing I can do right around here," she said.

"I can think of a few other things." His hand slipped into the jacket, and his eyebrows lifted. "*Damn*, Isabel. You're naked in there."

She couldn't stifle a laugh as she moved away. His expression told her he had every intention of whisking her back to bed. She welcomed the prospect, of course, but first she had something to ask him.

"What about this?" She held out the flyer.

He hesitated for a heartbeat. The piece of paper dropped from her fingers.

Dan propped one hip on the railing. His face was inscrutable. "The Yakima Suicide Race," he said.

She drew her hands into the sleeves of the jacket. "It has nothing to do with you, Dan. Right?" When he did not answer, she said again, "Right?"

"It's this afternoon," he said, not looking at her. "And I'm entered."

Isabel leaned back against the door and squeezed her eyes shut, hoping against hope that she'd heard wrong. Just the thought of grown men on motorcycles jolting down near-vertical slopes, leaping gullies and skirting cliffs made her nauseous.

"Dan," she said, dragging open her eyes. "My father *died* in that race."

"I know."

"Don't do it, Dan."

"One of the local wineries made the purse worth winning. It could keep me afloat through the summer, long enough to get the cash flow started."

"You won't need any business if you die in the race," she said fiercely. "I can't believe you'd do this to me."

"Will you listen to yourself?" Dan rounded on her. "Your father didn't do a damned thing to you. You've always regarded his death as a deliberate, personal affront. A reason to pretend you're not Indian at all, a reason to hide with your sterile Anglo foster parents and grow flowers on your sterile Anglo island."

His words sliced like cold metal into her. "I don't need this, Dan. I don't need you to say these things to me."

He advanced on her, anger blazing in his eyes, and braced a hand on the door behind her. "Maybe it's time someone *did* say them. Your father's death wasn't about you."

"And this race isn't about me, either," she retorted, glaring up at him, trying to tamp down her feelings of dread. "You're doing this because you blew the deal with Anthony, right?"

Dan said nothing. She took it as an affirmation. "You know," she said softly, "there's a sort of crazy gallantry in what you did. But there's nothing gallant about putting your life at risk."

His jaw tightened dangerously. "Isabel, don't do this. Don't make me choose."

"I can't make you do a damned thing," she said. "I never could."

Chapter Nine

"WHY ARE WE STOPPING HERE?" Isabel asked, noting a string of triangular colored flags stretched across the road in Thelma. Yakima Suicide Race, the banner proclaimed.

Resting his hands on the steering wheel of the pickup truck, Gary Sohappy held in the clutch and looked back at the straw-lined crate in the bed of the pickup truck. "I was just trying to decide what would be the best place to let the bird go."

"I don't think it can fly yet."

"Dan said it could." Gary shifted gears and continued down the only paved road in town.

"Dan's been wrong before." She looked at her watch. After their quarrel, she had insisted on coming to town to call Anthony. He had groused a little about having to reschedule a meeting, but he had agreed to meet her in front of the fire hall and take her back to the city.

The prospect left her cold and empty.

Dan had prepared for the race in stony silence. Like a knight of old, he had strapped on armor of black leather, adding shin guards, pads at his knees and elbows, and a helmet. He tried to kiss her goodbye; she turned away. Then she turned back in time to see him walking off with long, angry strides.

She opened her mouth to call to him, but no sound came out. He rode off on the motorcycle just as Gary arrived to take her to town, then to take the eagle into the wild and let it go.

One passenger into the wild, one back into her cage. The thought struck Isabel like a blow in the dark, and she gasped.

"Something wrong?" Gary asked.

Everything, she thought.

"Where does the race end?" she asked suddenly.

"Huh?"

"The race. I want to see the end of it."

"Same place it does every year. But I thought you had to meet somebody."

"Gary," she said, "I need to see the race."

He grinned. "Okay by me."

HER HANDS, clutching the door handle, were like ice as the truck bounced off-road and uphill. When the terrain became impassable, Gary parked and they got out. Tall grass swished and sighed in the breeze. Gary went around to the bed of the truck and opened the eagle's crate.

"Is she all right?" Isabel asked.

"I think so—ow! Her talons work just fine." Gary set the eagle on a large rock. The bird perched there, looking haughty and fierce, the breeze ruffling her feathers. Slowly, her wings unfolded.

Isabel held her breath. *Fly*, she thought. *Fly. You can do it.*

The bird let the wind sift through her feathers, then folded her wings back up.

"Not ready," Gary mumbled, clearly disappointed. "I brought my camera and everything." He scooped up the bird and began to climb the hill. "We'll have the best view of the race from Warrior Point," he said over his shoulder.

The cold numbness froze her hands once again, and no matter how hard she tried to drive the dark memories out of her mind, they came at her, as steady and inevitable as the tide.

She knew exactly where Gary was heading.

Because she had stood there and watched her father die. Her memories were as sharp and clear as slides viewed through white light. Her father and his friends were drinking beer. Not a lot—just the usual amount for an afternoon. Her mother laughed with them when her father teased his wife about her concern for his safety.

He kissed them both goodbye, his wife on the lips, his daughter on the top of the head. Isabel saw mirth in his eyes, but something else, too, something too subtle for her to grasp. Now she realized it was a restless hunger. A deep dissatisfaction.

Her father had never held a steady job. Running off on dangerous adventures seemed to be a way of proving himself. Defining who he was—not some reservation idler, but a man.

She understood none of this when she was a girl. She understood only that she had seen her father die.

A group of observers had gone out to the point, Isabel and her mother included. Isabel was standing, holding hands with her mother. The riders appeared in an explosion of dust and thundering hooves, pouring down a near-vertical gully, leaping a narrow, deep chasm before swinging in a hairpin curve down the side of the mountain.

Only, instead of making the hairpin curve, her father went over a cliff. Isabel stood in disbelieving silence, staring down at his broken figure and the unmoving horse beside him. She remembered one other detail of that moment in time. Her mother—quite deliberately and quite without malicious intent—dropped Isabel's hand.

Isabel's mother completely shut down. She had moved to the city and willingly surrendered Isabel to a foster home.

From that moment onward, confused and angry, Isabel pretended that the past did not exist. She eradicated from her character all Indian values and sensibilities.

Until Dan.

The thought of him drew a gasp of anguish from her.
"We're almost there," Gary said over his shoulder.
"I know," she muttered.

Dan had filled her with his passion and pride and vitality. She had been afraid of the Indian part of him, and perhaps she still was, but he had awakened her to the ancient songs and rhythms she had never quite been able to banish from her heart.

She had loved the tender, whimsical side of him. But she had never understood the dark side, the danger-loving side, the part of him that hungered for tests of his strength, his endurance, his mortality.

She saw the point looming ahead. Little had changed. A line of evergreens grew along a ridge. The valley was a deep cleft formed by the two mountains, with a rushing stream in between, and by gazing across the velvety green gorge, she could see the course the race would follow. It was more like the bed of a waterfall than a path, steep and curving and littered with rocks. And of course, there was the cliff, brooding and sheer, too stark to grow anything but the most tenacious of plants.

She stood and watched. Gary set the bird on the ground. The day was bright and sharply clear. The sound of the wind filled the air. And then she heard it.

The animal rumble of motorcycle engines. The riders were approaching the last and most dangerous leg of the race.

A curious thing happened. The eagle grew restless, bowing out her wings and rushing into the wind; then the bird flung herself off the end of the point. Isabel gasped and Gary laughed in wonder and lifted his camera to his eye. At first, the bird appeared to be falling, helpless, a horrifying sight. Then an eddy of wind caught her beneath her wings. With a high-pitched cry, she was soaring, soaring across the valley that was already alive with the thunder of the race.

DAN FELT A LITTLE SILLY wearing the windbreaker bearing the label of a Yakima Valley winery. It was white, and he never wore white, and besides, the zipper was faulty. But in return for their sponsorship, he got a few perks, including deep discounts on his supply of wine for the lodge.

Other riders were similarly garbed, their numbered windbreakers shouting ads for everything from motor oil to *masa harina* flour.

He knew he would win the race today. Number one, he needed the winnings. Number two, he was riding like the wind. There were simply days when this was true.

Smaller and more nimble than his Harley, the off-road motorcycle seemed an extension of his body, slanting and skating with elastic responsiveness beneath him. He could almost forget the look on Isabel's face when he had tried to say goodbye, hoping she would wish him luck.

She hadn't.

The flavor of danger filled his mouth with a sweetness that turned bitter when he remembered Isabel.

She seemed to think plunging into danger was his way of recoiling from intimacy, that after last night it was no coincidence that he was here today, putting his life on the line. She believed it was his way of avoiding emotional commitment.

He wanted to say she was wrong. But was she?

He set his jaw and prepared for the last and most treacherous part of the race. The windbreaker flew loose, the flimsy zipper breaking as he bolted down a rock-strewed ravine.

A movement caught his eye. He chanced a lightning glance upward and was amazed. A soaring eagle was circling the valley.

He wondered if it could be the eagle they'd rescued. If it was, that meant Isabel was *here*. Watching.

The loose jacket flapped madly. Dan swore under his breath and gritted his teeth, clearing his mind. He had to jump a gully and make a turn before he was in the clear.

He braced himself to soar across the gully. But then the unthinkable happened. The windbreaker caught a gust of wind and flew upward, obscuring his face, blinding him.

He never found a footing on the other side. He just kept going like a stone flung from a sling.

Chapter Ten

THERE WAS NO HOSPITAL in Thelma, so Dan was taken to the tribal clinic across the road from the fire hall. There was no regular doctor, either, but an emergency room physician from Olympia was on hand for the race.

Isabel did not even recall the frantic drive to town. The clinic personnel had barred her from seeing Dan; she had only glimpsed him as he was whisked past on a gurney. His eyes had been closed, his face pale.

They had promised to report back to her. With panic clawing at her insides, she paced the cool, antiseptic corridor, then finally stepped outside to lean against the cinder-block building.

She thought about praying, but no words would form. She thought about cursing, but that seemed so useless, like throwing stones at the moon. And so she covered her face with her hands and shuddered, wishing hard, wishing with all her might, that he would recover.

"Isabel?" A man's voice penetrated the swirling panic.

Her eyes flew open. "Anthony."

"Hey, I've been hanging around waiting for over an hour." He did not look angry. She had never known Anthony to get angry. He looked pleasant and smooth and artlessly handsome as always.

"Are you about ready?" he asked.

"I . . ." Her mouth felt like sawdust. "I can't go anywhere, Anthony. There's been an accident." She practically choked on the word. "I have to wait and see if—" She broke off and regarded him helplessly. "I can't go with you."

He raked a hand through his abundant dark hair. "Look, Isabel, this is getting ridiculous."

"I know," she said softly. "I know. You don't deserve this. You go back to town, Anthony. Never mind about me."

He held her lightly by the shoulders. "Babe, I'll wait."

Juanita Sohappy joined them, hurrying to Isabel. "Is there any news?"

"No," Isabel said faintly. "Not yet."

"I hope the white-eyes doctor knows what he's doing," Juanita said, using the language Isabel had never quite forgotten. She squeezed Isabel's hand, then went inside the clinic.

Anthony stared after her for a moment. "A friend of yours?"

"Yes. We just met, but she reminds me of the past, of people I used to know."

"This is really wild. People you used to know? Native Americans?"

She blinked. Her thoughts seethed and scattered like storm clouds. "I'm half-Indian," she said simply.

His hands dropped from her shoulders. He stared at her as if she had just sprouted antlers.

"Is that a problem?" she asked.

"Of course not." But his voice was taut, strained. "The problem is that you never told me."

"No. No, I didn't."

"Why in the world—" He made a fist and pressed it against the gray cinder-block wall. "What is it, Isabel? Did you think I'd find you weird or something?"

"I guess I didn't think much at all. I never told anyone."

"This is insane. We're supposed to be married Saturday. And here I am finding out things—important things—about you that you should've told me months ago. What else haven't you told me?"

Ah, so much, she thought sadly. About her father, her mother, all the things that had turned her into what she was when she had first met him—a bashful woman frightened of her past, intimidated by passion, seeking a way to belong.

And she wondered—she *made* herself wonder—if it was fair to expect Anthony to answer all those needs.

And that, after all, was the key. Neither Anthony nor Dan nor anyone could *give* her happiness. How naive she had been to think they could.

"Anthony," she said, her voice more steady than she could have wished. "I'm sorry. After I hear about…" Her voice broke. "About Dan, we'll talk."

"I'm not sure we need to." His lips thinned, and she could tell he was annoyed, but to the core of his being, Anthony Cossa was a kind and patient man. Kinder and more patient than she deserved.

A moment later, Juanita pushed open the clinic door. She did not say a word. She did not have to. The expression on her face said it all.

HIS GRANDFATHER would have called it a "true dream." Wispy images and sensations in Dan's head pulsed with vivid color. Drumbeats sounded in his ears, and he felt the heavy thud at the base of his neck.

Right where it hurt the most.

A coldness seized him, and he tried to dive back into the dream, into the colorful oblivion behind his eyes. But he could not will himself to slip away again. A horde of thoughts and regrets battered at him. He thought about asking for more of the painkiller that had gotten him this far, but that would only postpone the inevitable.

He had to open his eyes and face what had happened to him.

Correction, he told himself. What he had done to himself.

Minor lacerations, the doctor had reported. A few cracked ribs. It was a good thing he had been wearing a high-quality helmet. Too bad none of his safety precautions could protect his spine.

Possible nerve damage, the doctor had said with a look on his face that chilled Dan to the center of his chest. The physician claimed he could not render a prognosis until Dan was transported to a major hospital for extensive neurological evaluation.

But the doctor's expression, so studiously bland and gentle, said, *Sorry, buddy. You'll never walk again.*

Dan insisted on two things. That the doctor keep his condition strictly confidential. And that Dan receive the largest legal dose of painkiller the doctor could, in good conscience, administer.

The physician agreed to both requests without hesitation.

But now, Dan was emerging from his narcotic fog, and he had some decisions to make. First, the lodge. The tribal council would help him. Maybe the winery would keep things afloat until the guests started coming. And hell, if it came to that, Dan still had his voice. He could record something new, though he'd look pretty ridiculous singing flat on his back.

And then there was Isabel.... The pain lanced like lightning through him. He barely had time to compose his thoughts before she stepped into the room.

He hated himself for putting that expression on her face—that look of terror and pity and shattering grief. Her skin was pale and looked tautly drawn across her cheekbones. Her hair was mussed as if she had passed her fingers through it repeatedly in agitation. Her narrow hands were held clasped in front of her.

"Hi," he said. "I just woke up."

She nodded and stood at the foot of the bed, her gaze moving slowly over the apparatus that held him immobile. He was reminded of a time when their roles had been reversed, when she had been the patient. That was the beginning of the end for them the first time. Now, once again, their parting would take place in a hospital room.

"I would've waited all night if I had to," she said. "Would've waited a lifetime."

Dan let out a slow sigh. The bitter irony of it all ate at him. He had brought her here to make her see that they still loved each other, that they could make it together. And she had realized it, but the revelation had come too late. He knew she would stick by him through whatever ordeals he had to face in the coming months.

But he would never let her shackle herself to him now.

"I guess I deserve an 'I told you so,'" he said.

"I'd never say that." She moistened her lips.

The thought of never again tasting that beautiful, kissable mouth nearly drew a roar of anguish from him.

"How are you?" she asked, as he knew she would. "No one will tell me a thing. Exactly what's hurt? What's broken?"

"Nothing that can't be fixed," he lied. "Next year at this time, I'll be back in the race."

"You can't mean you'd do it again."

"Sure, I would." He troweled on more lies, saying anything—*anything*—to drive her away, to save her from loving a broken man. "I never should have come to see you again. You were right all along. I can't change. I'll always be wild and reckless. I'd drive you crazy."

She looked stricken. Tears brimmed in her eyes. "You're making me crazy now. I came to tell you I'd stay with you—"

"It's no good. It didn't work for us the first time, and it won't work now. It was stupid of me to think it would."

"But—"

"Go back home, Isabel," he said in a hard-edged voice. "There's nothing for you here."

She stepped back from the bed, clutching her stomach as if he had struck her. She swept him with a horrified gaze, taking in the huge iron device holding his head, the stiff cage around his middle. "I'm not leaving you," she whispered.

"I won't let you stay. We can't make it together. What happened today just proves it."

The pain that flashed in her eyes made him want to reach out, to beg her to stay, but he forced himself to say, "I never should have found you again in the first place. I'm sorry for that."

She looked at him for a long time. He thought she might cry, but she didn't. She squared her shoulders and lifted her chin, looking both fierce and fragile. "I won't force myself on you."

"Goodbye, Isabel," Dan said.

And when she turned away and walked out the door, he added in the faintest of whispers, *"I love you."*

Chapter Eleven

"IT'S WONDERFUL to see all of you," Isabel said, and she meant it. Sitting at her favorite garden café, enjoying a perfect Indian-summer afternoon, she truly did mean it. Six months after the disastrous bridal shower, Connie and Lucia had come over to Bainbridge Island for lunch.

Connie handed her a cream stock envelope. Somehow, Isabel knew before opening it what she would find.

It was an invitation to Anthony's wedding.

"We figured you'd want to know," Lucia said.

"You're right." Isabel smiled at them. Even after she had broken off the engagement with Anthony, his sisters remained friends with her. And Anthony surprised her by coming through with a contract for Dan's lodge. By all reports, the team had a spectacular weekend, hosted by Clyde Looking and Theo Sohappy while Dan was still laid up.

"I'm pleased for Anthony," Isabel said with conviction.

Connie touched the rim of her wineglass to the rim of Isabel's. "We figured you would be. But what about you, sweetie?"

In an odd way, Isabel cherished the hurt that she lived with night and day, the hurt she had endured since last April, when Dan had ordered her out of his hospital room, out of his life. Sometimes, that pain was the only thing that reminded her she was alive. Early on, she had tried to call, but again and again he refused to speak to her.

"I'm all right," she said, looking down, tucking a silky lock of hair behind her ear. She'd gone natural with her hair for the first time since high school, letting it grow in straight and stark black instead of using chemical perms and colors. Idly, she noted the blast of the one-fifteen-ferry horn.

Summer sales at the plant nursery had broken records. Of the three new staff members she'd hired, two were Native Americans, and one was an expert on traditional Indian herbs.

In a burst of energy, she had totally redone her cottage. Over the bed hung her pride and joy—a Yakima mat woven with the design of a soaring eagle crest.

On a good day, she avoided thinking of Dan for whole minutes at a stretch.

But most days, she dwelled on the time she had spent at his lodge, remembering every moment, polishing it up in her memory until it gleamed with the soft patina of a lost dream.

She had stayed in touch with the Sohappys. They told her little of Dan, only that he had gone to a hospital in Olympia for therapy and then returned home. The lodge was prospering thanks to the winery that had sponsored the race and to record summer visitors. Word-of-mouth recommendations kept the place booked solid.

From Dan, there was nothing but silence.

Isabel gulped back her wine and tried to focus on what Lucia was saying, but a faint sound kept humming beneath the murmur of conversation.

She gazed down the length of the café garden. Most of the plants had come from her nursery. The flower beds and trees burst with fall color.

The roaring grew louder, more urgent. Lucia stopped talking. Isabel stopped breathing as unbearable anticipation built in her. And then, right where the gravel driveway turned off from the road, he appeared.

He was an image out of her most intimate dreams. Clad in black leather. A bandanna around his head. Inky, flowing hair. Mirror-lens sunglasses. The Harley beneath him bucking and spitting gravel like a wild animal.

"It's Mr. Testosterone again," Connie murmured as the machine roared up the terraced garden path.

Isabel stood, clutching her wineglass in fingers numb with shock. The apparition skidded to a halt, jerked the 750 onto its kickstand and walked toward her. Long, loose strides with a limp that favored his right leg. Tall boots crunching on the path. Gold earring winking in one ear.

"This sort of déjà vu I can live with," Lucia whispered.

He yanked off the mirror glasses and stared at Isabel. His dark eyes dragged down the length of her, and she felt the touch of his gaze like a caress.

The wineglass slipped from her fingers, struck the grass and rolled under the table. "What are you doing here?" she asked.

He gave her the old cocky grin, the expression that used to make her go weak in the knees.

It still worked.

She was still drawn to his aura of seductive danger, the faint sulkiness of his full lips, the powerful body as well tuned as his Harley. The lean hips and broad shoulders that made her body flush with memories.

"I came to see you," he said. "And to say I'm sorry."

Her cheeks heated with stinging color as she moved away from the table. "'I'm sorry'?" she echoed. "You banished me from your life, and you think two words will cover it?"

"No," he said in a low, rough voice. "It'll take me a lifetime to make it up to you."

"You can start now," she said, folding her arms over her middle, not daring to let herself hope.

He gave her that lazy, Sunday-morning, stay-in-bed-all-day grin. "I figure it's now or never, Isabel."

She felt the rapt fascination of her friends, and from the corner of her eye, she saw Connie jerk her head, urging her to go with Dan.

Still uncertain, she took his hand, and they walked toward the Harley. She felt the unevenness of his gait. Rather than detracting from his physical grace, the limp shifted his weight in a way that was somehow wildly sexy.

He held out a helmet for her. She stepped back, dropping his hand and studying him. For the first time, she noticed a few extra lines around his eyes and mouth and a leanness in his face that had not been there before.

"I won't go with you until you tell me the truth, Dan. I want to know the real reason you stayed away so long. Why you never called." She eyed his right leg. "Just how bad were your injuries?"

He started to put on his mirror glasses, then seemed to think better of it. "Not so bad they didn't heal, Isabel."

"What about what you did to us?" she asked, forming the words around the ache of tears in her throat. "Will that heal?"

"Saying I'm sorry is only the beginning. When I sent you away, it was like cutting off an arm. Cutting out my heart, maybe. It was stupid, running you off when I had never needed you more."

"Then why?" she persisted. "I need to know."

"I thought I'd never walk again. I didn't want to saddle you with that."

She remembered the way he had looked in the hospital bed, immobilized by a stainless-steel scaffold. Realization hit her like a thunderclap—it hadn't been anger she'd seen in his eyes, but fear. "I can't believe you thought your physical condition would make a difference in the way I feel, Dan."

"Like I said, it was stupid. *I* was stupid. But I've had a lot of time to learn a few things."

"What sort of things?"

"That I don't need to take risks, to go looking for danger, to hide from my feelings. My reckless rebel days are over."

A rush of elation rose through her, and her mouth curved into a smile. "Well, it's about damned time. I'll hold you to that."

"I know." Without warning, he set down the helmet and pulled her against him so that she was engulfed by the textures and scents that had haunted her dreams all summer.

From the corner of her eye, Isabel saw Connie briskly fanning her face.

"Forgive me," Dan said, brushing his lips over hers, "for wanting to make sure I *could* heal before I came back to you."

"That *is* stupid," she whispered, entranced by the way he was kissing her, so lightly and gently that her head swam. "You should've told me."

"I'm telling you now," he said, still kissing her almost senseless.

"Telling me what?" she managed to ask.

"That I love you. That I want us to get married. Have babies. Grow plants and build picket fences and plan fund-raisers and go fishing—"

"Yes," she said, sliding her fingers through his long, silky hair, letting the bandanna drift to the ground.

"Yes to what?" he asked.

"To all of the above."

Dear Reader,

I don't think there is woman alive who at one time or another hasn't wondered what life would have been like if she'd ended up with another man: the one who got away, the one she just couldn't live with—or without— or the first one who truly touched her heart.

For most of us, first love takes place in high school. And though we mature and change a lot over the years, there is always something special about that experience. I wanted to write about those feelings in my story, *The Forgotten Bride,* and contrast the inexpressible joy of first love with the deeper satisfaction of mature love. Caroline and Reese run the gamut of emotions, from desire to contempt, and from bitterness to forgiveness. I hope you enjoy reading about their trials and tribulations as much as I enjoyed writing about them.

Janice Kaiser

THE FORGOTTEN BRIDE

Janice Kaiser

Chapter One

IT WAS her least favorite day of the year. And she thought it bitterly ironic that it should fall just before Memorial Day—a time when people went out of their way to remember. For most of Chicago, May 28 was an ordinary day. Sometimes it was hot; sometimes it rained. For Caroline Parker, it was a day she wished to forget. But there was no escaping it. Every year had a May 28.

"You okay?" Kitty said when she called first thing that morning.

"Yeah, I'm fine," Caroline told her.

Kitty Oslack was her best friend, and the only one who knew about May 28. "You sure?"

"Absolutely."

"I thought maybe we could go to lunch today."

Caroline couldn't help smiling. "You mean you want me to give you indigestion, like last year?"

"Somebody else's tears don't give me indigestion, Caroline. My own, maybe, but not somebody else's."

"It's sweet of you to think of me, but I'm okay. Last year was an aberration. Honest."

Strictly speaking, that wasn't quite true. The only reason last year had been different was that it was the first time she'd talked about it. Poor Kitty was dumb-founded when she had told her.

"We've known each other for, what, six years, and you're just now telling me this?" her friend had said. "Why on earth did you wait so long?"

"Because I'd rather not think about it," Caroline had told her. "And why would I talk about something I don't even want to think about?"

For the past fourteen years, whenever May rolled around, Caroline would inevitably start to feel the pressure build. By the end of the month, it was un-bearable. Some years she'd stay in bed on the 28th. Other years she'd work herself into a state of exhaus-tion. But last year Kitty had convinced her the best strategy would be to meet her feelings head-on. So Caroline had promised not to hide from the truth any-more.

"If not lunch, how about dinner?" Kitty said. "Or we can take in a flick. Daniel Day Lewis has to be on the big screen somewhere. If not him, Mel Gibson."

"Drooling over men is not my idea of a good way to spend May 28," she said. "Inventory will keep me busy. I probably won't even have time to think about it."

"Then how about if we do something tonight? For my sake," Kitty said. "Come to my place around seven. I'll fix spaghetti and we can take it from there."

"All right," she said with a laugh. "Spaghetti at your place."

"Feel free to bring a date."

"Yeah, sure, smart aleck. And I suppose you want me to bring someone for you, too."

"Wouldn't hurt."

At thirty-two, she was just a year younger than Kitty. Though her friend often moaned about the trials of spinsterhood, being alone didn't bother Caroline. She'd been burned once, and she didn't want to go through that again.

Ever.

Of course, few women reached thirty without getting hurt at least once, so she knew she wasn't unique. But her experience with Reese Claybourne had caused much more pain than the average broken relationship. He had given her his love, a baby, a ring, and then he'd taken them back, one by one, until she'd been left single, childless and alone. Not many seventeen-year-olds had been put through that particular gauntlet.

But time was a great healer. Over the years her memories of Reese had faded. She rarely thought of him anymore, though she knew she'd never forget Jennifer.

Every time Caroline saw a girl the age of her daughter, she remembered. And each year when May 28— Jennifer's birthday—rolled around, the pain would be almost unbearable. The loss was a scar on her soul.

Caroline sighed and glanced at the clock on the microwave. She didn't have much time, so she poured the last of her coffee down the sink, rinsed her cup and went to brush her teeth. The green eyes in the bathroom mirror were tired and puffy. Her soft brown hair was limp. Her skin lacked its usual glow. Part of it was not sleeping; the rest had to be mental. Late May was always the low point of her year.

Caroline dabbed her mouth with a hand towel and put on a smudge of lip gloss. That would have to do. At least she was presentable.

As she'd often told Kitty, owning her own business gave her a few benefits many people didn't enjoy—mainly that she didn't have to please anyone but herself, and her customers, of course. It also meant that Caroline worked harder than most people. But she loved her work and took it seriously, so she didn't mind.

Caroline had sunk the bulk of the money she'd inherited from her father into her gift gallery, Portabella, and she had worked darned hard to make it a success.

When she stepped out the front door of her condo, Caroline found that it was a warm and humid day. Thunderheads were building to the west. She'd heard on the radio that showers were forecast, so she made sure her umbrella was still in the back of her Honda, the car she'd bought when her dad's Ford finally died.

It wasn't far to her shop, but she hadn't even gotten as far as the Cherry Hills country club before it started raining.

It had been overcast on the day Jennifer was born, too. Caroline had a vague recollection of staring out the window at a gray sky, wondering if anyone would come to see her. No one did. Not even her father, though the home he'd sent her to was only a few miles away, on the north side of Chicago.

Caroline didn't like thinking about the birth, or that all too brief moment when the doctor had set the squirming newborn on her belly. Her eyes had filled with tears as she looked down at Jennifer. She touched the baby's cheek and her tiny hand, then they carried her daughter off, never to be seen again.

Her father came for her three days later. The ride back home was tense. "It will have a good life," Jim Parker said. "They've got money. That takes care of a lot."

"It" was the way he referred to the baby. The Claybournes were always "they." Her father handled problems by not talking about them. And to the day he died, that never changed.

The rain was coming down harder. Visibility was bad, made worse by the tears that poured down Caroline's face. She didn't want to hate her father or be bitter, but it was hard not to feel that way at times like this. Even so, when he'd died, there'd been forgiveness in her heart.

Caroline came to the shopping center on Vollmer Road where Portabella was located. She parked her car and got out, thankful for her umbrella. As she neared the door of her shop, she saw a girl huddled in the entry, using the protection of the overhang to stay dry. A backpack was at her feet, and the collar of her windbreaker was turned up at her neck.

If the girl wanted refuge from the rain, she could have gone only a few doors up and stepped inside the drugstore. Chances were she was from Homewood-Flossmoor High. Sometimes kids came over after school. In large numbers they could be a nuisance, though the isolated one who showed up during school hours was usually just cutting class and did no harm.

The teenager watched Caroline approach, a vaguely apprehensive look on her face. For a brief moment, Caroline wondered if the girl was up to something. Shoplifting was a problem for many stores in the area, though kids didn't come into Portabella often. Wrong kind of merchandise.

"Hi," Caroline said, coming to the door. "Get caught in the shower?"

The girl, whose dark hair was pulled back in a ponytail, nodded and seemed a little embarrassed. "Yeah."

She moved to the side as Caroline lowered her umbrella and took out her keys to unlock the door.

"I was looking in your window," the girl said. "You have some cute things."

The remark struck Caroline as curiously politic, especially from the mouth of a teenager. "Thank you." She turned the dead bolt.

"You own the place?" she asked.

Another surprising remark. Caroline glanced at the girl. "Yes, I do."

"Looks like a nice store. I saw by the sign you were about to open. Thought I'd browse, if you don't mind."

Caroline looked into green eyes that were not too different from her own. That, combined with the girl's age, made her think of Jennifer. The empty feeling in her stomach was stronger than usual, but that wasn't surprising. It was May 28, after all.

"I don't mind," Caroline said. "It's what I'm in business for. Come on in. Just let me get the lights on."

Caroline proceeded to the back of the shop, a wary feeling going through her. There was something awfully strange about a kid waiting in the rain to get into a gift shop like Portabella. Teenagers rarely bought upscale items or antique pieces.

The possibility of a robbery flashed through Caroline's mind. The girl's youth did not make it impossible. Only six months earlier the doughnut shop up the street had been robbed by two fifteen-year-olds pretending to have a gun. But a gift shop, especially at opening time, when there wasn't much cash around, was not a logical target.

She looked back from the counter at the rear of the store and saw the girl standing inside the door, her backpack dangling from her hand as she waited for the lights to come on. Caroline stepped into the back room, flipped on the overhead light, opened the light panel and turned on the shop lights. Returning to the sales room, she found the girl still at the door, gazing around.

Portabella was a first-rate boutique. The store had been written up in the suburban section of the *Tribune*. Art glass and giftware were her specialties, but she had a full line of upscale home accessories.

Over the years, Caroline had learned the importance of presentation. There was a lovely walnut armoire she'd gotten at an estate auction. The antique was for sale, but she used it to display her collection of custom-made throw pillows and cashmere throws. She also had a tasteful display of silk and dried-flower wreaths and centerpieces. Mrs. Mason, the woman she'd bought the shop from, had mixed antiques with newer merchandise and Caroline carried on the tradition, though she limited her stock of truly valuable antiques to small tables and the odd chair or sideboard.

The girl began moving slowly through the shop, taking things in with a mysterious reverence that seemed odd. And she also kept looking at Caroline in a way that aroused suspicion.

"Are you looking for anything in particular?" Caroline asked.

"I was thinking of a gift for my mother."

"Oh, how nice. A special occasion?"

"A birthday."

"Well, let me see," Caroline said, coming out from behind the counter. "Perhaps you can give me an idea what your budget is."

"I've got plenty of money. Anything up to a hundred dollars will be okay."

Caroline's eyebrows rose. "Well, that's a generous amount. It gives us quite a few options." She led the way to the armoire. "Does your mother like practical gifts?"

The girl hesitated. "I'm not sure."

Caroline blinked. "You aren't?"

"I live with my father."

"I see." *Just like Jennifer,* Caroline thought, then shook herself. "Well, something small and pretty is always appreciated—something in the it's-the-thought-that-counts category."

The girl laughed, and Caroline thought there was something about her mouth that was familiar. Almost as if she'd seen her before. *Don't be ridiculous, Caroline,* she told herself. *May 28 always makes you a little crazy.*

"Do you live in the area?" Caroline asked.

The girl hesitated. "No...I'm visiting...relatives," she said. "Uh...my name's Janine Wilson." She extended her hand in a self-assured manner that belied her age.

"And I'm Caroline Parker." She took the girl's hand. "I understand now why you aren't in school."

"We finish early at home."

"Where are you from, Janine?"

"Uh...out of state."

The girl was being evasive. And though she seemed harmless enough, that aroused Caroline's suspicions again. But Caroline kept her public mask in place and gestured toward a table of collectibles.

"You might find something here you like." She picked up a small enamel box. "These Battersea boxes make a wonderful gift for someone with discriminating taste. I have two left from Mother's Day." She handed the dark green box to the girl.

Janine looked at it, running her thumb over the word Mother written in flowing script on the lid.

"This one is pink, if you prefer a softer color," Caroline said, picking up another box. "They're both seventy-five dollars."

Janine glanced at it and shook her head. "No, I like this one. My mother's eyes are green—like yours."

Caroline swallowed hard. "It's my favorite, too."

Janine gave her the oddest look, her face hauntingly familiar. Caroline contemplated her, her mind full of questions that she shouldn't ask. So she kept to business.

"Would you like to take it?" she asked.

"Yes, I think I would."

"I'm sure your mother will be pleased."

They returned to the counter. Caroline removed the price tag from the bottom of the box, watching from the corner of her eye as Janine removed a wallet from a pocket of her backpack.

"May I wrap it for you?" Caroline asked.

"Sure."

Caroline got a small carton to put the box in and showed Janine several types of paper to choose from.

"You pick," Janine said, pulling a hundred-dollar bill from a wallet that was fat with bills.

Caroline began wrapping the gift, masking her surprise at the display of cash.

After a minute of silence the girl spoke. "Do you have any kids?"

Caroline sighed. *Why, today of all days, did someone have to ask that?* She was about to give her stock answer, when she remembered her promise to Kitty to meet her fears head-on. "Yes," she said. "One child. A daughter I've never seen."

"What happened?"

"Actually I prefer not to talk about it." She measured a length of gold ribbon.

"Sorry, I didn't mean to be impolite."

Caroline forced a smile. "Oh, you weren't impolite. Today's just not a very good day for me, that's all."

"I understand."

She finished the ribbon, sharpened a corner crease in the paper with her fingers and held the gift up for inspection.

"Nice," Janine said. "Really pretty."

Caroline wrote up the sales slip and took the girl's money, giving her change from the register.

"So, now I have something for my mother," Janine said. "Thanks."

"Thank you."

They looked at each other. A long moment of silence passed as Caroline thought of Jennifer, her own daughter. *This could be her,* she thought. She had an almost uncontrollable urge to say something about her pain. For a moment or two she fought it, then she felt her will snap like a dry twig.

"I'm upset because this is my daughter's birthday," she finally said, her eyes filling rapidly with tears.

"What happened to her?"

Caroline knew she had no right to dump her emotional baggage on this girl, but she couldn't help herself. "Her father's family took her away right after she was born. I've never seen her since."

"And now you're sorry?"

"*Sorry!* Hardly a day's gone by that I haven't thought about her."

"So, where's your daughter now?"

"New Mexico, I think. I'm not even sure."

"Don't you write to her?"

Caroline shook her head. "No, I can't."

"Why not?"

Caroline opened her mouth to answer, but the words weren't there. What was she doing? Why was she dragging this poor girl into her problems? Why was she torturing *herself* this way?

"It's a long story," she finally managed to say.

"My mother never asked to see me, either," Janine said solemnly, her eyes glistening. "I wish she had."

It was all Caroline could do to keep from breaking down again. She wanted the girl to leave. She wanted to retreat from her pain and pull back inside her cocoon.

"How old are you?" Caroline asked, biting her lip.

"Fourteen."

"That's how old Jennifer is," she said, her voice cracking. "Fourteen, and I don't even know what she looks like."

Tears were rolling down Janine's face. She wiped them away with her sleeve. Picking up the present, she examined it briefly, then pushed it across the counter toward Caroline.

"Here, this is for you."

Caroline blinked. "Wha—What about your mother?"

"I'd like for you to have it."

Caroline's head was spinning. "If you've changed your mind, I'll give you your money back." She turned blindly to the register.

Janine shook her head. "No, that's not what I mean. It's a gift for you."

Caroline stood dumbfounded, knowing what the girl was going to say before she said it. Realizing that she'd known all along.

"I'm not really Janine Wilson," the girl blurted out. "She's a friend of mine back home in Santa Fe. And the birthday I was talking about isn't my mom's, it's mine." She hesitated. "I'm Jennifer," she said with a trembling voice. "Jennifer Claybourne."

Chapter Two

CAROLINE FELT her knees buckle. She grabbed the counter as she tried to take it all in. This child was her daughter? Could it be true?

"You're...*my* Jennifer?"

The girl nodded, biting her lip. Caroline's brain was still struggling to process what she was hearing. Surely she'd heard wrong. This couldn't be happening. Could it? Then she realized what it was she'd seen in the face of the young stranger—a reflection of herself.

Caroline felt her way around the counter, keeping her eyes on Jennifer. The girl no longer seemed threatening. Nor did she seem like a self-assured young woman. She was just a child. *Her* child.

There was desperation in Jennifer's eyes as Caroline reached out and touched her face. Then they embraced, Caroline stroking Jennifer's head as they sobbed. Finally they pulled back to look into each other's eyes. "It's really you," Caroline murmured.

Jennifer nodded and laughed as she cried.

"What are you doing here?"

She wiped her runny nose on the sleeve of her jacket. "It's a long story."

Caroline took her arm and led her around the counter to the desk. She took a handful of tissues from the drawer and pressed them into Jennifer's hand, then took a few more for herself.

"Here, sit down," she said, turning the desk chair for the girl to sit. Then she pulled up another chair. They sat facing each other, wiping their eyes, smiling. "I've thought of this happening a million times."

"Me, too."

"How did you find me?"

"I looked in Dad's papers and found the address where you'd lived when I was born. The lady living there told me about your store."

"Mrs. Petersen. She's a customer."

"That's what she said. She didn't know where you lived now, and there were a bunch of Parkers in the phone book. So I came here."

"How did you get to Chicago?"

"On the bus."

"All the way from New Mexico?"

Jennifer nodded. "Yeah."

"Well, why didn't your father warn me?"

"Because he didn't know."

Caroline was stunned. "You mean you did this on your own?"

Jennifer nodded again.

She considered the situation, suddenly realizing that there was a lot more going on than she'd suspected at first. "Did you run away?"

Jennifer looked uncomfortable. "No. Not exactly. I came to see you. You *are* my mother, after all."

Caroline took her daughter's hands as they looked into each other's eyes. They were each biting their lips, mirroring each other.

"You're so pretty," Caroline whispered, "just the way I imagined."

"And so are you," Jennifer said, choking back a sob.

Caroline had to struggle to keep from breaking down again. She shook her head. "I still can't believe this."

"Me either."

"I feel so . . . unprepared."

"Yeah, I know."

Caroline reached out and caressed the girl's cheek—just as she'd touched the cheek of her newborn exactly fourteen years ago. "My God," she murmured.

"I've got to ask you something," Jennifer said. "Why did you give me away?"

Caroline felt her stomach knot. "I didn't give you away. You were taken from me."

Her eyes rounded. "How could they do that?"

"I was only seventeen and didn't have much choice. They had my father's cooperation. And I kept telling myself that it was for the best. Reese was your father.

You wouldn't be going with strangers. But by the time I stopped believing all that, it was too late."

"What do you mean, too late?"

"By the time I was old enough to do anything about it—out of college and financially independent—you were four or five. I had to decide whether or not it would be fair for me to disrupt your life. I didn't want to be selfish."

"Is that true, or are you trying to make me feel better?"

"It's true, Jennifer. After my father died, I asked the lawyer who handled everything to enquire about your situation. I was told your dad had recently remarried and that you were living with him and his wife. That meant you were in a stable family."

"Yeah, some family. Sandy is a real bitch."

Caroline blinked. "But what about your dad? Don't you love him?"

"Yes, but he doesn't understand me."

She squeezed Jennifer's hands. "I can't tell you how sad that makes me."

Jennifer lowered her eyes. "To be honest, I was pretty mad at you, too, even though I didn't know you. I figured you must have been worse than Sandy—otherwise they never would have taken me away from you."

Caroline felt her stomach knot. This was exactly what she'd been afraid of—that Reese and his parents would put her in the worst possible light, and she wouldn't be able to defend herself. "What did your father tell you about me?"

"He said you were really young when I was born and weren't able to keep me. He said you didn't have a mother to help you, that she'd died when you were little, and that's why I went to live with his parents."

"Did he say I was a bad person?"

Jennifer shook her head. "No, he just said it was all a big mistake."

Again Caroline felt a surge of anger. Reese had been a big mistake, all right, one that filled her with resentment to this day. But there was no way she'd tell Jennifer that. The very last thing she wanted to do was hurt her own child, so she held her tongue.

"Did your father tell you that we were married?" she asked.

Jennifer's mouth sagged. "You and Dad?"

"Yes. When we discovered I was carrying you, we ran off to Kentucky and got married. When our parents found out, they were livid. Your grandparents flew up here, and there was a terrible scene. They had your dad on a plane back to New Mexico before we even knew what was happening. We hardly got to say goodbye."

"And you never saw him again?"

"No. After the marriage was annulled, my father made me write him a letter saying I didn't ever want to see him again."

"That's really mean."

"My father meant well, but he was a bitter man. He never got over my mother's death and he became obsessive about me. I wasn't strong enough to fight him."

Jennifer reflected, her sweet face touched with sadness.

"So, things aren't so good between you and your dad and stepmother," Caroline said.

"Oh, they got a divorce when I was nine. Sandy's been gone for a long time."

"Then your dad's alone?"

"He is now that I left," Jennifer said.

The way she said it almost made Caroline feel sorry for Reese. And that was odd, because he'd been her nemesis for years and years. It was strange to think of him abandoned and alone. The way she'd been for years and years now.

"What about your grandparents?"

"Grandpa died a few years ago, and Grandma lives in town. I see her lots. She's always been nice to me. But I'm kind of mad at her now, too."

"Why?"

"Because she takes Dad's side on everything."

Caroline was beginning to see there was serious trouble at home. This visit of Jennifer's was motivated by more than just a desire to see her mother, more than simple curiosity. There was a deeper problem.

"And I gather your father doesn't know you're here," she said.

Jennifer shook her head. "No. It's none of his business."

Caroline heard the bitterness in Jennifer's voice. It was clear that her daughter was running from something. "Would you like to talk about it?" she asked gently.

Jennifer considered the question. "Maybe later."

Caroline nodded. "I guess there's still a lot of time separating us, isn't there?"

"Yeah. But I came because I wanted to see what you're like."

"I'm glad you did," Caroline said, patting her daughter's hands. "I hope I won't be a disappointment."

"You're a lot more normal than I expected."

"I'm pleased to hear that . . . I guess."

"I was afraid you'd be strange or awful. I even thought you might be mad at me."

"Why would I be mad?"

Jennifer regarded her closely for several moments. "Would it be okay if I stayed here for a while? Don't feel you have to let me or anything. But it'd be nice if I could for a few days, if you don't mind."

"I'd love for you to stay with me, but I'm concerned about how your father would feel about it."

"We don't have to tell him I'm here."

"I'm not so sure. He's undoubtedly worried. And the police may be looking for you, too."

Jennifer's expression turned wary. "So, what do you want to do?"

Caroline stroked her chin. "I think we ought to tell him you're here. We can also say you'd like to stay for a few days. I can't see why he'd object to that, do you? After all, you're fourteen."

"Yeah, but Dad's been pretty crazy recently."

Caroline saw her opportunity. "Why? What's the problem, anyway?"

Jennifer gave her a tentative look, lowering her eyes. "We had a big fight."

"What about?"

"Carlos."

REESE CLAYBOURNE RODE east on Calle Estado in his new Ford pickup, gripping the steering wheel like a bronco rider clinging to the reins, barely aware of how fast he was driving. It had been that way for four days now, ever since Jennifer had disappeared. He had been so distracted, he'd hardly remembered to eat.

Coming to Bishop's Lodge Road, he turned north. The Mendez place, he'd been told, was ten or twelve miles outside of Santa Fe—only twenty miles or so from his family's ranch, close in geographical terms, but a world apart in most other senses.

He'd been assured by the head of the state police himself that the Mendezes had no information on Jennifer's whereabouts, but they were about the only people in the county he hadn't spoken with, so he figured why leave a rock unturned? Hell, there wasn't anything he wouldn't do to get his precious child safely home.

As he drove, Reese searched his mind as he had so many times the past few days, wondering what he might have done differently. Jennifer was far too young to be involved with a boy of eighteen, so he couldn't give her his blessing. Carlos was decent enough, but Reese knew what it was like to be in love at that age. And Jennifer wasn't even as old as Caroline had been. Three years made a lot of difference at that age, even if seventeen wasn't exactly grown-up, either.

It was not surprising that Caroline had come to mind a great deal the past few days. There was even bitter irony in the fact that he should find himself in a position not too different from Jim Parker's fifteen years earlier. During those god-awful days in Chicago, he'd hated Caroline's father but he'd also resented his own dad for using the Parkers the way he had.

"Be thankful you have parents who are willing and able to bail you out of this mess," his father had told him. "You should be thanking your lucky stars your

mother's willing to spare that girl the burden of raising a child, not to mention giving you another chance
at life. What we're doing might seem cruel now, but no
two kids have been given a bigger gift, believe me."

At the time, Dan Claybourne made something
wrong seem entirely reasonable. Caroline would be
able to get her education at their expense, sparing her
father the financial and emotional burden. She could
marry and have a family when she was ready for it.
"Backing off, that's your gift to her, son," his father
argued. Still, Reese wasn't convinced until he got the
letter from Caroline saying she never wanted to see him
again. "We both know the only reason we married was
because I was pregnant."

That he couldn't deny. Oh, he was sure he loved her.
But a teenage summer romance was hardly a basis for
marriage. If that wasn't clear then, it became clear soon
enough. By the time he was in his second semester of
college, Caroline Parker was just another sad chapter
in his life. Not that he forgot her—his guilt wouldn't
let him, and Jennifer was a constant reminder. But that
emotional dash to Kentucky to get married had been
the foolish act of children. If hindsight hadn't proved
that, Jennifer's rebellion certainly brought home the
point that teenagers could show phenomenal lack of
judgment. Maybe fate was paying him back.

Leaving the outskirts of Santa Fe, he knew it was no
time to dwell on the past. The life of a young girl hung

in the balance. Even if the Mendez family didn't know where Jennifer was, their son had to have an inkling. Deep down, Carlos had to be a factor, somehow, some way.

The larger homes and ranchettes along Highway 590 had given way to the more modest rancheros and chicken farms, as some folks called them. Many, though not all, were owned by Mexican families. Reese had looked into the Mendezes when Carlos first started coming around. The father, Raul, drove a truck for the state highway department, and the mother worked part-time as a domestic while raising five kids. The oldest daughter was in college, the first in her family to make it. Carlos had plans for college, too, but in Reese's one conversation with the boy, he discovered the kid was unfocused. Carlos was thinking of a hitch in the army to get his education paid for, which seemed to Reese to be a pretty decent idea.

Over the past month things had changed between Jennifer and Carlos. Their relationship seemed to transform from casual dating to something more serious. It took a while for him to catch on, but the kids seemed to be headed in the direction he and Caroline had gone.

"Why can't you leave me alone!" Jennifer had screamed when he told her he didn't want her seeing Carlos anymore. "You're ruining my life!" Those words led to a crying fit and Jennifer's day-long exile in her room.

"The girl's got her mother's spirit," his mother told him when they talked on the phone about Jennifer. "You've got to be firm with her, honey."

Jennifer's adolescence had taught him that the line between firmness and tyranny was not easily drawn. Ironically his major concern from the time she first showed interest in boys was that history would repeat itself. It seemed now that was exactly what was happening—or something nearly as distressing.

Reese slowed his truck to check the number on the next few mailboxes along the edge of the highway. Coming to the Mendez mailbox, Reese pulled off the road and went along the dirt driveway leading to the house. It was adobe and not large, though not as modest as many he'd seen farther back in the hills. He parked behind an old panel truck and climbed out. Three or four chickens were pecking in the small patch of lawn. An old gray cat lay on the porch. Reese pushed his Stetson back on his head and ambled with long strides toward the front door, bypassing a tipped-over tricycle along the way.

A plump woman of about his own age, or perhaps a bit older, met him at the door. She looked at him suspiciously with large dark eyes. "*Señor?*"

Reese removed his hat. "Morning, ma'am. My name's Reese Claybourne. I was wondering if I might speak with Carlos."

The woman's expression turned grim. "My son is not home."

"When do you think I might find him in?"

"One minute, please. My husband, he will speak with you." She pushed the door open. "Please come in."

"Thank you, ma'am, but I won't intrude on your family, considering I've come uninvited. I'll wait here, if that's all right."

"As you wish."

She went inside. Reese put his hat back on and looked back across the highway at the snowcapped Sangre de Cristo Mountains off to the northeast. The high desert could be as inhospitable as it was beautiful. Having been born into relative affluence, and having spent his life in a big, comfortable ranch house, he always admired and wondered at the people who survived a Rocky Mountain winter in these little adobe houses, some of which didn't even have plumbing and running water.

Inside the house he could hear a TV. His Spanish was good enough to make out that the program was a soap opera.

Two small children poked their heads around the corner of the house. When he glanced at them, they giggled and disappeared. After another minute or two the screen door opened, and a slender man with a belly that protruded slightly over his belt stepped onto the porch. He had on jeans and boots, and a fresh white shirt. He had a thin mustache, and his jet black hair was neatly combed.

"Good morning, Mr. Claybourne. I am Raul Mendez. My wife, she says you want to speak with our son Carlos."

Reese took the man's outstretched hand. "Yes, Mr. Mendez. I was hoping he might help me find my daughter. She's been missing for several days now. Since they're friends, I thought Carlos might know something that would be useful."

"Yes, I am aware. The police have been here twice. Carlos knows nothing."

"Would you mind if I spoke with him?"

"No, but he's in the south and won't be back for some days. I had a call from him last night. He's with relatives."

Reese noticed a smudge of shaving soap on Raul Mendez's ear and realized he'd probably been shaving. "Is he aware Jennifer's missing?"

"He thought she would leave home because she was very angry, but he doesn't know where she went."

"It isn't possible they might be together?"

"I asked Carlos this, and he swore to me he does not know where your daughter is. I believe this is true. My son does not lie to me."

"I'm sure he doesn't, Mr. Mendez, but you can imagine my anxiety."

"I have two daughters myself, Mr. Claybourne."

"Then you know."

"Yes, but if Carlos knows nothing, he knows nothing."

Reese looked off at the distant mountains, then scratched his neck. "Would you have any objection if I spoke with the boy?"

"Carlos will come home in a few days. I am not sure when, but I will have him come to speak with you."

"I'd be much obliged, Mr. Mendez. Well, forgive me for intruding. My apologies to your wife."

"Thank you."

Reese turned and headed for his truck. He hadn't gone more than a few steps before Raul Mendez called to him. Reese stopped and faced the man.

"I don't know if it means something," he said, "but Carlos told me that the last time he saw your daughter she was very emotional and spoke of her mother."

"Her *mother?*"

"That was what he said."

Reese pondered the news, thinking there must be a mistake. Jennifer hadn't spoken about her mother in months, though he'd sensed that as she grew older, what had happened was becoming more of an issue. He nodded.

"Thank you."

"Good luck, *señor.*"

Reese saluted the man with a casual wave and got back in his truck. He backed to the highway.

Instead of returning to Santa Fe, he decided to go to the ranch. As he drove, he thought about Raul Mendez's comment about Caroline. Jennifer couldn't be with her. She had no idea how to get hold of her. Besides, Caroline would have called if Jennifer had showed up in Chicago. On the other hand, how could he be sure?

CAROLINE WATCHED Jennifer look around her small but well-decorated living room. After a moment her daughter turned toward her and smiled.

"It's really nice."

"I'm glad you like it."

Caroline had decided to close up her shop and take Jennifer home. After waiting years to see her daughter, there was no way she'd put her on the back burner till closing time. Besides, her customers were loyal. If they missed her, they'd come back. She gestured toward the small brown suede sofa.

"Make yourself at home and I'll get you something to drink. What would you like? Orange juice? Milk?"

"Do you have coffee?" Jennifer asked.

"Coffee?"

"Dad always had some on the stove whenever he was home, so I started drinking it last winter—in the mornings, anyway."

"What kind of food does he feed you?"

Jennifer laughed. "I wasn't neglected. I always got vegetables."

"But did you eat them?"

"Sometimes."

Caroline wagged her finger at the girl, then caught herself. "Lord, I'm sounding like a mother, aren't I?"

"You *are* a mother."

Caroline went over, took the girl's head and kissed her on the forehead. "Yes, and it feels wonderful."

"For me, too."

Caroline patted her cheek, emotion welling up again. "At the risk of sounding too much like a mother, I really think I should call your father."

Jennifer's expression turned sullen.

"Unless you'd rather do it yourself," Caroline said.

"No, you can . . . I guess."

"He'll be relieved to know you're safe. I'm sure he's been having visions of you dead in a ditch somewhere."

"No, he thinks I'm with Carlos. And to tell you the truth, I'm glad. He deserves to worry about that."

"I'm sure he loves you, Jennifer."

The girl's expression confirmed Caroline's suspicions that this crisis was no small thing. Caroline put on a pot of coffee, then she got a pad so she could write down the number she was to call.

"I don't know whether he'll be at our house in town or at the ranch," Jennifer said, "so I'll give you both numbers. My guess is he's at the ranch."

Caroline jotted down the numbers, then went to her room to make the call. She'd been so focused on dealing with Jennifer and seeing to her welfare that she hadn't thought a lot about Reese. As she sat on her bed and picked up the bedside phone, she remembered with a sick feeling that the last time she'd spoken with him she was seventeen.

She took a deep breath and dialed the number at the ranch. As it rang, her heart started pounding. After about four rings, a woman with a Spanish accent answered.

"Is Reese there, please?"

"One moment."

There was a pause, then Caroline heard the woman's voice.

"For you, *señor*, it is a woman."

Those words made Caroline wonder about the women in Reese's life. Jennifer had said that he was single, but she hadn't said anything about his love life. He'd been a charmer at eighteen. There was every reason to believe he still was, though of course she had no way to be sure.

As she waited, her mouth went dry. Her fingers trembled. She heard someone taking the receiver on the other end, then his voice.

"This is Reese."

She forced a careful breath. "Reese...it's Caroline. Caroline Parker."

There was dead silence. It seemed to last forever. Then he said, "She's there."

"Yes," Caroline replied, "she's here."

Chapter Three

"IS SHE ALL RIGHT?"

"Yes," Caroline said, drawing an uneven breath, "she's fine."

"Thank God."

There was a silence on the line. Caroline didn't know why, but she was about to burst into tears. This was a lot harder than she had thought.

"What happened?" Reese asked. "Did she just show up on your doorstep?"

"At my shop, yes."

"How'd she know where to find you? It would have taken me some effort."

"She seems to be resourceful."

Another silence.

"I'm sorry this happened, Caroline," he said. "I take full responsibility."

What could she say to that? She didn't want an apology. Didn't he realize what this meant to her, what an emotional roller coaster she'd been through?

"I...hope it wasn't too traumatic," he said, his voice clearly apologetic.

"I wasn't prepared—let's put it that way."

"I'm really sorry." He cleared his throat. "Listen, I'll come pick her up right away. I've got access to a private plane. I can be there in just a few hours."

"I don't know that Jennifer's all that eager to go home. She's asked to stay here awhile. I knew you'd be worried and that's why I called. But the problem between the two of you is hardly resolved."

"Hmm." He cleared his throat again. "Are you saying you want her to stay there for a while?"

"I'm saying she's upset and asked to stay."

"I see."

Caroline was in agony. This was Reese Claybourne she was speaking to, the man who'd been so pivotal in her life, the man who, in her mind, had always been something of a black knight, the agent of so much sorrow and regret.

"How do you feel about having her there?" he asked.

"How do I feel? My God, she's my child! This is the first time I've laid eyes on her since the day she was born! How would you feel?"

She choked back a sob, clamping her hand to her mouth as her tears flowed. This time they were as much tears of anger as release.

"I feel terrible about this," he said. "I really do."

Caroline bit her lip, trying to regain control. "It's all right," she managed. "It's not your fault."

"What concerns me a little is school," he said. "She's already missed a week, and exams are coming up."

"I thought school was already out."

"No, she's going to have to go to summer school if she doesn't get back in the classroom pretty quick." He hesitated. "Maybe I should talk to her. Would you mind putting her on the line, Caroline?"

She was glad because it gave her an excuse to get off the phone. "I'll see if she'll speak to you. Just a minute."

She put down the receiver and went to the front room, where Jennifer was sitting hunched over, almost hugging herself. She looked up with trepidation.

"Your dad would like to speak to you."

Jennifer frowned, then got to her feet. "Why am I surprised?" she mumbled as she went off toward the bedroom.

Caroline dropped into a chair with a sigh, glancing around. Only a few short hours ago she'd left her condo, marking another anniversary of one of the most emotional days in her life, never dreaming for a moment that today she would not only see her daughter, but speak with Reese, as well. In the future, May 28 would carry additional significance, but at this moment she couldn't say what sort of memory. There was joy, but would there also be more pain?

From time to time over the next several minutes, Caroline could hear Jennifer's voice, but not her words. There were some pretty emotional things being discussed; that was obvious, but beyond that she couldn't say. Then Jennifer returned, teary eyed.

"He wants to talk to you again."

Caroline got up and returned to the bedroom. She picked up the receiver lying on the bed and took a deep breath to fortify herself.

"Yes, Reese?"

"I've got Jennifer half-convinced to come on home, but I'll need your help."

"What do you want me to do?"

"Come with her."

"What?"

"She said she'd come back right away, tomorrow, if you'd come with her."

"I can't leave Chicago, Reese. I've got my business to run. I've got responsibilities."

"I know it's asking a lot, but you'll not only be helping Jennifer and me, it'll give you an opportunity to spend time with her, see the sort of life she lives. After today I'm sure you'll want some reassurance on that score. I know I've made a lousy impression, and you must be concerned."

"That's not the issue."

"What is the issue?"

Caroline took a moment to gather herself. "If you knew what a shock this has been . . . Not only am I seeing my daughter for the first time, now you're asking me to fly to New Mexico with her."

"Do you have employees who can look after your business for a few days?"

Caroline rolled her eyes. Either the man didn't realize the complications of running a small business or he didn't care. Most likely the latter. The Claybournes always insisted on getting their way. "There are a couple of women who work for me part-time, but that's not the only consideration, Reese."

"If you'd rather not, I certainly won't force the issue. I just thought it would ease things for Jennifer, and benefit you, too. She seems really to have taken to you, Caroline."

"Funny thing, isn't it?" she said ironically.

"Look, I didn't mean to be flip. This conversation is as hard for me as it is for you. I had no more idea it would happen than you did."

She drew a ragged breath. "I'm not being critical. It's just that . . . well, I'm upset."

"Would you like to talk to Jennifer about it before you decide and call me back?"

Caroline closed her eyes and tried to think. The reason she was hesitating was because of Reese. Spending time with Jennifer wasn't the problem, nor was leaving town. Caroline asked herself if she had a duty to have a good look at her daughter's life up close. There was no denying that things at home were in a state of turmoil, but could she help? Just as importantly, was she up to it?

"Hang on a second, Reese," she said. "I'll be right back."

Putting down the phone, she went back to the front room. Jennifer was waiting, anguish and uncertainty etched on her young face.

"Jennifer, do you really want me to go back to New Mexico with you?"

"I won't go alone," she said, shaking her head, her expression turning hard, almost defiant.

"What about school?"

"I don't care about it."

She could see the girl was determined to fight her father. "So what can I do to be of help?" she asked.

"You can talk to Dad."

A hard knot formed in her stomach. Once again she was smack in the middle of a crisis with Reese Claybourne. Ironically it was over the same issue as before—their child. Last time she had been too young to assert herself. She'd been at the mercy of the judgment of others. This time was different. Turning, she returned to the bedroom.

"Okay, Reese," she said, "I'll bring Jennifer back and I'll stay a few days to help sort things out, but my offer comes with a condition."

"What's that?"

"If Jennifer and I decide we want to be part of each other's lives, I expect you to cooperate."

He hesitated for only the briefest of moments. "How can I say no to that?"

CAROLINE AND JENNIFER HAD some coffee and split a pastry. Reese called back half an hour later to say he'd arranged a private plane. He explained that made the most sense because Santa Fe didn't have a commercial airport, which meant flying into Albuquerque and a lot of hassle. Reese's friend not only had his own jet, but an airfield that would accommodate it. "You can leave first thing in the morning from Midway Airport and be at the ranch for lunch," Reese said.

After the call Jennifer wanted to take a bath, so Caroline got her a towel and showed her to the bathroom. Then she took the opportunity to call Kitty and tell her what had happened.

"My God," Kitty said, "talk about serendipity."

"It's the most incredible thing. And Jennifer's an angel, an absolute doll. I'm sure there are other sides of her that I'll get to know in time, but she's just wonderful."

"They say mothers are partial to their offspring, so you can hardly be objective."

"She's almost exactly the way I pictured her."

"I'm really happy for you, kid."

All that afternoon she and Jennifer talked. They told each other about their lives—their hopes and dreams. And the more they shared, the closer they felt to each other. Caroline could hardly believe how natural it seemed to be together.

In a silly fit of whimsy, they decided to bake a birthday cake for their dessert. They had a lot of fun, laughing when they both ended up with flour on their faces. A few hours together, and they were already acting like mother and daughter.

When it finally came time for bed, they hugged and told each other how happy they were. Caroline was afraid to go to sleep for fear she'd awaken and it would all have proved to be a dream.

Morning, however, brought Caroline a different reality—Reese Claybourne. The day before, she and Jennifer had talked a lot about the girl's difficulties with her father, about their arguments over Carlos. Caroline was relieved to know that most of their troubles were recent. From what Jennifer said, it was clear that Reese was suffocating Jennifer as her own father had suffocated her. But at least Jennifer admitted that they'd had a good relationship until Reese "freaked out over Carlos," as she put it.

They rushed to the airport and found the jet waiting. The pilot, a taciturn man in his forties, took Caroline's suitcase, stowing it in the cargo compartment. In a matter of minutes they were on their way.

For most of the flight Jennifer was fairly quiet. She spent a lot of time reading the fashion magazines Caroline had brought along. She didn't seem particularly nervous or upset. Caroline was the one who was suffering, especially during the latter part of the flight, as they neared their destination.

Knowing they were getting close, Jennifer put her magazine aside and seemed to turn her mind to what lay ahead. "You must have really loved Dad if you married him," she said, indicating her mind was on the impending reunion.

"Of course. At least I thought I did," Caroline replied.

"You mean you didn't really?"

"Our love was real enough. But love's not everything. When you're young, you have a lot of hurdles to get over. Marriage is not easy even for people in their twenties and thirties. People change a lot over the years, Jennifer. I'm not the person now I was at seventeen."

"What are you saying—that you and Dad would have gotten a divorce?"

"Who knows? We might have been lucky, but the odds are against it."

"Maybe I love Carlos more than you loved Dad."

They were the first words that showed just how serious she was about the boy. Sure, Jennifer was a kid, but Caroline knew that teens could take their love life very seriously.

"Time will tell," she said. "But maybe there is an important message in what happened to me."

"What?"

"Don't get pregnant!"

Jennifer laughed.

"It sounds funny, I know, but it could be the most important advice you ever get."

The engines of the jet changed pitch, and Caroline felt a sudden well of anxiety. She'd always been certain she'd never see Reese Claybourne again. But now, incredibly, they were about to be reunited.

THE JET CAME DOWN into a mountain valley between two ranges, the snowcapped peaks below them at first, then at the same altitude as the plane. Caroline watched the reddish earth rising below them, a magnificent panorama of stark beauty. And then the runway suddenly appeared and the jet dropped some more, finally touching down.

Caroline took Jennifer's hand, giving it a squeeze. She felt nervous and wary, as if *she* were the child. The puckish look on Jennifer's face told Caroline she was curious, maybe even bemused at the thought of her parents meeting again after so many years.

Though she'd had the entire flight to think about it, Caroline wasn't sure what to expect. Over the years she'd had hundreds of imaginary conversations with Reese Claybourne, most of them contentious. Now, ironically, he was beholden to her. She was bringing his daughter to him, though she knew that giving the girl up this time was different. Jennifer had already made it clear she wanted them to have a relationship. All that remained was to see if Reese's apparent acceptance of that fact was genuine.

They'd taxied toward some outbuildings at the edge of the landing strip—a small hangar, a garage and what might have been a storage shed. At first she didn't see anyone. Then she spotted a man in a cowboy hat who was leaning against the fender of a pickup truck. He was in jeans and boots and wore sunglasses. He was too far away for her to be sure it was Reese, though his general physique matched that of the eighteen-year-old boy she remembered.

Jennifer looked past her, out the window. "There's Dad," she said with resignation. "At least he didn't bring Grandma."

The jet, a bit closer now, stopped and the engines died. Caroline again looked at the man, asking herself if that stranger could really be the man who'd fathered her child—the one who'd married her, then quickly abandoned her, leaving her a forgotten bride.

Jennifer stood up and stretched. Caroline glanced back out the window and saw Reese amble toward the plane. The pilot, a methodical, efficient man, had scarcely said a word. He had the cabin door open and was lowering the steps. Jennifer slung her backpack over her shoulder and moved toward the door. Caroline grabbed her carry-on bag.

The girl had followed the pilot down the steps and looked back at Caroline, who'd arrived at the door. She was struck by three things—the scent of the high desert air, the bright sunshine and the mix of emotions elicited by the man approaching the plane.

"Go ahead and say hello to your father," Caroline said. "I'll be along."

Jennifer went a half a dozen steps or so, stopped and reluctantly allowed her father to embrace her.

"I might be the bad guy," Caroline heard him say, "but you can afford a better hug than that, can't you?"

Jennifer complied, but without enthusiasm. Reese watched her approach, even as he continued to hug his daughter. His face was familiar, even behind the sunglasses. He looked like the much older brother—or the father, even—of the boy she'd run off with those long years ago.

Jennifer ended the hug and turned to face her. Reese just stared at her, his lips bending into a slight smile. She remembered the mouth, remembered it vividly.

She had purposely dressed in an understated way in designer jeans and a simple white cotton blouse. Reese removed his hat, his smile broadening.

"Hello, Caroline."

"Hi, Reese."

She was relieved when he offered her his hand. She wasn't about to hug him, whether Jennifer had or not. They had no relationship, only a past.

"Thank you for coming," he said simply. "I know it wasn't easy."

He let go of her hand. Caroline nodded, acknowledging the remark. Jennifer moved a bit closer to him, and he slipped an arm around her shoulders, all the while keeping his eyes on Caroline.

"How come you never told me Mom was so pretty?" Jennifer asked.

"Oh, I told you, sugar. You just don't remember. How else do you think you got so pretty yourself, if it wasn't from your mom?"

"Still a flatterer, I see," Caroline said.

"You remember that about me."

"I do now."

He grinned. Reese was as masculine and handsome as they came—and so much more manly than the image she'd carried in her head all these years. He'd filled out and was no longer the thin, wiry kid she'd known. There were touches of gray in the dark hair at his temples. And he was a bit weathered, like a man who spent lots of time outdoors. Generally he had a mature, confident look about him that only came with living.

Reese put his hat back on and reached for her bag. "Let me carry that for you."

"That's all right, I can manage."

He didn't insist, but seeing the pilot approach with her suitcase, he took that instead. The pilot bid them goodbye, and the three of them headed for the truck. Caroline walked on the other side of Jennifer so that the girl was between them.

"How was your flight?" he asked, slipping his hand under Jennifer's ponytail and giving the back of her neck a squeeze.

"Faster than the bus," she said.

"You little rascal." He gave her ponytail a light tug, then his expression grew sober. "I suppose you have no idea how scared to death we've all been."

"All I did was go to see my mother," she replied with a sideways glance at Caroline. "What's so bad about that?"

"If you'd told me, I'd have put you on a plane to Chicago and saved us all a lot of trouble."

"This way you get to see her, too," Jennifer said. "You should be glad."

"Maybe I am."

Caroline gave him a less than amused look, enough to indicate she didn't consider this a joking matter.

"You look good, by the way, Caroline," he said to her. "The years have been kind."

"Thanks."

"Prettier than I remember. Jennifer's right."

Caroline didn't know how to respond, but she was saved from the need to when they reached the truck. Reese put her suitcase in back, then opened the passenger-side door. Jennifer climbed in the cab. Reese took Caroline's arm and helped her up, closing the door behind her.

As he went around to the driver's side, Jennifer leaned toward her. "Dad's impressed with you, I can tell." She giggled as Reese got in the truck.

"You two got secrets?" he asked, looking at each of them in turn.

"Just the usual mother-daughter ones," Caroline said airily.

"Sounds like you've made up for lost time."

"There was a lot to make up for," she replied.

It wasn't exactly a frosty retort, but Reese got the message. There was still bad blood between them, and a past not easily forgotten. It was a message she wanted him to get. Loud and clear.

Chapter Four

THE AIRSTRIP WAS LOCATED on a plateau that ran along the flank of a mesa. The narrow asphalt road they followed wound through small stands of junipers and piñons toward the bottom, where tall, pale green cottonwoods lined the creek bed.

Caroline looked out the truck window with awe at the rugged beauty of the country. But even the majesty of the high desert could not keep her from being very aware of Reese. When she'd known him years before, they'd talked about New Mexico some, but he hadn't struck her as a cowboy. He'd been just like the other kids, except for that little bit of swagger he'd had even then. Yet for some reason, she was sure that the man she was seeing now—the sexy cowboy—was the real Reese Claybourne. This was the man in his element.

She half listened as he bantered with Jennifer, enough to satisfy herself that their relationship was basically sound. She had been concerned about Jennifer's home life, but it was clear now that running away had a lot more to do with the clash over Carlos than their general relationship.

"Ever been in this part of the country before, Caroline?" Reese asked, seeming to want to include her in the conversation.

"No, first time in the Southwest."

"God's country. But then, lots of people claim that."

"New Mexico has had some associations for me that weren't the most pleasant," she said, seeing no point in mincing words.

"I guess I should feel fortunate you're even being civil to me. I can't be one of your favorite people."

"All that's long past," she said. "I'm here now because it is important to Jennifer." She put her hand on the girl's knee. "And I liked the idea of being able to spend more time with her."

"I hope you stay a long, long time," Jennifer said.

"I don't know about that, but a few days would be nice."

"Dad, can I visit Mom again? Like later this summer, maybe?"

"Have you two been making plans?"

"We've talked generally," Caroline said. "I told Jennifer a lot depends on conversations you and I need to have."

"I'm not eager to play the role of the heavy," he replied. "This reunion between you two was plainly overdue."

It was about eight miles to the Claybourne ranch. Reese pointed out where his property began, explaining how he'd taken over total management of the operation soon after his father had had his first stroke. Then, upon his father's death, his mother had moved into Santa Fe, turning everything over to him. He'd already cut back the size of the cattle operation and shifted resources into other assets.

"Jennifer and I spend most of our time in town because of her school, so I've invested heavily in commercial real estate," he explained. "Mostly in Santa Fe and Albuquerque. But being a Claybourne, the ranch remains a special place."

"Our house in Santa Fe is really nice," Jennifer chimed in.

"You got your city-girl side from your mother," he chided. "When I met her, she'd never been on a horse. Still true, Caroline?"

"That's right."

Reese grinned. "Guess we'll have to do something about that."

"We can take her riding, Dad," Jennifer said.

"How about we let your mom get acclimatized before we go lining up activities for her. The first order of business is to make her feel at home."

Caroline had to smile at the show of hospitality. What she didn't know was whether Reese's attitude was motivated by fear, genuine southwestern friendliness or guilt. This visit had to be as uncomfortable for him as it was for her.

Before long they left the highway, driving through a plane of verdant sage and grasses that were speckled with wildflowers and juniper. The carpet of green ended at the base of the barren sandstone buttes bordering the valley. On a rise at the edge of the hills, Caroline could see a low, rambling ranch house in a stand of shade trees.

"See, there's the house," Jennifer said, pointing.

The enthusiasm in the girl's voice told Caroline that home wasn't such an awful place. Jennifer had been holding back some to let her father know that issues remained unresolved, but her feelings about her situation were generally positive. Caroline was glad. She didn't want that worry on top of having to deal with Reese.

After a few more minutes of driving, they climbed the driveway to the ranch house. Made of heavy timbers and adobe with a tile roof and covered with flowering vines, the place had a welcoming feel about it, somewhat like an oasis in the desert. There was a good-sized lawn out front, offering an impressive view across the valley. A gardener was at work in the flower beds as they drove up.

Caroline climbed out of the truck, amazed that she found the Claybourne hacienda so hospitable in appearance. In her mind it had been a forbidding place hidden behind barbed wire, where the vile Claybournes had taken her child. Jennifer, climbing out behind her, waved to the gardener, who had turned from his labors to watch their arrival.

"Hi, Miguel!"

The man waved back. "Welcome home, *señorita!*"

Caroline inhaled the aromatic mountain air, taking in the vista. She glanced around the grounds again. Shadows from the trees fell across the house and much of the lawn, a sharp contrast to the brilliant southwestern sun.

Reese had gotten her suitcase from the back of the truck and stood waiting for her to come around. Jennifer had gone on ahead.

"You've got a lovely place," Caroline told him.

"As you'll see, I'm in the process of renovating, somewhat to my mother's chagrin. But I warned her not to let go unless she really wanted to. I figured there was no point in having the place unless it was truly mine."

As they made their way to the front door, a middle-aged Hispanic woman appeared, greeting Jennifer with a big hug. By the time Caroline and Reese got to the overhanging porch, the woman was bubbling with joy, tears in her eyes. Reese introduced her as Lorena, their housekeeper.

"So good to meet you, *señora,*" Lorena said. "Now that I see you, I understand why Jennifer is so beautiful! Welcome, welcome."

Reese gave Caroline a grin as they went inside. He set down her suitcase in the entry hall, then took off his hat and glasses. He turned to her, and their eyes met for the first time.

His utter familiarity was startling. Over the years Reese's features had dimmed in her mind. In a way he'd almost become an abstraction. But gazing into his deep blue eyes brought back the boy from the past. Only now the boy was a man.

"Why don't I let Jennifer show you around?" he said. "You'll want to see her bedroom, I'm sure. And she can show you to a guest room. After you've had a chance to freshen up, we can have lunch. I don't know about you, but flying always gives me an appetite."

Jennifer professed to be hungry, too. Lorena had fixed a special meal at Reese's instruction, he said, and they'd be eating soon. Caroline took Jennifer's hand, and they headed down the long hallway, through the sprawling house. Caroline couldn't help feeling excited as she glanced around the rooms they passed. It was incredible to think she was visiting the Claybourne place as a welcome, virtually honored guest.

They went to the guest room first, a spacious, pleasant, if somewhat plainly decorated room. Then Jennifer took Caroline to her own room, a virtual suite. There was a lovely old-fashioned dressing table that had been painted a soft pink and a matching chest of drawers. In the sitting area there was a large TV with a VCR and comfy chairs, perfect for Jennifer and a girlfriend to watch movies. Caroline noted, though, that the room seemed barren of personal things.

"Most of my stuff is at our house in town," she explained, "but I really like this room. It was Dad's when he was growing up. It's the best thing about the ranch, besides Lorena. She's real nice. Mrs. Barfield's our housekeeper in town. She's nice, too, but she can't help me with my Spanish like Lorena can. And I like Lorena's cooking."

It pleased Caroline that Jennifer was so eager to share the joys of her life, as well as her tribulations. Jennifer sat on her queen-size bed and looked at her mother.

"So, what do you think of Dad after all these years?"

Caroline couldn't blame Jennifer for being curious. "I'm relieved he's so kind to you." She hesitated. "He *is* like this all the time, isn't he? I mean, he isn't on good behavior just because I'm visiting."

Jennifer shook her head. "Dad's pretty neat—about everything except Carlos. As soon as he found out I was seeing him, he came unglued. Maybe if you talk to him, he'll change."

Caroline sat on the bed next to her daughter. "Jennifer, I don't know enough about things to offer opinions. Maybe I've earned the right to say what I think, but short of your father mistreating you, I don't know what I could say to him."

"You can tell him not to do to me what your father did to you, can't you?"

"I'll talk to him about it to see where he's coming from. I can promise you that much."

"Do it sooner rather than later."

Caroline took the girl's hand. "Honey, I hope you don't think I can change things, because I might not be able to. If I see a way to be helpful, I will. But I've got to be honest with you. I'm not even sure what's right in this situation."

Jennifer was clearly disappointed, but she wasn't going to complain. It seemed she was willing to wait and see how things played out.

Jennifer wanted to call a few of her friends before lunch, and so Caroline went to her room to unpack. Then she wandered back through the house, noting that one or two rooms had been stripped down for painting and remodeling.

She found Reese, freshly washed and his hair combed, sitting in a big leather chair in the family room. He got up when she entered.

"Settled in?" he asked.

"The room is very nice." She glanced around. "You have a lovely place."

"It's becoming mine."

She looked out the large windows at a small flower garden in back. "I can see why you like it."

"Lunch will be ready before long. Can I get you something to drink? Beer? Wine? Juice? Coffee?"

"No, thanks, I'm fine."

"Well, sit down, make yourself at home."

Caroline took a seat on the leather sofa, choosing the end farthest from his chair. She crossed her legs, feeling a bit self-conscious now that they were alone. Reese was watching her, the faintest of smiles on his lips. She looked back at him, holding his gaze until it came into her head that this was the man she'd actually been married to for about two months, though they'd only spent one night together—their wedding night. The awareness of that made her turn away.

"So," she said, making conversation, "this is where you'd come from when you visited Chicago that summer."

"Yes, the family spread."

"Funny, I knew you'd grown up on a ranch in New Mexico, but the image of you I've carried in my mind is not of a...cowboy. I don't even remember you wearing boots."

"I didn't. Part of me wanted to fit in...part was trying to reject my father, the classic man-on-horseback if ever there was one."

"And so, here you are."

"Well, I haven't come full circle, if that's what you're suggesting. But like most people, I've come to be more accepting of who I am." He looked around.

"Besides, a tie doesn't work in this environment—though believe it or not, I do own a tuxedo."

Caroline thought that'd be an interesting sight to behold, though she didn't say so. Their eyes met again. Her cheeks began to color despite her best efforts to act casual.

Reese finally broke the silence. "I don't suppose you want to hear about the guilt I've felt over the years."

She didn't expect him to be so direct. "Actually I don't. The only reason I came is because of Jennifer. As far as you and I are concerned, we're best off if we forget the past."

"I understand."

"I'm not sure you do, Reese."

"That's sort of why I wanted to talk about what happened. I thought it might be easier, being under the same roof and all, if we could . . . let's say agree to disagree amicably."

"I think we did that fifteen years ago. I don't hate you, if that's what you're concerned about. And if it's forgiveness you want, you've got it."

"Why do you not sound very convincing?"

"Maybe it's you, Reese," she said.

"Yeah, my guilt."

"Our parents engineered things. Not you."

"But I didn't prevent it from happening, did I?"

"I really do think we should change the subject," she said.

Reese leaned back in his chair, crossing one booted foot over the other. "Then let me thank you for rescuing Jennifer. I feel damned lucky she fell into your hands. The way the world is these days, anything could have happened."

"I'm certainly no expert on kids, but Jennifer seems pretty levelheaded for her age."

"Except when it comes to Carlos."

"Do you think she's truly serious about him, or is she just reacting to you?"

Reese contemplated her. "Were you that serious about me, or were you reacting to *your* father's protectiveness?"

"I was seventeen."

"True, but kids are more precocious these days. Anyway, I remember what it was like to be eighteen. That's what concerns me, if you want to know the truth."

"And now that the shoe's on the other foot . . ."

He smiled and nodded. "Yes."

"If it was anybody but Jennifer, I'd say you deserve it."

He contemplated her. "Maybe I'm not forgiven, after all."

"New subject," she said.

He leaned back, contemplating her again, his hands folded over his belt buckle. "All right. Tell me why an attractive woman like you never married."

"Obviously I chose not to."

He rolled his tongue in his cheek, thinking. She knew exactly what was going through his mind.

"Don't worry, Reese, it has nothing to do with you. I'm not bitter toward all men or an emotional cripple. I just never met anyone I wanted to marry." She recrossed her legs.

"I'm glad you were able to forget me. I can't really say the same."

She blinked. "What do you mean?"

His expression turned thoughtful. "I've thought of you many times over the years, wondered how you were doing, if I ought to send you pictures of Jennifer or something. But I never was sure if that would be a favor or a cruelty. I didn't know what was right."

She heard the regret in his voice . . . and the determination. Caroline sighed. "You obviously won't rest until I tell you how giving Jennifer up affected me. Well, what can I tell you? A week hasn't gone by that I haven't thought about her, prayed for her, worried about her. May 28 is the darkest day of the year for me. I dread it. Every time it rolls around, another little piece of me dies all over again.

"So, yes, Reese, I guess a part of me does still hate you, and hates the Claybournes. But at the same time I know you were a victim, too." She looked down at her hands, then up at him. "There. Are you happy now?"

His eyes were dark with sorrow. "Maybe we're finally getting to what needs to be said."

"Maybe we are."

There was a very long silence, during which she felt the same old pain. But she also sensed his humility and shame. That stirred up new and unexpected emotions in her.

"That night at the Indiana dunes when I got you pregnant, I was terribly selfish," Reese said softly. "I told myself I loved you, so it didn't matter what happened. That soft lake breeze on our naked bodies felt like heaven, and it was beckoning. I just didn't give a damn about anything but having you."

Caroline sat stony silent, listening to his mea culpa.

"I can't think of that night without realizing it was a high point in my life in more than one way—special not just because of Jennifer, but because of the way I felt about you. What I'm trying to say is the suffering that followed has never diminished what we had."

A well of emotions rose in her. Caroline's eyes shimmered. "I'm glad you can say that," she said with a trembling voice. "I certainly can't."

She got up and went to the window. She did not want to be having this conversation. She did not want to relive what had happened.

Reese kept mercifully quiet, allowing her to calm down, get control of her emotions. She watched a hummingbird in the garden until it flew away. Knowing it was up to her to set the tone of future conversations, she faced him.

"Look, you're obviously more comfortable talking about the past than I am," she said. "As far as I'm concerned, we've gone on with our lives, and the only reason we're even speaking to each other now is because of our daughter. Please, let me be, Reese."

Caroline glanced up and saw Jennifer at the door. Reese turned and saw her, too.

"I was thinking it was kind of neat having both of my parents together under the same roof," Jennifer said. "But maybe I was wrong."

Chapter Five

LORENA SUDDENLY ANNOUNCED that lunch was ready, beckoning them to the dining room. Caroline and Jennifer walked ahead with Reese following. Caroline put her arm around the girl's shoulders, and Reese heard her say, "Don't worry, honey, it's not your problem. You can have a good relationship with each of us."

Jennifer glanced back at him. Reese nodded. "Your mom's right."

They sat at the table, Reese taking his place at the head, Caroline and Jennifer on either side of him. Lorena went off to the kitchen. Reese looked at each of them in turn. "This is an historic occasion. It'd be nice if we could put our differences aside and try to enjoy it, don't you think?"

Caroline and Jennifer looked at each other.

"Am I the only one who feels that way?" he asked.

"No," Caroline said. "You're right."

He picked up his glass. "Then let's drink to . . . understanding . . . tolerance . . . and good times."

Jennifer picked up her glass, and Caroline did, too. They all touched glasses.

"I'm glad you're here, Caroline," he said. "Welcome."

He saw a flicker of emotion cross her face, but she didn't say anything. Jennifer was watching her mother and seemed pleased.

Reese suggested they make plans, pointing out that Monday was a school day, so they only had the weekend before Jennifer needed to put her nose to the grindstone.

"Oh, Dad . . ." she moaned.

"Let's make it a positive, sweetheart. Maybe your mom can visit the school. We can stay here at the ranch for the weekend and spend the week in town. While you're in class, your mom can see Santa Fe and some of the local sights."

"But I haven't even studied for my exams."

Reese turned to Caroline. "You finished college, didn't you?"

She raised an eyebrow. "Yes."

"Then look at it this way, sweetheart. You've got two college graduates to tutor you. If we all work together, we ought to be able to save you from having to go to summer school." He winked at Caroline. "What'd you study in college?"

"English."

"Perfect," he said. "I've got math and science covered. All we've been lacking is expertise in the humanities."

"You seem to have it all figured out," Caroline said wryly.

"Dad always does," Jennifer said grumpily.

"Is that bad?" he asked his daughter.

"Maybe everybody doesn't always want to do things your way."

"Then why don't you and your mother decide what we do this weekend."

Lorena entered with a serving cart, drawing Jennifer's attention. The housekeeper had made tamales, enchiladas and burritos, as well as beans, rice and a salad. Jennifer cheerfully gave Caroline a minilecture on Mexican cuisine, with commentary from Lorena. Reese took it all in, but mostly he enjoyed the opportunity to observe Caroline, marveling at the woman she'd become.

She had the same perfectly sculpted profile he remembered—a straight, patrician nose that tipped up ever so slightly at the end, a mouth that signaled resolution if not strength. She was sleeker now, and the wide-eyed innocence had been replaced with a quiet savoir faire. She struck him as understated, but she had substance. She wasn't flashy, but there was a simple elegance about her that appealed to him.

What was most surprising—or maybe it wasn't—was how she affected him. The moment she'd climbed out of the plane, he'd had that same feeling all over again—the one he'd had when he'd first set on eyes on her. He and his cousin had gone to an end-of-the-school-year dance in Chicago, and that's where he'd first seen the green-eyed brunette in the simple sundress, her hands folded demurely in front of her, her eyes shyly lowered as she stood off by herself. There were flashier girls there that night, but there was something about Caroline's quiet beauty that had drawn him to her.

He asked her to dance to a disco tune. And when a slow number came on after that, he kept her on the floor. She had come alone because her girlfriend was sick. Her father had dropped her off without realizing that.

They danced with each other all night. When eleven came, she told him she had to go. Her father was really strict, she said, but before she left he got her phone number. The next day he borrowed his cousin's car and went to see her. Sitting in her front room while her father was at his pharmacy, they talked for hours. Before he knew it, he was head over heels in love.

Reese shook off his revery and realized he'd been gazing at Caroline. She'd obviously noticed him watching her and gave him a half smile as Lorena took his plate to serve him.

"What would you like, *señor?*"

"The works, Lorena."

Caroline was politely waiting for him to be served. Jennifer had already plunged in.

"Go ahead and eat," he said.

"I'll wait."

When Lorena placed his plate before him, Caroline picked up her silver. Reese asked the housekeeper to bring him a beer and Caroline one, too, if she wanted it. She declined.

"Still like to dance?" he asked her.

"I haven't in years."

"Your mom was quite a dancer, Jennifer," he said. "We met at a teen dance in Chicago."

"You told me that once, a long time ago."

"I'm sure I'm remembering it more fondly now than I did then."

A vaguely alarmed look crossed Caroline's face, and Reese realized he had to be careful. Fortunately Jennifer seemed to have missed the nuance.

"So, was Dad a good dancer?" she asked Caroline.

"As I recall, yes."

"We danced once, didn't we, Dad?" Jennifer said.

"Yes, the time I chaperoned your spring dance in junior high."

"It was pretty funny," Jennifer said, "because he was doing these weird things with his feet. But Miss Crawford, the social-studies teacher, did the same kind of dance, so they looked all right together."

"It's not easy being an old fuddy-duddy," he said.

Caroline smiled briefly, but then fell quiet. Reese sensed he'd touched a nerve. Maybe she was thinking of the times she'd missed, the lost years. He could see then that his many crimes against her would not be easily forgotten. He might be facing an impossible task.

IT WAS NEARLY DARK by the time Caroline woke up. After lunch she'd gone to her room for a nap because she'd felt overwhelmingly drowsy. Reese had told her the altitude did that and it would take a day or two for her to adjust.

Lying on the bed, gazing out the window at the twilight, she realized she'd dreamed of Reese, partly as a boy, partly as the man he'd become. She couldn't remember exactly what had happened in the dream, but there had been a lot of anxiety. She recalled that he'd made her dance with him, that she'd been upset, especially when he kissed her.

Caroline sat on the edge of the bed, feeling numb. She went to the bathroom and splashed some water on her face to remedy the puffiness. Then, pronouncing herself presentable, she got a dress from the closet, slipped it on and went off to see what everyone was doing.

Jennifer was not in her room, and the house was very quiet. As she passed by the sitting room, she glanced in and saw a white-headed woman in a chair by the open window, smoking a cigarette. Caroline stood there for a moment before the woman turned and looked at her.

"Ah, there you are, Caroline. Did you sleep well?"

She realized that it was Reese's mother, Marian Claybourne. She'd only seen her once, years ago, when Marian and her husband had come to Chicago to talk to her father. It wasn't so much the woman's face—which was only vaguely familiar—as her manner that Caroline recognized.

"Hello, Mrs. Claybourne." She entered the room. "I had a nice nap, thank you."

As she approached, Marian held out her hand.

"Forgive me for not getting up, but I have a bad hip." She gestured toward the cane leaning against the arm of the chair.

They shook hands.

"Please sit down." The old woman, excruciatingly thin yet regal in her bearing, took a final drag on her cigarette before stubbing it out. "Reese doesn't approve of smoking in the house, but he and Jennifer are out tending to the horses, so I took the opportunity to cheat. I hope you won't betray me."

"Of course not."

Marian Claybourne measured her with milky gray eyes. "So you've grown up to be an attractive young woman. Reese said as much, but I thought I'd see for myself. That's the advantage of being an old matriarch—you can come without being invited." She looked Caroline over. "My granddaughter has quite an affinity for you, I understand."

"I *am* her mother, Mrs. Claybourne."

"Indeed you are."

Caroline wasn't sure whether Reese's mother was registering disapproval at her presence or just being cantankerous. She'd always thought of her as the moving force behind Jennifer going to the Claybournes and had consequently considered her a witch. It was odd to be sitting next to her now, looking into her eyes.

"Reese says you've been civil," Marian said. "I admire you for being broad-minded. I don't know if I would be if I were in your shoes."

"I've tried to forget the past."

"I suppose this sounds like self-justification, but things look very different from the perspective of years. What might seem cruel now was perfectly sensible back then."

"I'm more concerned with the future than the past."

"Yes, I would imagine." The woman picked up the leather cigarette case lying next to her on the table, then, apparently thinking better of it, she put it back down. "Tell me, what are your plans for the future? Regarding Jennifer, I mean. Reese was vague on your thinking."

"I hope to see Jennifer. We both would like a relationship, but I can't be more specific than that because I don't know."

Marian Claybourne regarded her again. "I understand you own a business."

"Yes, a gift boutique in the Chicago suburbs."

"You're unattached, I take it."

Caroline did not like getting the third degree, especially from the woman who was largely responsible for taking her child from her. But as Marian had implied, she was used to having her way. That evidently included being able to question the mother of her granddaughter as she pleased.

"I'm unattached at the moment, yes."

"What's your position regarding this Mexican boy Jennifer's taken up with?"

"I don't have a position. I don't know enough about it to form one. I'm here because Jennifer wanted me here. And I also wanted to satisfy myself that she was in a happy home and being raised properly."

Marian was clearly taken aback by Caroline's pointed remark, but refrained from commenting. Instead she gave in to her desire for another cigarette. She took one from the case and lit it. "I hope you don't mind me smoking," she said after the fact.

Caroline shook her head. Marian drew on her cigarette.

"It's hard for a man to raise a girl alone," she said, exhaling a cloud of smoke, "even with the help of servants and a mother to look over his shoulder. At a certain age, a mother is almost indispensable." She tapped her cigarette on the edge of the ashtray. "Reese and Jennifer will be coming in soon, so let me be direct.

What would be the prospects of you relocating your business to Santa Fe?"

Caroline blinked. "Why would I do that?"

"To be near Jennifer."

Caroline shook her head. "Is this some kind of test?"

"No. I played a major role in taking Jennifer from you. I'd like to play a role in returning you to her life. I would happily bear all your expenses—personal, as well as business, if you'll relocate here."

Caroline tried to digest what she'd just heard. Marian watched her with flat gray eyes. Smoke curled around the old woman's head as she waited impassively for Caroline to speak. Caroline shifted in her chair.

"Mrs. Claybourne, I'm sure you have the best intentions, but I don't consider my relationship with Jennifer your business. I make all my own decisions. I'm not the seventeen-year-old girl I was the last time we met."

"My only concern is for Jennifer's welfare."

"That's my only concern, too."

They heard voices coming from the back of the house, and Marian stubbed out her cigarette. "They're coming," she said. "Give my offer some thought. Take a few weeks, or months, if necessary."

Caroline glanced toward the door, lowering her voice. "Why are you so sure it would be a good thing for Jennifer if I moved here?"

"It's partly selfish. I'd rather Jennifer go across town to see you than to Chicago. I may have been born and raised in New England, but the Southwest is my home and this is where I want my family to be."

Reese suddenly appeared in the doorway. "Well, look who's having a chat."

"You're right about her, son," Marian said. "Caroline has become quite a young woman."

Reese gave Caroline a crooked grin. "You seem to have won everybody's hearts."

"It isn't what I set out to do, believe me."

Jennifer came along just then, a glass of milk in her hand. "Lorena said you're staying overnight, Grandma."

"Yes, I invited myself. I thought tomorrow evening you could come back to Santa Fe with me, to save your father the trouble of bringing you into town for school Monday."

"Mother, we're planning on going into town anyway," Reese said.

"Yes, but this way you and Caroline can have some time alone to discuss the future. You don't mind do you, Jennifer? It's in your interest."

Reese looked at his daughter.

"I sort of wanted to spend as much time with Mom as I could," she said.

"It's just one night," Marian said. "We won't have to leave until after dinner."

"And Caroline and I can pick you up after school on Monday," Reese added. "We'll help you get ready for your exams, if you need it, and then we'll go out to dinner wherever you and your mother would like."

Jennifer shrugged. "Okay, but are we going on a ride tomorrow?"

"Sure, if that's what you want to do."

"Needless to say, I'll be staying right here in this chair," Marian said.

"Caroline, you up to your maiden voyage on horseback?" He poked his tongue in his cheek.

She looked at the three of them. "You know what? You folks ought to open a dude ranch. You offer gourmet lunches, tours of Santa Fe and even rides on horseback. With all that hospitality, you'd make millions."

Reese chuckled. "Not a bad idea. I wonder who we could get to run the gift shop?"

AFTER DINNER THAT EVENING, which Caroline found oddly tense with Marian present, the old woman retreated to her room to read. Caroline, Reese and Jennifer played Sorry in the family room. Caroline won with a little help from her daughter.

"Is this a man-versus-woman thing, or do mothers and daughters just enjoy ganging up on fathers?" Reese asked.

Caroline looked at her daughter. "What do you think?"

"Men against women," Jennifer said. "Must be."

Reese laughed. "If so, it's got to be genetic. I didn't teach you that men are the enemy. Or is it something you learned in school?"

Caroline noticed a sudden dark look cross Jennifer's face. "What's the matter?" she asked.

"I just remembered. I've got to read a novel and do a book report for English. It's due Monday."

"Is there a book here you can read?" Reese asked.

"Yes."

"Why don't you get started, then?"

"Can I still go riding tomorrow?"

"Let's see how fast you read," he said. "You've got a few hours till bedtime. And you can get up early in the morning."

Jennifer got up from the game table. "Ugh. I hate school."

"It's only bad when you fall behind," Reese said. "Cheer up. You've only got one week of hard work ahead, and there's lots of help available."

Jennifer kissed each of them and went off to her room. After she was gone, Caroline and Reese regarded each other across the table.

"This is strange," Reese said, "us being together like this, I mean."

"Yes, it is."

He rested his chin on folded hands. "Let me ask you something. If our parents hadn't pressured us into splitting up, do you think we would have stayed together? Could this have been our millionth game of Sorry rather than our first?"

"I doubt it."

"Why?"

"People change so much from when they're young. I know I certainly did. Jennifer's even younger than we were, granted, but can you honestly picture her still caring about Carlos ten years from now?"

"No, of course not."

"Our parents probably thought the same thing about us. And they were probably right."

Reese acted a little surprised. "You're saying they were justified in doing what they did?"

"No. Disapproving of a relationship is one thing, but destroying one is another. Anyway, that wasn't what you asked. It was whether we'd still be together. All I said was that the odds are against it."

"Which brings me to my next question," Reese said. "Have you ever seen the high desert by moonlight?"

Caroline laughed. "Now there's a non sequitur if I ever heard one."

"Not as much as you might think. Grab a sweater and I'll show you what I mean."

Caroline was a little leery, but also curious. She got a sweater from her room, and they went outside. As they walked across the lawn, she looked up at the blanket of stars overhead.

"My God," she said, peering up at the heavens, "look at that."

"Beautiful, isn't it? All you have to do is get up in the mountains where the air is clear and there aren't any city lights and, bam, you discover what nature can really offer."

"It's incredible."

Reese laid a hand on her shoulder as they walked. "You're really sounding like a city girl."

"I *am* a city girl."

They came to the edge of the lawn, which gave a wonderful perspective of the valley. The moon was bright enough that she was able to see the muted greens and reds and browns of the landscape. The barren hills looked like mottled plaster of paris under the moonlit sky.

"I suppose you take this for granted," she said.

"It was all I knew growing up."

They gazed out at the vista as a cool night breeze rose, fluttering her hair. Caroline hugged herself against the chill. Reese put his arm around her, lending his warmth. She didn't object, choosing to interpret it as a kindness rather than a familiarity.

"Except for that one summer I spent with my cousin in Chicago," he said. "That summer took me to a different world, one that's stayed with me over the years."

The slight tremor in his voice signaled he wasn't just making conversation. Her awareness of him became more acute, and she shivered slightly, feeling uncomfortable. Reese rubbed her back, and she wondered if she should move away.

"A part of me never left Chicago," he said, his voice tinged with nostalgia.

Caroline did turn from his embrace then, taking a half step back. "Reese, why are you saying things like this?"

"Because it's true."

"Is that a good enough reason?"

"I think it is." He reached out and touched her face, drawing his fingers slowly across her cheek, then along her jaw.

Caroline froze. She was both mesmerized and horrified by his touch. Yet she neither moved nor said anything. She just peered into his eyes—the eyes of the boy who'd made love with her on that sandy dune on the shores of Lake Michigan. There'd been stars out that night, too. And a cool breeze. She recalled how they had wrapped themselves in an old blanket, the cocoon they'd shared against the intrusion of the world.

Love. Had there ever been such love, and could there ever be such love again? She'd wondered that in the silent musings of her aloneness in the years since then.

Summer love. The one and only fairy tale she'd ever lived ... until ... the clock had struck twelve.

Reese moved toward her slowly. She shook her head, but he took her face in his hands and kissed her anyway. For a long moment she stood rigid and still. Then her body began to bend, slowly curving into his, her lips parting to accept his kiss, her arms enclosing him as his enclosed her—together again in their cocoon, holding each other as they had before.

But then she remembered. She remembered who she was, where she was and who was kissing her. Tearing her lips from his, she worked her hands between them and pushed him away. The desert air washed over her, chilling her burning face.

The word *no* was on her lips, but she couldn't say it. She couldn't say anything. Tears flooded her eyes, making his face shimmer in the moonlight. Biting her lip, she turned and ran across the lawn to the house.

Chapter Six

CAROLINE AWOKE late the next day, having spent a miserable night. She dreaded seeing Reese because she hadn't been able to decide what their kiss last night had meant.

She found Jennifer in the family room, reading *Pride and Prejudice*. The girl had gotten up really early and had been reading furiously.

"I decided having to go to summer school would be the pits," she said. "Anyway, I want to go see you in Chicago this summer."

Caroline caressed the girl's cheek. "Where is everybody?"

"Dad's gone with Ben to check one of the herds, and Grandma's giving Miguel instructions about the flower garden."

"She likes to be in charge, doesn't she?"

"Dad lets her be bossy about the flowers because Miguel's the one on the receiving end. But he draws the line there."

Caroline sat on the arm of the chair. "So, how are you and Jane Austen doing?"

"I'm almost done, but I'm not sure what to say in a book report."

"That was one of my favorite books. Want to come into the kitchen while I have some coffee, and we can talk about it?"

They went off and had a good conversation about *Pride and Prejudice*. Caroline used the occasion to point out how sensible Lizzy Bennett had wound up with Mr. Darcy, whereas her impulsive younger sister had run off with a soldier whom the family had to bribe before he'd make an honest woman out of her. It was clear that Jennifer had seen through her casual comment, but they didn't argue over it.

By the time they finished talking, Lorena had scrambled Caroline's eggs. As she ate, Jennifer told her that Reese had promised they could go for a ride and picnic if she'd finished reading her book by twelve o'clock.

"Would you be terribly upset if I didn't go with you?" Caroline asked.

"Oh, you've got to come," Jennifer moaned. "That's the whole point."

Caroline decided it would be unfair to punish Jennifer because she was uncomfortable around her father, so she relented.

By eleven-thirty Jennifer had finished her book and written the first part of her report. Reese had returned to the house by that time, and Caroline ran into him in the hallway.

"Regarding last night . . ." she began.

He gave her an affable grin and said, "Sentimentality is hell, isn't it? Thanks for indulging my weakness so graciously."

"I hope you don't think—"

"I think you're a hell of a good sport to put up with me, Caroline. I promise to be on my best behavior from here on out, which I know is what you want to hear."

She gave him an uncertain look.

"But we've got to figure out how we're going to outfit you for our ride," he went on without skipping a beat. "You brought jeans. That's a start. Jennifer's got I don't know how many pair of boots of various sizes lying around, so unless you've got huge feet, we should be able to accommodate you. And there's a closet full of hats. That's a necessity because the sun can be brutal down here."

Caroline laughed, shaking her head. "If you don't open a dude ranch, Reese, you're really missing your calling."

He gave her cheek a pinch. "We'll talk about that later. Meanwhile the posse will be meeting in the living room in, say, twenty minutes. Tell Jennifer her job is to get you outfitted. I'll get our lunch from Lorena and see that the horses are saddled and ready. Any questions, Miss Parker?"

"No, sir."

Reese took her hand and kissed it. Then he gave her a sly wink and went off.

RATHER THAN HEADING into the hills, Reese planned on a leisurely ride along the valley floor. It would be easier going for Caroline, and there was a stand of cottonwoods by the stream where they could picnic.

They met in the front room. Caroline looked cute as hell in Jennifer's old boots—"half a size too small, but wearable"—and a hat that was half a size too large. Jennifer had tied a big red bandanna around her mother's neck for effect. No self-respecting cowgirl would wear designer jeans with cowboy boots, but that was easily overlooked, considering she was a greenhorn.

Reese made her turn around, as much as to admire the pleasing curve of her derriere as to evaluate her readiness for riding. "What do you think, Jen," he said to his daughter, "too pretty and fragile for the Wild West?"

"Stop, you two," Caroline protested. "I've got 'city slicker' written all over me and I know it."

They went to the barn, and Reese showed Caroline how to sit in the saddle and how to use her knees and feet, as well as the reins, to give commands. "It's important to be assertive," he said. "If the horse senses you aren't in charge, he'll take advantage of you."

"Sort of like a man, eh, Reese?"

He tipped his hat. "Walked into that one, didn't I?"

They mounted up and headed for the trail. Jennifer trotted on ahead while he and Caroline continued at a leisurely pace.

Reese looked over at the woman who'd once been his bride, admiring her. She wasn't much of a horse-woman. She needed to learn to relax in the saddle. She needed the right kind of jeans and a hat that fit her. She needed lots of practice before she'd look at home. But a deeper truth came to him with sudden clarity—Caroline was just where she belonged. He wasn't sure why, but he felt it in his bones.

Odd how the perspiration on her lip and the smudge of dirt on her cheek seemed just right. On the down-side she was wary of him. Maybe a part of her still hated him. But he wanted this woman. Fate had brought them together for a reason, and he wasn't going to make the same mistake twice.

CAROLINE SAT ON THE LOG, munching her lunch as she watched Jennifer toss stones into the stream. There was a lot of young woman in the girl, but also a lot of child. Reese sidled over and sat next to her.

"We produced quite a young lady, didn't we?" he said.

"Yes. I've only known her a couple of days, but it feels like she's mine as much as if I'd had her with me all along."

"I'm glad, Caroline. Real glad."

She considered telling him what his mother had said the previous evening, but decided it wasn't the time. Her feelings were muddled. From minute to minute she seemed to be pulled in opposite directions. For the time being the smartest thing seemed to be to avoid serious conversation of any kind.

"I'm glad I got to see you in your natural environment," she said. "I have a different mental image of you now."

"A better one, I hope."

"You like this life, don't you?" she said.

"There's nothing like a spirited quarter horse beneath you and the wind in your hair, Caroline. Believe me."

"You're a terrible romantic, aren't you?"

He pushed his hat to the back of his head and took a bite of apple. "I'm surprised you're just figuring that out now."

She smiled, then she got up. "I think I'll go see what Jennifer's up to." She ambled down to the stream. When Jennifer didn't notice Caroline's arrival, she gave her daughter's ponytail a tug. Jennifer turned and hugged her.

"I'm so glad you came back with me," she said. "Dad's been nicer."

"Has he?"

"I think he wants to impress you."

Caroline glanced back toward the log where Reese was seated. "I'm not sure that's a good thing. What happens after I'm gone?"

"I've been wondering the same thing," Jennifer said.

An hour later, on their way back, Caroline felt adventurous and urged her horse to gallop. By the time they reached the ranch house, she was more than a little sore and decided a hot shower would be a good idea.

After spending a good while under the soothing stream of water, she lay down to rest and, without intending to, fell asleep. A few hours later Jennifer came to wake her.

"Dinner in twenty minutes," the girl said.

Caroline, who was in her bathrobe, propped her head up on her pillow. "I enjoyed our ride this afternoon."

"Me, too. I wish I'd found you sooner. Like ten years ago."

Caroline took Jennifer's hand. "We can't think of the years we missed. We have to think of the time we'll have together."

"Grandma said you might move to Santa Fe. Is it true?"

Caroline felt a sudden stab of anxiety, mixed with a little resentment. Marian had no right getting the girl's hopes up like that. "She suggested I consider it," Caroline replied carefully, "but I've got a home, a business and a life in Chicago. For the time being we should think about you visiting me."

"Well, I hope you do move here. It would be great."

Jennifer went off and Caroline was left alone to think. Marian Claybourne was trying to manipulate her. Again. Although Marian seemed to have no evil intent this time, Caroline had been badly burned once by the woman and she was in no hurry to embrace her now.

At dinner Reese's mother was more than civil; she was almost solicitous, which made Caroline all the more suspicious. Nothing direct was said about the future, but the issue hung in the air. After dinner they went to the living room to talk. Marian and Reese had a cognac while Caroline and Jennifer drank coffee.

Reese was obviously indulging his mother, but Caroline could tell he was losing patience with her overbearing ways. But she'd called for her driver to pick her up, so they didn't have long to put up with her.

"I can't tell you how touching it is to see the three of you together," Marian said, beaming.

Caroline had to bite her tongue. How nice that Marian was happy at last. She could only conclude that the old woman was afraid—afraid because she knew that Caroline now had leverage when it came to Jennifer.

Mercifully Marian's driver arrived, and they said their goodbyes. "Perhaps I'll see you later this week," Marian told Caroline. "Do think about my proposal." The last word she said in a whisper, though the others must have heard.

Caroline gave Jennifer a hug, as did Reese. "We'll pick you up at the main entrance tomorrow after school," he told the girl.

"Bye."

Reese went with them to the limo, while Caroline lingered at the door. As the vehicle pulled away, she waved. Reese joined her and they went inside.

"Will you have a cognac with me?" he asked.

Caroline started to decline, but then thought, why not?

They went to the family room, and he got their drinks. Reese had no sooner handed her the brandy snifter than Lorena informed Reese that he had a phone call. Caroline waited alone, sipping her cognac. He was back in a few minutes.

"That was Carlos," he announced. "I'd asked his father to have him call me. He's coming over. I thought you might like to meet him."

"Sure."

"It won't take long, but I do need to talk to him."

"Fine."

Reese gave her a friendly, appraising look. "So, how's your backside?"

"A little sore."

"Tomorrow you'll feel it in your legs, but it won't be bad. If we'd taken an all-day ride, it'd be another story."

He turned toward her, bending his knee on the cushion and casually resting his arm on the back of the sofa. She could smell the pleasing masculine scent of his body. There was a vaguely seductive look in his eye.

"I'm glad we'll have a little time alone together," he said.

"Are you?"

"Yes. If we're going to share a daughter, we should be better acquainted."

It was the most definitive statement he'd made about the question of Jennifer's future. Caroline knew they were in uncharted waters and that they'd have to feel each other out before any decisions could be made. But all in all, everything felt pretty good so far—except, perhaps, where Marian was concerned.

"I hope my mother wasn't too heavy-handed," he said as though he had read her thoughts. "Old habits die hard."

"She means well," Caroline said, trying to find something positive to say.

Reese asked her about her shop, and she gave him an account of how she'd learned the ropes from Mrs. Mason, and then bought the woman out. Caroline was surprised at how knowledgeable he was about retailing. When she pointed that out, he explained that he'd been a partner in an art gallery in Santa Fe for several years—mostly a silent partner—and had picked up some insights along the way.

Soon Carlos Mendez arrived, and Reese brought him into the family room. He was a tall, slender boy, well-groomed, with coal black eyes, long lashes and an easy, charming manner. He seemed nervous, but had presence and knew how to talk to adults. Caroline could see why Jennifer was attracted to him.

After pleasantries, Reese suggested to Carlos that they take a little walk to discuss some things. Before leaving, he refilled Caroline's glass and put some soft music on. Carlos bid her goodbye and left with Reese.

The whole thing seemed innocent, but Caroline couldn't help wondering what was up. Reese could do what he wanted, of course, and his business with Carlos didn't concern her. Still, their meeting struck her as a bit odd. In fifteen minutes Reese was back, apologizing for abandoning her.

"I'm used to being alone," she said. Then she added with a smile, "I've always thought of myself as decent company and I rarely get bored."

He grinned, sipping his brandy. "I admire you, Caroline," he said with a touch of reverence. "I really do."

"Why's that?"

"For becoming what you are. For doing it alone."

"I haven't done anything special. I just live my life."

"It's not as easy to do as you make it sound. Not successfully," he said. He touched his glass to hers.

They sipped their cognac in silence for a while. Caroline was very aware of his proximity and the eyes that were always on her. The brandy made her feel warm and languorous, but Reese had the opposite effect, making her feel uncertain and on edge. It seemed to her awfully inconvenient that she was attracted to him, but there was no point denying it—at least to herself. What bothered her most was that she couldn't tell what he was thinking.

Caroline usually didn't drink, but she let Reese fill her glass again. He absently toyed with her hair, and it was obvious he was becoming seductive. But she felt mellow and didn't mind. In fact she was starting to like his attention. Being with him reminded her of the afternoon he'd come to her house, the day after they'd met. They'd talked for hours, and he'd eventually kissed her. She'd known he would, but he'd refrained from rushing it.

It was the same now, although the kiss had already taken place the night before. At the time, it had upset her, but in retrospect it didn't seem so bad. Maybe it was the brandy.

Reese grazed her cheek with his fingers. "Hear that?"

"What?"

"The song on the stereo."

Caroline listened. She recognized that it was Dionne Warwick, but not the name of the song, though it was familiar. "What is it?"

"'I'll Never Love This Way Again,'" he said. "We danced to it the night we met. Don't you remember?"

"Yes, now that you mention it, I do."

"I can't hear it without thinking of you."

Reese got up and went to the stereo, resetting it to the beginning of the song. He returned to the sofa, holding out his hand. "Is it too corny to relive an old memory, or will you dance with me?"

Caroline felt herself color, much as she must have at that dance fifteen years ago, all prim in her little cotton dress, her heart fluttering. She let him pull her to her feet, folding naturally into his arms as he embraced her.

Reese held her firmly, even more purposefully than he had that first time. Caroline inhaled his scent as she pressed her cheek against his neck. They swayed to the music, and she found herself surrendering to the moment.

The easy friction of his chest against her breasts, the heat of his body and his warm breath in her hair were arousing. His hand tightened around her waist. A recollection of the first time they made love—less than a week after they met—came to mind. They'd driven to the Indiana dunes, supposedly for a swimming party. But they'd wandered away from the group to be alone... and they'd made love. Thinking about it, Caroline sighed.

Reese must have noticed and sensed it was time, because he lifted her chin to kiss her. She kissed him back, surrendering and taking. She let herself get carried right back to her youth. She was in Reese's arms, and the memories of her greatest happiness were in her heart again.

"Oh, Reese," she murmured as they kissed more fervently.

The next thing she knew, he'd lifted her into his arms and was carrying her through the house. She gave herself up to it, hardly thinking until he set her down on his bed.

The room was dark except for the moonlight coming through the sliding door. Her thoughts were gathering, but far more slowly than events were unfolding. Reese had taken off his boots and was unbuttoning his shirt as he looked down at her, his face barely discernible in the shadows.

The questions, the uncertainty, were in the back of her mind, but they stayed there, unexpressed. She lay very still. Reese sat on the bed beside her. Leaning over, he kissed her sweetly on the lips.

"You had a smudge of dirt on your cheek this afternoon when we were riding," he said. "Seeing it made me fall in love with you all over again. I have to admit, though, I think it happened even sooner…maybe even when you first stepped out of the plane.''

She ran her fingers through his hair, remembering the texture of it, the feel of his cheekbone under her thumb. ''We shouldn't be doing this,'' she whispered.

He tapped her nose with his fingertip. ''Says who?''

''Says common sense.''

He bit at her lip as he kissed it. ''To hell with common sense.''

He undressed her, then finished undressing himself. She waited quietly as he opened the nightstand drawer and took out a small packet. They looked at each other, remembering, but neither of them spoke.

In a few moments Reese stretched out next to her and took her into his arms. Caroline could feel the wind off of Lake Michigan coming through the open sliding door of his home in New Mexico, the sand under them soft as satin. The heat of her desire was fifteen times mellower, fifteen times more intense than when she was an innocent girl.

They made love with the same mindlessness as they had that first time. There was only this need, this moment, this craving to be fulfilled.

She did not experience orgasms as a girl and had only on rare occasions since. But with Reese she came with a wild abandon that she could barely understand and could not control. It took her as he took her, with inevitability. She writhed under him, her insides pulsing even after he was spent.

Caroline lay suspended in the timeless moment, aware only of her pounding heart. Reese slowly came to life, kissing her shoulder, then the corner of her mouth. He rolled onto his back beside her, grasping her hand and pressing it against the moist skin of his stomach.

"God, Caroline," he said with a sigh, "what an utter fool I was to ever let you get away."

She lay still, in the grip of her contentment. Then she moaned softly, drifting slowly toward sleep, the cool air washing over her.

"I want you to come to Santa Fe . . . to be near Jennifer and me," he said with surprising insistence. "Move here," he said. "Be part of our lives."

His words hit her with the sort of shock that always came with an abrupt awakening. It was as if she were emerging from a wonderful dream—except she was fully aware that what had happened was real. She could hear Marian Claybourne saying, *I'll pay your expenses, Caroline. Everything.*

"What about the expense, Reese?" she murmured, hiding her wariness.

"I'll take care of it. Don't worry about anything. Just come."

Caroline lay very still, evaluating what was happening. Reese had seduced her. She was beginning to see it was for a purpose. He, like his mother, wanted her in Santa Fe. Things would be safer for them with her here. The Claybournes weren't fools. It was one thing to take a baby from a seventeen-year-old girl, another to try to keep a fourteen-year-old from her mother.

"It would please Jennifer if I moved here, wouldn't it?" she said, waiting for his response.

Reese squeezed her hand. "Are you kidding? She'd love it."

"And it would be more convenient."

"She'd have her mother and I'd have you."

"Would you, Reese?" she said, trying to hide her indignation. "Would you really?"

He rolled his head toward her, having detected she was upset. "What's the matter? Did I say something wrong?"

"I just wonder if you aren't being presumptuous."

"About what?"

"About what this means."

He lifted his head, his face screwed up with perplexity. "Caroline . . ."

She sat up, then started fishing for her clothes on the floor.

"What's the matter?" he insisted.

"Isn't it strange—if I'm inconvenient, you get rid of me. If I can be useful to you, you'll fall all over yourself making me feel welcome. Jennifer needs a mother right now, and since you can't hire one for her, you try to buy the real one."

"Caroline, what in the hell has gotten into you? Why this sudden outburst?"

"It's sudden because I just woke up," she said, fastening her bra. "Last time my father made me take it lying down. Well, not this time, Reese. I love Jennifer and I want her in my life, but it's going to be on *my* terms, not yours."

She quickly stepped into her panties and then her dress.

"I don't know what makes you think I'm manipulating you," he said, sitting up on the bed, "because I'm not."

She started to walk away, but he grabbed her wrist. "You've got to listen to me," he said, barely controlling his anger.

"Let go of me."

He kept a firm grip on her arm. "Something I said or did obviously upset you, but you're dead wrong about one thing. This...our making love...had absolutely nothing to do with Jennifer. If I was wrong to make love to you, it's because I was thinking too much about myself, what I wanted, and not enough about the consequences."

"Well, congratulations, Reese. Maybe you *are* growing up, after all. Another fifteen years and maybe you'll be a decent human being." She jerked her arm free and stomped from the room.

Chapter Seven

"BUT WHY DO YOU HAVE to leave now?" Jennifer demanded.

"Honey, something has come up, and I have to get back to Chicago. I wish I could stay until you finish your exams, but I can't."

They were standing in front of Jennifer's school. Kids were walking by, talking and laughing, getting in cars or heading for buses or the student parking lot. The girl looked over toward her father's pickup, where Reese sat passively waiting.

"But I was really looking forward to us being together," she said. "School's almost out."

"I know, Jennifer. All you have to do is buckle down for a couple more days, then you'll be free for the summer. As far as I'm concerned, you can come see me whenever you wish. When you've worked it out with your father, let me know and I'll send you a ticket."

Jennifer had a skeptical look on her face. "Can't you come back after you do whatever you have to do? Grandma said she was sure you'd be moving here."

"I'm sorry, but your grandmother assumed too much. I can't move here. But that doesn't mean we can't be together. You're old enough to have a say in where and how you spend your time." She looked at her watch. "But I have to get going. Your father's going to drop me off at a hotel where I can get a shuttle to the airport."

They started walking toward the pickup truck.

"How come we aren't taking you to Albuquerque?"

"Because you've got to get home to study, and the bus will get me there in time for my flight."

They came to the truck, and Caroline opened the door. Jennifer climbed in. Caroline got in after her.

"Dad," Jennifer lamented, "how come we're letting her go?"

"Your mom's got responsibilities, sugar," he said, starting the engine. "Besides, she's her own boss."

Caroline was glad Reese was being civil about her decision. That morning he'd tried to talk her out of going. They'd argued again, but she made it damned clear she wasn't changing her mind. It didn't matter what his intentions had been in seducing her, she told him. The point was, she wasn't going to make the same mistake twice. They did agree on one thing, though— they were not going to let her departure mess up Jennifer's exams. They would play down any sign of a rift, and both of them would make it clear that Jennifer was free to visit Caroline anytime during the summer that she chose.

They rode in silence. Caroline, who hated leaving her daughter more than anything, took Jennifer's hand.

"Are you ever coming back?" Jennifer murmured, evidently sensing that something was wrong.

"I might," she said, trying to sound upbeat. "Maybe sometime I can come pick you up, and we can go on a vacation together. That would be fun."

"Do you hate New Mexico? You don't like the ranch, is that it?"

Caroline pressed Jennifer's hand to her cheek. She hadn't known it would be this difficult. She'd thought a promise of spending some time together over the summer would pacify the girl. "Honey..."

"We've got to be fair to your mom, Jennifer," Reese said. "I twisted her arm to make her come here in the first place. As it is, we're lucky that she was able to get away for a few days without any notice."

"Call me as soon as school's over," Caroline said. "Or call me during the week. Anytime you want to chat, pick up the phone. And it's fine to call collect."

"That's not necessary," Reese said. "She can call you whenever she wants."

They arrived at the hotel. Jennifer's eyes were glassy, and Caroline's were teary, too. It was even more obvious to her now that coming had been a mistake. Reese had obviously counted on the fact that her emotions wouldn't allow her to leave—Santa Fe would prove to be an emotional trap. The part she hated most was that he'd played with her feelings for both Jennifer and him.

Sure, he cared for her. Probably some of his feelings for her were truly genuine. But she didn't want to be wanted for the sake of convenience. She wanted to be wanted for herself.

Caroline had spent the night wondering how enthusiastic Reese would have been toward her if Jennifer had disliked her as much as she'd disliked Sandy. Get rid of whoever's a problem and buy whomever you need—that was the Claybourne way.

Caroline embraced her daughter, and they exchanged tearful kisses as Reese climbed out of the truck. Then Caroline got out, as well. She dabbed her eyes with a tissue from her purse, then went around to where Reese had set her suitcase and carry-on bag on the sidewalk.

"The bus will pick you up right here."

"Fine."

She looked at him and he looked at her.

"I'm sorry, Caroline," he said, tipping back his hat. His eyes shone with emotion. "I didn't mean for it to work out this way."

"I didn't, either. I'm sorry, too."

"I hope in time your feelings toward me will soften."

"It was a mistake to try to relive the past, Reese, whatever your intentions. Love is a lot more than an old song and a few memories."

"You're right about that," he said.

They studied each other a moment longer, then Reese offered his hand.

"There's one common bond we'll always have," he said, "and that's Jennifer. I'd like to think we can work together in her best interests."

"I would, too."

Reese took off his hat and gave a sad smile that brought fresh tears to her eyes. He took a half step back, then got in the truck. Jennifer was looking out the rear window, her cheeks streaked with tears. As the truck pulled away, the girl waved, and Caroline waved back, watching until the pickup disappeared around the corner. It was the second-worst day of her life.

CAROLINE TALKED with Jennifer twice that week. Her exams were going well, despite the time she'd missed. She would not be getting all A's, but she'd pass. They talked about summer, and Caroline mentioned a lake in Wisconsin she used to go to with her mother when she was little. "I haven't been back since, but it might be a fun place for us to go," she said.

"Sure," Jennifer replied, "it'd be fun doing anything with you."

Their conversations allayed Caroline's biggest concern—that her abrupt departure would harm their relationship. There was no telling what spin Reese might choose to put on it, though there was no sign that he'd taken advantage of it to her detriment.

"I'm seeing Carlos tomorrow, after my last exam," Jennifer confided. "He called, and we're going to meet in the plaza."

Caroline wasn't sure why Jennifer had shared that particular confidence, unless the girl had sensed her alienation from Reese and had assumed that made her an ally. "Does your father know?"

"He doesn't have to know everything. I'm not a child."

"No, of course."

Caroline felt a sudden well of doubt. She wanted to be supportive, but she didn't want to encourage a dangerous course of action. Meeting Carlos after school was nothing in itself. But where might it lead, especially if it was in defiance of her father?

"Call me Friday, after you see Carlos," Caroline said. Jennifer promised she would.

They talked about other things, then Caroline got off the phone. She still felt uncomfortable. Things were getting complicated and, whether she wanted to or not, she was being pulled into the vortex of her daughter's stormy life. She considered calling Reese, but decided against it. She had Jennifer's confidence, and that would enable her to serve the girl's interests best.

When Caroline didn't hear from Jennifer Friday evening, she began to get worried. At nine o'clock she telephoned and spoke with Mrs. Barfield, Reese's housekeeper in Santa Fe. The woman told her that Jennifer had come home that afternoon all upset, then left a short time later with her backpack, giving no explanation.

"Does Reese know?"

"Yes, ma'am. That is, I called the ranch and told Lorena. Mr. Claybourne was out on the range dealing with some sort of emergency. Lorena was going to try to get word to him."

Caroline called the ranch next and got Reese. He'd just gotten home and heard the news.

"I don't know where she is," he said, obviously upset, "but the first thing I should probably do is contact Carlos. I'll go to the Mendez place now."

"I don't know if you're aware, but Jennifer met Carlos this afternoon after school."

"How do you know?"

"A couple of days ago she told me she was going to be seeing him. I probably should have let you know about it, but I thought keeping her trust was more important."

"What's done is done," he said. "But I'd better track her down. As soon as I know anything, I'll give you a call."

Caroline hung up, feeling dreadful. She paced nervously back and forth, wondering if she'd contributed to the problem. God, what if Jennifer and Carlos had done something foolish? One thing was becoming clear—mothering from afar was not an easy proposition.

Around eleven that night Caroline's intercom buzzed. She couldn't imagine who'd be at her door at that hour. She went to the intercom.

"Yes?"

"Mom, it's me. Can I come in?"

Caroline was shocked. She met her teary-eyed daughter in the hall. They embraced.

"How did you get here?"

"I flew. But I only had enough money for a one-way ticket."

Caroline pushed back the girl's dark hair. "Honey, why didn't you let me know? Your father and I have both been frantic."

"Mom, I hate Dad," she sobbed. "I just hate him." Her lip quivered. "Dad gave Carlos a car and some money to join the army so that he can get his college paid for."

"What?"

"Carlos told me everything. Dad bought him off!" She began crying again as Caroline led her into the apartment. "I hate them both!"

They went into the apartment, and Jennifer dropped into a chair, her backpack at her feet. She wiped her nose with the sleeve of her jacket. "I want to live with you," she said, her eyes hardening. "I want to stay here and go to school."

It was midnight before Caroline reached Reese to tell him Jennifer was with her. He was relieved, saying he half expected it after talking to Carlos.

"Reese, she's really mad," Caroline told him. "Livid is more like it. I think you turned the screw one too many times."

"I did it for her, Caroline. Carlos's father was pleased. The boy's going to get an education. Everybody wins!"

"Especially you."

"What do you mean, *me?*"

"Doesn't this business sound at all familiar?"

He cleared his throat. "If you're talking about us," he said, "you're wrong. This is completely different. Jennifer's only fourteen. I have responsibilities to her."

"Yes, but I'm not sure manipulating people is the best way to meet that responsibility. It's not enough to mean well. Can't you see that? Everything you do is calculated for effect. Everything."

"Caroline, if you think making love with you was an attempt to manipulate you, you're wrong! Dead wrong!"

"I think we've got a more pressing problem than that to worry about right now, don't you?"

"All right," he said, his voice low and full of emotion, "what shall we do?"

"I'll keep Jennifer for a while. At least she's finished school, and we have the summer to figure things out. I have no idea how long it will take her to get things into perspective, but time away from you should do you both good."

"Does that apply to us, as well?"

"Reese, you and I are not the issue! What happened the other night was an aberration."

"An *aberration?*"

"Just let go, will you, please?"

He didn't speak for several moments, then he said, "Call me when you and Jennifer have decided what you want to do. It seems my attempts to resolve things keep falling short."

CAROLINE LOOKED OUT over Lake Michigan from her vantage point at the top of the dune. Jennifer was wading in the lake, seemingly enjoying herself, but Caroline knew a dark shadow hovered over her happiness. The past two weeks had been bittersweet. They'd cherished their time together, but things had been different since Reese's letter and the legal documents had come.

The letter, which she'd been carrying around with her, was addressed to them both, though Caroline knew it had mainly been written to her. As the balmy breeze caressed her face, gently tossing her hair, she gazed down at her daughter. Yet it was Reese who was in her thoughts.

Unable to help herself, Caroline dug into her purse and took out his letter, as she had so many times the past week.

Dear Caroline and Jennifer,

The past few weeks I've learned some things about myself that I just hadn't been able to see before. Caroline, when you said, "It's not enough to mean well," I realized I'd been living my life under a misapprehension.

Jennifer, I realize now that what I did with Carlos was wrong, regardless of my intent. My actions showed a lack of respect for other people and set a poor example. Caroline was right, I was repeating mistakes my parents had made. I should have found a way to solve the problem with you, not for you.

My family's sins against you, Caroline, are unforgivable for the pain they've caused. You were denied your daughter for fourteen years. I might have been young when she was first taken away, but when I was old enough, I made no attempt to right the wrong.

Under the circumstances, it only seems fair that your rights as a mother be restored. I have had my lawyers draw up papers that give you joint custody with me. If this is satisfactory, all you need do is sign and return the enclosed documents. As far as where Jennifer will live and go to school, I defer that decision to you and her. I will provide whatever financial support you feel you need.

These small steps cannot begin to right the wrongs I've committed. I don't expect you to forgive me, but I hope to earn at least a small measure of your respect for trying to do what is right. Despite the mistakes I have made, one thing remains true— I love you both and always have.

> Love,
> Reese

Caroline put the letter away. Every time she read it, there was more forgiveness in her heart. Of course, that had undoubtedly been his intent in writing it, but if he was sincere, what was wrong with forgiving him? And there was nothing to be gained from Jennifer being alienated from her father. Caroline wanted to see them reconciled, for both their sakes.

Down at the water's edge a couple of teenage boys passed Jennifer, obviously trying to get her attention, but she ignored them. The poor thing was heartbroken over Carlos. But she was young and she would heal. Dozens of crushes lay ahead of her.

Jennifer turned from her solitary play and climbed up the dune until she reached their blanket. She plopped down next to Caroline, looking disheartened.

"Looks like the boys are more interested in you than you are in them," Caroline said.

"I don't care about boys," the girl said. "I don't care about anything."

Caroline felt sorry for her. She was obviously having a rough time. "It's not easy to go to a place where you don't know anyone and start over. I think that's why I've always stayed here."

Jennifer picked up a handful of sand and sifted it through her fingers.

"You know, having you here has been wonderful. But if you decide you want to be with me for the next school year, it won't be like this all the time."

Jennifer looked up. "What d'you mean?"

"Only that you and I have been on good behavior up till now. But sooner or later I'm going to do something you won't like... maybe set down a rule or tell you you can't do something. I want to be your friend, Jennifer, but I have to be your mother first."

"Yeah, I know. But it won't be like Dad."

"Maybe not. Time will tell. Still, it won't be easy."

Jennifer brushed her dark hair back from her face and stared out at the lake. Caroline saw the same sadness in her eyes that she'd seen in Reese's when they'd said their last goodbye. It brought a lump to her throat.

"You miss your friends at home, don't you?"

"Sort of," Jennifer said, resting her chin on her knee. She drew a heart in the sand with her finger. "I wish I'd met Carlos here. At least you'd have let me see him. Not bribe him to go in the army like Dad did."

"No, I wouldn't have done that. But I would not have necessarily encouraged the relationship. At least not until you were ready."

Jennifer looked at her with surprise. "You wouldn't have let me see Carlos?"

"With groups of kids it would have been fine, but I agree with your dad that you're still too young to date a boy that much older. Your father's mistake was the way he handled it. There was room for compromise."

"I thought you understood, because of what happened to you."

"I understood you needed to be part of the decision process. You needed to be trusted. Rules are important, but they have to be reasonable and fair."

Jennifer continued playing with the sand, but Caroline could almost see the wheels turning. Finally Jennifer lay back on the blanket and stared up at the puffy clouds.

"I wish you and Dad were still married and that you both were my parents. This last year would have been different."

"A lot of things would be different."

"Are you sure you don't want to move to Santa Fe?" Jennifer asked, almost pleading.

"Listen, Jennifer," Caroline said, "I don't want you to think you've got obligations toward me, because you don't. You have friends, a home, a school, a life in Santa Fe. At your age those things become as important as family. If you want to live there and go to school there, I understand. We can still see each other summers and holidays."

Jennifer was silent for a long time. Caroline stared out at the lake, remembering how, all those years ago, she and Reese had watched the dusk fall until the water and the sky were black. She remembered how they'd clung to each other in their cocoon under the blanket, in their own little world.

"Maybe I'll go back home to talk to Dad," Jennifer said. "If I do, will you come with me? Just for a few days to make sure Dad's really changed?"

"I don't think that's necessary, honey."

"Please. For me."

Caroline smiled. There was so much of Reese Claybourne in her daughter—not that that was surprising. Caroline shook her head, marveling. What was it about the Claybournes that made it so hard to say no to them?

Chapter Eight

WHEN THEY PULLED UP to the ranch house, Jennifer gave her mother a meaningful look before she got out of the rental car. Caroline jumped out of the driver's side and hurried around the car, where she took Jennifer's hands. Just then the front door opened and Reese appeared.

Jennifer waved and called to him. "Hi, Dad." She gave Caroline another desperate look. "Are you sure you shouldn't be with me when I talk to him?"

"Very sure. I think it's important that you deal with him."

Jennifer nodded and headed toward the house. Reese stroked her head as she passed him and went inside. He peered out at Caroline.

"Aren't you coming in?"

"No, I think I'll sit out on the lawn and let you two talk."

Reese looked disappointed but he didn't object. "There are some things I want to say later, Caroline."

"Okay. I'll be out here."

She found a lawn chair in a shady spot and sat down to look out across the valley at the white-topped mountains. The caps had shrunk considerably over the summer. Only the highest peaks were still dusted with snow. The thin mountain air was hotter than it had been at the end of May.

She heard the door open and glanced back toward the house. Lorena appeared. She made her way across the lawn.

"I thought maybe you would want a cool drink, *señora*," she said, putting a tray down on a small table nearby. "You like lemonade?"

"That sounds good. Thank you."

Caroline took the tall glass Reese's housekeeper offered. The woman glanced back toward the house.

"I never did hear so much crying and laughing from a father and a daughter," she said. "They are...baring the soul, as you say."

"That's good," Caroline said.

"If you want to know what I think, you are a good influence, *señora*."

"I hope so."

The housekeeper went back in. Another fifteen minutes went by before Jennifer came running out of the house, a big grin on her face.

"I'm going to stay for the school year," she announced happily. "Dad and I made a deal. And he arranged for us to see a counselor. He's going to try to understand me, and I promised to try to understand him."

Caroline smiled as she got to her feet. "Wonderful," she said, hugging the girl. "It sounds like things are working out for the best."

They were brave words, but there was a catch in her voice as she spoke. Having Jennifer in her life had changed things. She liked being a mother. Yet she'd prepared herself for the inevitable, because she knew that this was the way it should be, as long as Reese and Jennifer could come to an understanding.

"Dad said I can have a pre-school party, so I'm going to call my friends and see who all can come. Tiffany will help me organize it."

Caroline patted Jennifer's cheek affectionately. Then she looked up to see Reese coming across the lawn toward them.

"I'll talk to you later," Jennifer said, turning back toward the house. She gave her dad a high five as they passed.

Reese ambled up, looking as happy as Jennifer had.

"Sounds like you two have patched things up," she said as cheerfully as she was able.

"I owe you a tremendous debt of gratitude," he replied.

Caroline shook her head. "No, I want her to be happy. Besides, you did me a big favor letting Jennifer be with me for the summer."

Reese gestured toward another chair near her. "Can we talk for a few minutes?"

"Yes, if you want."

He pulled the lawn chair up next to hers and settled into it. For a moment he gazed off across the valley, then said, "By my reckoning, our accounts are square. You have free access to Jennifer, whenever you want it. We have joint custody, and neither of us owes the other a thing except continued goodwill. Would you agree?"

Caroline nodded. "Yes, I think so."

"Then would you agree I have no reason to manipulate you?"

The question perplexed her. "What do you mean?"

"Caroline, let me be brutally frank. I want you to stay here with me. Not for Jennifer's sake. For mine."

She was immediately suspicious. "Were you and Jennifer inside plotting?"

"No, I swear I didn't even hint that I was going to say this to you. I didn't want her to be disappointed if you said no, and I didn't want you to feel any extra pressure. I only wanted you to know this is a request coming from the heart."

She shook her head as emotion flooded her.

"Before you answer," he said, "you should know that I haven't been able to get you out of my mind. When I saw you last May, I realized that the greatest tragedy of my life was allowing our parents to separate us. You said the odds were against the marriage working because we were so young. Maybe that's right. But

I do know the love I feel for you now is not immature. We're both adults and we can put the mistakes of the past behind us, if we just try."

Her eyes filled with tears. She chewed at her lip to try to keep from crying.

"I know I'm asking a lot," he went on. "There's a risk that it won't work. You called me a romantic once, and maybe I am a romantic fool, but I want us to have another chance at love."

She looked into his eyes, seeing that boy who, the night she told him she was pregnant, had said, "We're getting married. I don't care what our parents think. Damn it, we're getting married."

The bright New Mexico sun filtered through the trees, playing on Reese's face. She gazed at him, feeling her resolve drain away. Was it weakness, or was it love? Was it a quick cure for her needs, or a glorious second chance at happiness?

"There's that little problem of us living a thousand miles apart."

"You went to Kentucky with me once, can't you come to New Mexico now?"

"I was pregnant."

"Well, I was in love and I wanted you to be my wife."

Caroline put her face in her hands. She half cried, half laughed. "Reese, this is crazy. It's as crazy as us running off to Kentucky like we did."

He reached over and took her hand. Caroline looked down at his fingers, and her heart flooded with warmth. He pulled her hand to his lips and kissed it.

"You weren't wrong to say : ˑs last time. Only the circumstances were wrong."

"Why am I even considering such a foolish thing?" she said. "We both can't be fools."

"Maybe you feel the same way I do," he said, looking into her eyes.

She squeezed his hand as hard as she could, feeling anger and love. "I don't know whether to love you or hate you."

A big grin spread across his face. He rolled his tongue through his cheek, then chuckled. "Don't fight it."

"Easy for you to say."

"Come on, Caroline," he said, his eyes pleading and laughing. "I love you. Always have, always will."

CAROLINE STEPPED into the tiny, enclosed garden outside the chapel. The air was fragrant with spring flowers. Once again it was late May, but it was a May like no other. She glanced down at her beige silk suit and the pearls Reese had given her for a wedding present. She was nervous.

All morning she'd been flashing back to that town in Kentucky and the little house where they'd found the justice of the peace, a brusque man with a smudge of catsup on his shirt from breakfast. He'd summoned his wife and daughter to act as witnesses. In scarcely ten minutes she'd become Reese Claybourne's wife. It had seemed so right, not because she was carrying his child, but because she loved him.

His proposal that day she'd returned with Jennifer to Santa Fe had been almost as compelling as that first one. "How about May 28?" he'd said. "For sentimental reasons. We can have wedding cake and birthday cake both. And maybe if that date is twice as good in the future, it will help make up for all the bad ones in the past."

She had asked for time to think it over, and Reese could do nothing but agree. After all, such a move would mean making a lot of changes—selling her business and condo, starting over. Besides, Caroline wanted to be sure she wasn't making a mistake. So she'd decided to relocate to an apartment in Santa Fe first to see how the three of them adjusted to being in close proximity. If all went well, then she'd consider his marriage proposal.

Right from the first, things had gone well among the three of them. She and Reese worked hard to present a united front to Jennifer, and thankfully she responded. The only fly in the ointment was Marian Claybourne. Caroline simply did not trust the woman.

Then, in early November, a week before Caroline's birthday, Marian asked her over for dinner. Caroline was sure the old woman had something up her sleeve, but to her complete surprise, Marian went out of her way to be kind. After dinner she gave Caroline a present, and that in itself surprised her. But she was overwhelmed when she opened the package to reveal a beautiful diamond bow pin.

Marian told her that her husband had given it to her for a wedding present, and it was her favorite piece of jewelry. Caroline protested that she couldn't accept such a valuable gift, but Marian insisted that it was only right that she have it since Caroline was the mother of her only grandchild, whether she married Reese again or not.

Then Marian Claybourne hugged her, saying that she knew she didn't deserve it, but if Caroline could find forgiveness in her heart, she'd do her best to be worthy of it.

Caroline was deeply moved by the abjectness of Marian's apology. And though they never referred to it, things were a lot different between them after that.

At Christmas, she agreed to make the engagement official. Jennifer was ecstatic, and Reese seemed overjoyed and somewhat relieved. They really became a family after that. Caroline rarely went to her apartment, staying either at the house in town with Reese and Jennifer, or at the ranch. All they were waiting for was May 28.

The door of the chapel opened, and Jennifer stepped into the garden. She was wearing the pale blue dress they'd picked out together. Reese and Caroline agreed she was the perfect bridesmaid, though Jennifer was more concerned how Jason Kroll thought she'd look. Although Reese hadn't been thrilled, it was agreed the boy could attend the wedding and reception.

"If he's that important to you," Caroline had said, "he's that important to us." Reese had dutifully nodded, even though his fatherly instincts were obviously screaming no.

"Everybody's about ready, Mom," Jennifer said.

Caroline stepped inside the reception room where she and Jennifer had dressed. She and her daughter faced one another and clasped hands.

"I don't know which of us is more nervous," Jennifer said, sounding almost giddy.

"I am, definitely," Caroline replied. "The man waiting out there to see you is one among several boys you'll know in your life. The one waiting for me is the man I'm going to spend the rest of my life with."

"Yeah. But you know, you've already married him once."

"True."

They embraced, picked up their bouquets and went to the door. Lorena signaled for Jennifer to take her place. The music began, and she started down the aisle. Then Caroline stepped to her mark. She peered into the chapel. Kitty was there, grinning, along with their other friends and Reese's relatives, but Caroline's eyes went right to the man waiting for her. His smile was so broad and happy it beckoned her to his side.

The first notes of the wedding march sounded. Caroline took a deep breath and started walking down the aisle, thanking God for her good fortune. It was Jennifer's birthday and her wedding day. May 28, the most wonderful day of the year.

Dear Reader,

I've always felt a strong connection with the women who came before us—our grandmothers, great-grandmothers and even farther back to those women who found their way in a world without the Equal Rights Amendment, the vote, or even the status of a valuable human being.

They raised families, gave generously of their love, their idealism and their spirit, and most of them never even wondered how to find time for themselves. Yet the paintings and photographs they left behind show us how beautiful they were without the benefits of collagen cream and lip liner, how beautiful their clothing was, and how skillfully it was adorned.

I took a fashion history class while researching a historical novel and was fascinated by what nimble fingers could bring about: lace created on a hairpin, flowers embroidered out of ribbon, ruffles, pleats, ruching, scalloped edgings and beading that took years to complete!

When asked to take part in this collection of wedding stories, I immediately caught sight in my mind's eye of a very modern and busy heroine affected, as I have been, by the charming fashions of a bygone time. I added a meddlesome mother, an unforgettable ex-husband, a setting on the forever beautiful Oregon coast and a parade of wedding dresses out of the past to offer you a glimpse of *The Bygone Bride*. Enjoy!

Muriel Jensen

THE BYGONE BRIDE

Muriel Jensen

Chapter One

I *HAVEN'T* LOST IT.

Delaine Porter sipped at a bottle of mineral water and paced moodily around her drawing table. Her steps traced a broad circle, as though the table at the center were a hostile entity from which she must keep her distance.

After three weeks of trying to develop something new for her unique line of giftware—and failing—the table had become her enemy.

Delaine looked around her new studio, the one she'd always wanted. It had every amenity, and took up the third level of a restored Victorian on Boston's historic Back Bay. The success of the designs with which she'd launched her business four years ago had made it possible for her to purchase the beautiful house.

She continued to be amazed at how much her life had changed in that small span of time. She'd gained confidence in her ability, and an office in New York. The name of Delaine Designs was on the back, the bottom or the front of almost any item that could be purchased in a gift shop, from greeting cards to underwear. She'd become a household name.

After years of poring over this same drawing table, she'd achieved success beyond her wildest dreams.

She'd also lost a few things along the way, but who didn't? That was the price of fame.

She barely acknowledged the aching feeling in her chest. That was where her love for Max used to be. But that place was empty now, and she'd learned to live without him.

What she couldn't live without was the creativity that flowed from her brain through her fingers to the paper. Work defined her now. She had to be able to continue.

She marched back to the table and firmly set her bottle of water on the tabaret beside it.

"I have *not* lost it!" she said aloud, taking a little comfort in hearing the denial.

Then she smiled wryly as she straddled the stool. She sounded like a woman trying to convince herself that her virginity remained intact.

The doorbell pealed loudly through the house.

Delaine groaned at the interruption, then ran lightly down two flights of stairs, hoping it was Dorchester Deliveries with her art supplies.

She yanked the door open, an anticipatory smile on her lips—and felt it freeze there in stunned disbelief.

It was not Dorchester Deliveries.

It was the Dastardly Duo; her mother and her sister.

Delaine felt tension close around her stomach like a fist. No. *No.* She didn't need this now. Her family managed to stay on good terms only because her divorced parents and her sister lived in San Francisco, while she stayed on the other side of the continent.

"Sis!" Jalisa hugged her briefly, then walked into the house. She raised her eyes to admire the plaster medallion in the middle of the living room ceiling. "Wow," she breathed.

"Hi, Lisa," Delaine said.

"Dee, darling!" Allie Winfield wrapped her daughter in a perfumed embrace. Delaine couldn't help but notice that the skirt of her mother's white crepe suit stopped well above her shapely knees.

Allie's overwhelming embrace made Delaine feel as though someone had dropped a radio in her bathwater. Her mother was all electric energy, sparking impulse, vibrant emotion.

"Hi, Mom," she said, suddenly realizing how much she enjoyed the physical contact. She hadn't been held by anyone in more than a year, she remembered absently. The simple pleasure surprised her.

But her mother was trouble. She always had an idea. And her ideas always drew everyone in the vicinity into their whirling vortex. Delaine didn't have time for that now. Her career was in crisis.

Allie pulled away and smiled delightedly. Delaine saw her own features reproduced in her mother's bright blue eyes, her straight nose, her softly rounded chin. But Delaine's blond hair was dark as honey, thick and usually caught carelessly back in a ponytail. Her mother's was salon enhanced to platinum, side parted and fell smooth and straight to her shoulders.

"So how's my little marketing wonder?" Allie asked. "I swear, you can't go anywhere without bumping into your work." She quickly hugged her again, then followed Jalisa across the living room, her eyes perusing architectural details. "I like to think your success is all because I never made you clean up your art projects. Remember how they were always all over the dining room table, the floor of your bedroom, the coffee table?" She threw her arms open. "Isn't this the most magnificent room?"

It was. Delaine had been captivated by it when the realtor had first brought her into the house. But now she sometimes wondered what she'd been thinking when she bought it. It was too big for her. And she spent most of her time upstairs in the studio.

Jalisa turned to smile at her. "You've become such a star. I'll never escape your shadow now."

Delaine swatted at her arm. Her sister had their father's dark hair and eyes, dramatic Audrey Hepburn eyebrows and a smile that she used discriminatingly. She dressed conservatively in jeans, a white shirt and a cotton blazer, which matched her more serious nature. Last year at this time Delaine had gone west to see her graduate from Berkeley with a journalism degree.

Allie and Jalisa proceeded through the house on their own, and Delaine had little recourse but to follow, accepting their praise, listening politely to their suggestions, then grudgingly leading the way to the third level when they insisted on seeing her studio.

Her mother and her sister looked foreign in the all-white room with its wide windows looking onto romantic Comm Avenue. Allie was too elegant, and Jalisa too serious.

Jalisa wandered around, looking at the designs Delaine had tacked on the walls around the room, some of them old, some new. Having her work posted all around her used to help her create. But it hadn't helped in the past few weeks. Nothing had.

Allie leaned over Delaine's drawing table and studied the half-finished design of children and animals she was working on. The drawing didn't have it. Delaine didn't know what it was lacking; she just knew something was. Every little figure was perfectly executed, but somehow there was no warmth in it, no life.

She waited for her mother to observe its deficiency. The woman had an uncanny ability to discern what was bothering Delaine and point it out with loving but brutal honesty.

But she simply turned from the table, perched on the stool and smiled at her. "This is a wonderful house."

Jalisa went to the window and looked out at the view. "Is Max's boat somewhere out there?"

Delaine felt a clutch of panic. Max. She'd never explained about Max. Oh, God. She didn't want to have to deal with that now.

She smiled evenly and said, with no audible sign of distress, "No. He gave it up about a year ago. No time."

She had no idea if that was what he'd done, but he'd talked about it—before they stopped talking altogether.

Jalisa accepted that without question and fell into an old wicker chair with a red-and-white-flowered cushion.

Wanting to divert the conversation from Max, Delaine looked from her mother to her sister. "All right, what's up? I know you haven't come all this way just to admire my new house."

"Actually we haven't," Allie admitted. She stood and wandered slowly across the room, arms folded, high-heeled pumps clicking loudly on the vinyl tiles.

Delaine knew that walk. It was the President-of-the-Junior-League walk, the fund-raiser-of-the-year walk, the Governor's-Board-on-Historic-Interiors walk. It meant she had an idea.

Delaine's suspicion was confirmed the next instant when Allie spread both arms and said with a wide smile, "Lisa and I have a great idea!"

Jalisa quickly denied responsibility. "It was *your* idea, Mother."

Delaine had been right. She went to the small refrigerator across the room and removed three bottles of flavored iced tea. She placed them on a wooden tray that bore one of her birds-and-flowers designs, along with three ceramic mugs from the same series.

"We're going to start a bridal magazine!" Allie announced. She selected a bottle of raspberry-flavored tea and hooked her index finger into the handle of a mug. Her grin broadened. "Doesn't that sound like an adventure?"

Delaine, leaning down to offer the tray to Jalisa, turned in surprise, causing her sister to lose her grip on the bottle, juggle it, then save it just before it collided with the floor.

Jalisa straightened with a sigh of relief and a scolding glance at Delaine.

"Sorry." Delaine handed her a cup, then carried the tray to a low table on which a few magazines and the morning paper were spread out. She sat before it in the wicker sofa that matched Jalisa's chair.

"A bridal magazine," she repeated. It did not sound like an adventure. It sounded like an exercise in personal and financial disaster. But she hated to rain on anyone's parade. "I . . . guess that could be an adventure. I imagine you've researched this and concluded there's a need for it and you can do it."

Allie laughed and poured the drink into her mug. "Of course not. I just *want* to do it. And you know how I am. When I set my mind to something, I'm invincible."

Delaine glanced worriedly at Jalisa, who rolled her eyes and shrugged helplessly.

"Mom." Delaine put her unopened bottle of tea aside. "There are several well-respected bridal magazines on the stands—"

Allie sipped her tea and gave her a scolding look over the top of her mug. "I know that, of course. But we have a different spin on it."

"And what's that?"

"We're going to call it *Bygone Bride,* and we'll feature only period dresses. Remember Clarinda Goodwin from Girl Scouts?"

Delaine nodded. She'd make her troop Indian costumes the Mohawks would have admired.

"She's designing a bridal line with everything from medieval-court dresses to fifties gowns. We're going to start with hers, but a lot of designers are putting period dresses into their bridal shows. Just think, Dee." Allie's eyes lost focus, obviously envisioning her masterpiece as it existed in her dreams. "With all the pressures on the modern bride, she has to take herself back in time to capture the romance she hopes to find in her wedding. And Jalisa has some good ideas on how to present the fashions—less portraitlike and more theatrical, dramatic."

Delaine had to concede that it did seem to have a more interesting edge than the average bride magazine, but the capital required to launch and support such a venture still concerned her.

"Mom," she said, trying again, "I know Daddy sees that you're comfortable, and that you've got a bundle on your own, but this . . . well, we're talking a lot of money. You'll need models and photographers and advert—"

Allie nodded, seeming not at all concerned. "I've been 'marketing' charities all my life. I've dealt with newspapers, convention facilities, contributors and socialites the world over. I have connections the French don't even know about."

Delaine smiled at the feeble joke. "Let's hope so, because one of them may have to put you up before this is finished. Mom, think. What do you know about this?"

Allie put her tea aside and stood again. She strolled across the room, this time her pace relaxed, a little arrogant and all female.

Delaine knew this walk, too. It was the spoiled-heiress walk, the so-your-father-thinks-he-can-leave-me-for-his-secretary walk, the don't-you-dare-suggest-I-can't-do-it walk.

"My friends have always used me as a fashion and style consultant," she said with no attempt at modesty. "I think it's time I put that skill to use. And we had the good fortune to bump into an up-and-coming photographer while we were picking out gowns at Clarie's. He was there working on her catalog. He's willing to work with us for less than scale for the exposure." She swept a hand toward Jalisa. "We have a brilliant young creative director/copy writer/cum dogsbody and a pair of gorgeous models." She patted her elegantly styled bob. "And, of course, I'm qualified to do hair and makeup."

Delaine stood and went to take hold of her mother's arms. "Mom, do you have any idea what those models will cost you?"

Her mother smiled smugly. "I was hoping they'd cost me nothing more than a few days at the beach house."

Delaine tried to make sense of her mother's words and failed. She gave her a gentle shake. "Why should models who get hundreds of dollars an hour be happy with a few days on the Oregon coast?"

Jalisa joined them wearily and rested her forearm on Delaine's shoulder. "Because that's where we're planning to have our first shoot," she said, then looked her sister in the eye, "and the models she has in mind are her daughter and son-in-law."

Daughter and son-in-law. Delaine repeated the words to herself, striving for coherence. Allie had only two daughters, and Jalisa wasn't married. That meant she wanted to use *her*. Her and Max. Max, from whom she'd been divorced for a year without ever telling her family.

Chapter Two

DELAINE OPENED HER MOUTH to reply, torn between offering the scores of practical reasons why the project wouldn't work, and simply admitting honestly that she'd found the son-in-law her mother revered so highly in the arms of a secretary.

But she was saved from doing either by a subtle beep from her mother's watch.

"Oops," Allie said, turning in a circle to look for the purse she'd left on the floor near the stool. "Have to take my pill. Bathroom?"

Delaine walked her to the far corner of the room, which boasted a small but serviceable bathroom. She closed the door on her, then turned to stride toward her sister with a frown.

Jalisa met her in the middle of the room, both hands raised in a halting gesture. "I know, I know," she forestalled her in a loud whisper. "The whole thing is crazy. But you have to agree to help us! Mom's determined to do this, and if we have to hire models and pay for an exotic location shoot, we might not have more than one issue. Please, Dee."

"Lisa, I can't believe..."

Jalisa nodded again. "I know. But Mom *needs* to do this."

"What do you mean? Why?"

Jalisa looked heavenward in supplication. "Oh, I took her with me to a charity ball I was covering for the *Haight Herald* and Daddy was there, getting lots of attention from a group of gorgeous young things and she . . ." Jalisa shook her head. "You'd think a couple who's been divorced for thirteen years would get over each other, wouldn't you?"

Delaine put an arm around Jalisa's shoulders. Each of their parents was wonderful, but it had seemed that containing them within a marriage caused too much turmoil. Curiously their divorce, when Delaine was thirteen and Jalisa nine, hadn't seemed to end the turbulence.

Though continually busy and productive, Allie had seemed lonely without their father. Yet every time he appeared at the house to visit or take the girls for the weekend, the fireworks began.

Conversely the same man who was a loving, indulgent, warm and amusing father turned into an arrogant and argumentative man when dealing with his ex-wife.

Delaine had never understood it; she'd only known it had made her miserable for a long time. Until a year ago, when she'd acquired her own personal misery to deal with.

Jalisa, fortunately, had yet to fall in love. Unfortunately, though, that meant she had no personal grief to distract her from worrying about their parents.

"Anyway," Jalisa continued with a sigh, "she's been like a demon ever since. I don't know if she's trying to put him out of her mind, make herself feel young or what. But she's determined to launch this new career and has talked about nothing else for weeks. And all her denials about having researched it are a lie. She's got the demographics all worked out, advertising sales reps in all major metropolitan areas and an office on Russian Hill."

Delaine put a hand to her forehead. It was beginning to ache. "Do *you* really want to do this?"

She shrugged a shoulder. "The *Herald* laid me off because there's a budget crunch and I was the last one hired. So, I need a job." She made a face. "I know Mom would never let me starve, but you, Mom and Dad are so successful and accomplished, I don't want to seem like the good-for-nothing in the family."

Delaine laughed and hugged her. "Lisa, I'd like to help, but I don't know anything about modeling."

Jalisa rolled her eyes. "With those looks, you don't even have to. How come you got Dad's savvy, Mom's looks, and I took after Grandma Salvatore, who sold dried tomatoes in Sicily?"

The bathroom door opened, and Allie came out to join them, smiling eagerly over their laughing embrace. "Does this mean you've talked her into it, Lisa?"

Jalisa reached back to the coffee table for her bottle of tea. "Not exactly. She claims she doesn't know how to model."

Allie sat Delaine down on the wicker sofa. "It's going to be so simple," she said. "All it'll take is three days, four at the most. You and Max don't even have to *model*. What the two of you have is so special, it's obvious to everyone around you. And it'll be obvious to the camera. I can see it all in my mind, and the photographer's in complete agreement with me. Just think of it as a long weekend at the beach where you'll get to wear pretty clothes and relax with your husband. Then, when the eight-page spread comes out in *Bygone Bride* featuring Delaine and Max Porter, it'll be good publicity for you, and it'll help Jalisa and me. What do you say?"

Delaine looked into her mother's optimistic smile and just barely bit back the truth. *I say I'm divorced!* was on the tip of her tongue. *Max and I split up in the heat of anger, and all I've seen of him in the last year has been photographs in the community section. Far as I can tell he sees a different woman every night.*

Then her mother wrapped her arms around her. "Come on, Dee. I need your help. Do this for me."

That was it. Even Delaine in a career crisis couldn't deny her mother anything when she used four-millimeter guilt.

She was vacillating when her mother kissed her cheek. "Call Max, Dee," she implored. "Call him right now and see if he'll do it. Lisa and I have to fly back to San Francisco in the morning."

Delaine went to the cordless phone on her desk, pulled up the antenna, pushed the On button, thinking all the while that she hadn't called Max at the office in over a year. Would she even remember the number?

Then she watched in fascination as her long index finger tapped out the digits without hesitation.

"Teal, Burgess, Gaines and Porter," a cheerful young woman's voice said. Delaine recognized it instantly. "Good afternoon."

This was bizarre, surreal. But her mother and her sister had wandered back to the wicker sofa and were watching expectantly.

Delaine perched on the stool. She needed to sit down. "Hi, Nicki," she said as though she'd spoken to her just yesterday. "It's Delaine. Is Max with a client?"

There was an instant's hesitation, then the receptionist responded with careful courtesy and a hint of curiosity. "Delaine? Delaine! Uh ... hi. No, he isn't. I'll put you through."

MAX RECLINED in his high-backed leather chair, feet crossed and propped on the corner of his desk. In his lap were his notes on the Browder-Wing merger and half a bagel on a paper plate. Between his thumb and forefinger he waggled a pen.

His phone buzzed and he reached for it, his attention still snagged by the numbers on the page.

"Max?"

Everything inside him stopped. No. Couldn't be. And when he didn't respond, convinced he must have mistaken the voice, it said again, "Max?"

He lowered his feet to the floor, losing his notes and bagel to the tobacco brown carpet.

"Max, darling? Are you there?"

Darling? She had gone two rounds with him in the lobby of this very building, thrown his clothes out a second-story window to land in a snowbank, spoken to him only through her lawyer during the divorce and had been silent ever since. And she was calling him *darling?*

The line was heavy with silence.

"Max?" she prompted.

"Hello, Dee," he finally said coolly.

"Guess who's here?" she asked. Her voice was high, theatrically cheerful.

He began to suspect there was some sort of performance underway on her side of the conversation.

"Mom and Lisa!" she supplied, though he hadn't tried to guess. "Isn't that great?"

They'd had three and a half years of heaven together, followed by several months of hell. Since then, he'd had a year of abject loneliness. He knew her very well. Under the cheer in her voice he heard fear.

All the old protective instincts rose in response, but he reminded himself that just a year before, she'd listened to lies and walked away from him without even asking to hear his side. The knight in shining armor within him put aside his lance.

When he made no response, she continued, sounding more and more desperate. "You'll never believe what they're doing? They're going to start a magazine!"

Then he couldn't help himself. Airhead Allie and Jaded Jalisa? "A magazine?"

Apparently thrilled by even that small reply, Dee began to chatter. "A bridal magazine! Isn't that... interesting? They're starting small, but they have big ideas, and some of them are really clever. And guess what?"

She waited for him to ask.

He didn't.

"They need our help."

Contracts drawn up? he wondered.

"Not your help as a corporate lawyer," she said as though she were reading his mind. It startled him that she could still do that. "It's kind of complicated."

There was a moment's hesitation, during which he heard her small intake of breath, then she asked in that same pseudocheerful voice, "Do you think you could come home early? They have to fly back first thing tomorrow morning."

Max leaned back in his chair and propped his feet up again. He tapped the pen against his thigh as the situation finally became clear. She'd never gotten around to telling her family about the divorce.

Her attorney had asked him right after the decree not to mention the divorce to her family if they were in touch with him. She'd intended to find the right moment to do that herself. Apparently she hadn't.

So, in the intervening year, with three thousand miles between Delaine and her mother and sister, their busy lives hadn't crossed closely enough for anyone to notice that she no longer had a husband.

Until now.

So. He was in a position of power. He liked that. And he wasn't above using it.

"Why, darling," he replied, seesawing the pen from finger to finger. "I no longer live with you. And I like it that way."

A second ticked by. "Could you pick up takeout from Madino's on the way?" she asked intrepidly. But he heard the panic rising in her voice. "Or would it be easier if we came by for you and ate out?"

He played with the pen and thought. He was crazy to even consider this. He owed her nothing. Still, a day hadn't gone by in the past year that he hadn't thought about her—and remembered what their life together had been like before the temp service sent Paulette Bristol to his office.

All right. He had to establish a bottom line. "For the sake of argument, let's say I understand the problem and help you out here." He heard that small intake of breath again. "What's in it for me?"

He let the question hang there with all its selfish and suggestive inferences.

"A long weekend on the Oregon coast," she replied without hesitation. There was that same cheerful lilt in her tone for the audience on her end of the line, but a definite frost at the heart of it was aimed directly at him.

He had a few theatrical tricks of his own. He sighed heavily. "Nice as that sounds, I'm in the middle of merger contracts and I can't just—"

"Well...what do you suggest?" she interrupted. "That is, if you don't want Madino's?" she added quickly. She wanted her mother and sister to believe they were back to discussing food.

He wrapped the pen in his fingers and pressed the top of it with his thumb. He was surprised when it snapped in half. He tossed it onto the desk.

"I'm not suggesting anything," he replied. "I'm just telling you I'm not putting myself behind in my work to travel three thousand miles to spend a long weekend with you behaving like an icicle. I endured that for the last few months of our marriage, thank you very much." He paused, surprised to find temper building in him. He'd thought he'd gotten over being angry.

"Look," he went on. "I know you hate to admit to anyone that you failed at anything, but it's a fact of your life, Dee. Maybe you should try telling your mother the truth, rather than trust that we can pretend that we still love one another."

"Mom would never be able to digest that," she said with a light laugh. "Why don't you just bring home the *pupu* platter for four from the Red Dragon? Mom and Lisa can explain their plans to you, then if you can't fit it into your schedule, they'll just have to understand. Fair enough?"

Clever woman. His refusal to participate in whatever her mother's magazine scheme was would absolve Delaine of responsibility in it, and she could escape both having to do it and having to tell the truth about their divorce. She would simply pretend to be married to him tonight, then her mother and sister would head back home in the morning.

But she'd had things her way from the moment she'd walked into his office and found Paulette in his lap. This was his chance to turn the tables.

He seldom considered his role in the demise of their marriage, because he remained convinced it *had* been all her fault. Still, had he made her listen to him, even if that had required holding her down while he did so, they might be together today.

But his feelings had been hurt that she'd listened to lies and never asked him what happened. And that she'd filed for divorce without telling him she intended to.

She'd made a prideful mistake.

But so, he supposed, had he.

And there were moments, sometimes in the middle of the night, sometimes in broad daylight and without warning, when he regretted it.

"All right," he said finally. "I'll be there in an hour."

She hesitated. "Do you...? I...ah..."

It took him just an instant to grasp the problem. "Yes, I know where to find you. I had to sign off the papers on the old place when you sold. It had your new address on it."

She sounded relieved. "Good. We have tea and coffee and wine, so we should be all prepared. See you in an hour."

"Right," he said. "Bye, *Darling.*"

The line went dead.

Max hung up the phone, folded his hands behind his head and leaned back with a groan.

You should have told her to take a flying leap, he told himself. You should have told her there wasn't a chance in hell you'd come to her rescue. Who do you think you are? Lancelot, St. George and Richard Gere all rolled into one?

No. He knew who he was. He was Maxwell Wallace Porter. The man who still loved her.

Chapter Three

WHEN DELAINE HEARD Max coming up the walk, she
hurried to unlock the front door while her mother and
sister struggled, laughing, in the kitchen with a bottle
of wine and a corkscrew. Her heart thudded and her
palms were damp.

This is ridiculous, she thought. *I used to be married to
him.* But she'd had erotic dreams about him almost
every night since their divorce, and she had a horrible
fear that he would read that in her face.

The dreams were always so vivid. She could feel the
hair on his chest against the tips of her breasts, his
broad hand splayed between her shoulder blades, his
muscled legs entangled with hers while he plundered
her mouth with his.

Just the memory of her dreams caused her to utter a
little moan and to feel a single shudder in her femininity, reminding her even more clearly of how he'd always made her feel.

Unfortunately Max chose that moment to shoulder
the door open.

He had a smile in place and a welcome for his in-laws
on his lips. But instead, he found himself face-to-face
with Delaine, and she wore a look of desperate long-

ing. For him? He was startled into stillness. It was the same distracted, out-of-focus look he'd seen on her face countless times when he'd brought her to climax. It usually accompanied a series of little gasps, eloquent shudders and sometimes even a tear or two. And it always ended with her arms wrapped around his neck, and a long, warm sigh breathed against his throat.

He fidgeted, aware of an uncomfortable pressure in his groin.

Then Delaine focused on him, and he saw distress in her eyes. Had his hands been free, he would have put one to her cheek in comfort. But he had his briefcase in one hand and the *pupu* platter for four in the other.

A burst of laughter from the kitchen shattered the moment, and her expression changed abruptly. It was now a combination of the cold accusation he'd seen on her face during the last six months of their marriage and a kind of feverish desperation he didn't completely understand. He would have thought it related somehow to her need to make her mother believe they were still married. But it seemed to go deeper than that. She appeared vaguely off-center, a little disoriented, as though she'd suddenly looked up and discovered she was lost.

"Dee, is that Max?" her mother called from another room.

Delaine's eyes darkened threateningly, and her chin angled in stubborn defiance. That was another look he remembered well.

"You will tell her you're busy!" she whispered angrily, taking a fistful of the front of his white shirt. "That you don't have time to go away for a long weekend. Do you hear me?"

Anger simmered inside him. It annoyed him that it only exaggerated his desire.

Over her head he saw Allie and Jalisa enter the room.

"Hi!" he called with a welcoming smile. "What a great surprise!" Then he took advantage of the fact that Delaine still held his shirtfront and leaned down to plant a kiss on her lips as a reminder that he hated being told what to do.

It was more than chaste, but he didn't let it go too far. He didn't want to overplay his role.

When he raised his head, Delaine flashed him a glare just before Jalisa took the platter and Allie shoved her older daughter aside to walk into his arms.

"So, WHAT DO YOU THINK?" Allie asked. She'd explained her new project and her plans for the shoot. The platter was down to one crab puff. She popped it into her mouth with no apparent pang of conscience. "Four days relaxing on the beach. You'd have to work a few hours in front of the camera, but you can really think of this as a short vacation. We want to start working a week from Friday morning. So we'd need you there Thursday." She sat beside him at the table and put an arm around his neck. "Tell me you'll come."

Delaine gave him a warning glance from across the table. She didn't want to do this. There were pale blue shadows under her eyes, and he wondered idly if she'd been working too hard, not sleeping well. He wouldn't be surprised. In the first glow of grand success, she'd probably signed a contract someone should have looked over for her first.

It was clear she expected him to refuse her mother's invitation. In fact, her eyes demanded that he refuse. That was all he needed.

"Sure," he said to Allie, smiling blandly into Delaine's glare. "We'll do it."

"But you said . . ." Suddenly panicky, Delaine began to repeat the argument he'd given her on the telephone.

He reached across the table to catch her hands. "I know, darling. But your deadlines and my clients always come first. It's time we did something for ourselves." He squeezed her fingers in warning. "And for Mom and Lisa."

Jalisa, seated beside Delaine, stood and leaned across the table to kiss his cheek. "Thank you, thank you! Now I'll be among the employed again. And if you have to work, why not do it at the beach?"

He pinched her chin. "My sentiments exactly. How's your love life these days?"

She rolled her eyes. "Don't ask. Action's been slow. Very slow."

Delaine tidied up the table and made a fresh pot of coffee while her family and her ex-husband caught up on their lives. As she worked, she privately called Max every kind of a rat, though she had to admit he'd done a skillful job behaving as though they were still married.

He had asked her mother and sister only those questions he wouldn't already have learned through Delaine. When Jalisa mentioned having missed him at her graduation, he apologized profusely for his absence and explained that he'd intended to come home but had been socked in at Heathrow at the time.

Jalisa frowned and said, "Delaine said you couldn't get away from the office."

Delaine panicked for an instant, but he replied smoothly, "Now that we have a London office, I have as much trouble getting out of that one as I do this one."

Any discrepancy in their stories vanished, and Jalisa moved on to another subject.

So on the one hand he was helping her sustain her charade. But on the other he'd just done precisely what she'd asked him not to. He was forcing them into four days of intimate proximity at the family beach house, where the pretense would have to continue.

She closed her eyes and groaned at the prospect. If anything could kill her creativity permanently, that should do it.

Then her mother walked into the kitchen, yawning, and another, more immediate problem claimed her attention.

"Dee, I'm dead on my feet," Allie said. "And I'm so relieved you two have agreed to do this that all the starch seems to have gone out of me. Where do I sleep?"

Sleep. Of course. She had to put her mother and sister up for the night.

And that meant she had to do the same for Max. It would shatter the performance if he left to sleep at his own apartment.

This was rapidly going from bad to worse.

Delaine settled her guests in two separate rooms on the second floor while Max carried their bags up from the living room.

He'd shed his jacket and rolled up his shirtsleeves. He seemed annoyingly at ease. She concluded from the grin he gave her over the top of her mother's head that he was aware of the sleeping dilemma.

Delaine found him thirty minutes later in the kitchen. Her mother was already asleep, and her sister was showering.

"I suppose you think you're very clever," she said without preamble.

He turned with a mug of coffee in his hand to lean against the counter. He'd cleaned up the kitchen, she noticed, but refused to give it a moment's thought. She didn't want her anger diluted by the thoughtful gesture.

He considered her, his eyes dark and lazy. "If I were clever, I wouldn't have come tonight."

"Then why did you?"

"Because you sounded desperate."

"I never got around to telling them about the divorce," she admitted grudgingly as she went to pour herself a cup of coffee.

"So I gathered."

She fell into a chair at the table with a sigh. "I wanted to tell her, but she was carrying on about how good we look together, how we have something the camera will see." She gave him a dry look over her shoulder. "How we'll be the perfect romantic bridal couple to launch the magazine. Lisa thinks she's fixated on the idea because she saw my father surrounded by young women at a charity ball."

Max sat opposite her at the table. With his white shirt and clean good looks, he did look like a full-page ad for the casual groom.

"Maybe it won't be as hard as you think," he suggested, sipping at his coffee. "In fact, I bet it'll be a cinch."

"Really." She rested her chin on her hand and asked, openly skeptical, "Why?"

He shrugged as though it should be obvious. "Because the pressure's off. We know it only has to last a few days, then we won't have to deal with each other anymore. So all we have to do is behave like affectionate acquaintances until it's over. We can pull that off, can't we?"

She met his gaze steadily. "We'll be forced to share a room. I seem to recall that the last few months we spent together, you found me . . . unappealing."

He held her gaze long enough that she lowered her eyes.

"As usual," he said, "you misread the situation. I found you consumed with your work, often absent, preoccupied, suspicious, judgmental and closeminded." He recited that litany with merciless ease. Then he added with sudden weariness, "But never unappealing."

That revelation unsettled her. She straightened in her chair, struggling for composure. If he could handle this situation, so could she. It didn't matter that there was all this . . . this *stuff* between them, that it didn't feel as over as it had when she'd left him, that she could look across the kitchen table at him and remember in vivid detail the times they'd sat over breakfast after a night of lovemaking and looked into each other's eyes, remembering.

Heat filled her cheeks. She looked at Max to find that he had been perusing her face and noted the change. His eyes locked on hers, and a small, grim smile quirked his lips. "That's just the kind of look your mother will expect to see," he said, pushing away from the table. "But for safety's sake, you'd better not turn it on me. Where's our bedroom?"

"Second floor," she said. "Far end of the hall. I sleep on the window side."

He put his cup in the sink. "Will I find a pair of men's pajamas if I look around?" he asked.

She turned sideways in her chair, trying to form a casual reply. He made acting casual so difficult. "Sorry. You'll have to sleep in your underwear."

He arched an eyebrow. "No men friends?"

"Several," she replied. "They just don't sleep here."

"Do you sleep there?"

Delaine found it interesting that he asked—and that he seemed to be persisting to get an answer. It gave her the first feeling of control she'd enjoyed since he'd walked in the door. She took considerable pleasure in it.

"*With* them, you mean?" she asked in wide-eyed innocence. "On occasion." She reached across the table for a napkin so that she could look away from him. She didn't want him to see that she was stretching the truth.

She had slept with Jon Fielding—or rather, beside him—at an Artists for America weekend flea market and camp-out. The ground had been hard, her sleeping bag soggy, and her companion had been in his own bag. Its only redeeming feature was that the proceeds had gone to feed the homeless. Despite that, she thought the situation close enough to allow her to answer in the affirmative.

"You aren't going to ask for details, are you?" she asked, using her napkin to wipe at a spot on the table-top. "The man who's been squiring a different woman every night for the past year?"

Mistake. She knew it before she'd finished, but it was too late to stop. Now he had the upper hand again.

He took a step closer to the table, hands in his pocket, smile interested. "How do you know that? Been keeping tabs?"

She shook her head, leaning an elbow on the back of her chair. "I always have newspapers spread around to catch the paint. And you're always *in* the paper with some young woman or other. If you're not careful, they're going to age you before your time."

Another mistake. She sounded petty and spiteful when she'd wanted to sound as though she didn't care.

"Not true," he denied with a grin. "I can provide proof of continued virility at any time."

"No, thank you." She smiled brightly, desperate for him to leave the room. "Good night. There's an extra blanket in the closet and more towels under the bathroom sink."

"Aren't you coming up? What if your mother decides to look in on us?"

"She's asleep."

The kitchen door swung open suddenly, and Jalisa stood there in a short terry robe, her luxurious hair piled up on top of her head. There was only a four-year difference in their ages, but Delaine felt as though the past year had tipped her into middle age.

"There you are," she said to Delaine. "Can I borrow some moisturizer? I forgot mine."

Delaine frowned at her. "Of course. Second shelf, my medicine cabinet. But you're twenty-two. Why do you need moisturizer?"

She came into the room to pat Delaine's face. "So I can look like you at twenty-six." Then she giggled. "Just kidding. You guys better get to bed if you're going to drive us to the airport. Flight leaves at seven."

"Right." Delaine avoided Max's eyes, but was forced to endure his casual arm around her shoulders as they walked upstairs with Jalisa following.

Delaine ducked away from him to lead the way into her bathroom.

Jalisa followed and frowned at the contents of the medicine cabinet when her sister reached for the moisturizer. "Geez. You don't leave any room for Max's stuff."

Delaine handed her the bottle and closed the cabinet. Max leaned a shoulder in the doorway, awaiting her reply with interest.

"He's just so naturally gorgeous," she said, spreading her arms wide with dramatic overstatement, "he needs no artifice. And, of course, I'm willing to share Band-Aids and deodorant."

He acknowledged her quick thinking with a twitch of his lips. "If you ladies are finished," he said, stepping into the small room, then urging them out with a sweep of his hand, "while I do remain naturally gorgeous, good grooming still requires a shower." He rapped Jalisa on the top of her head as she passed him. "See you in the morning, Lise."

The house was quiet and the room was dark fifteen minutes later when Delaine felt the mattress dip with Max's weight. The fact that she was extremely tired and that he remained firmly on his side prevented her from feeling uncomfortable with his presence.

"Good night," she said softly. Then after a moment she added grudgingly, "Thank you for coming over."

"Sure," he replied after a moment. "But you're going to have to tell your mother the truth sometime."

"I know. I just didn't want to deal with it now."

"Then relax. Everything'll be fine."

She wanted to believe that. She really did. But nothing had been fine in a long time. She couldn't imagine it would start being fine now.

Chapter Four

"GOD," MAX SAID as he turned the rental car they'd picked up at the airport onto the gravel driveway just outside of Blue Bay Beach. A weathered sign bore the name Winfields. "This is still one of the most beautiful spots on earth."

The driveway wound down at a gradual slope to the glass-and-cedar lodge-style home Delaine's father had built twenty-five years earlier. It stood on a dune that sloped farther down to a crescent-shaped beach and the beautiful blue bay it embraced. Giant rocks had been strewed at random by some long-ago eruption. The ones farther out served as a rookery for puffins and other water birds.

Flowers bloomed around the house and in hedges alongside the driveway.

Max had always loved the city, and never felt the urge common among many city dwellers to find some quiet country spot and settle down. But he did love it here. The Oregon coast was less sylvan and bucolic than wild and unpredictable. It wasn't a cozy country atmosphere, but elemental, even a little threatening.

He liked that about it. A man stayed on his guard here.

A sigh escaped Delaine as they pulled up behind Allie's parked pale green Mercedes. He couldn't tell what it meant. She'd been polite but quiet on the ninety-minute drive from the airport.

Her mother and sister, the plump Latino housekeeper and a lanky young man Max didn't recognize were already pouring out of the house, converging on the car.

There were hugs, greetings, laughter.

"Señor Max!" Fernanda said excitedly. She barely topped five feet and was almost that round. They'd been great friends when he'd been married to Delaine. "Is good to see you! And Delaine. How you are?"

"Great!" Delaine was almost surprised to discover she wasn't lying. As a child, this beach house had always been her favorite place. Her parents had fought less here, her little sister had seemed less obnoxious and Fernanda's good spirits could brighten up any teenage funk.

The summer after her parents had divorced, she'd sat on the deck through a rainstorm and come to terms with the change in her life.

And when she'd brought Max here to meet her mother for the first time, sharing it with him had been like inviting him into her cocoon. When she'd seen that he loved it, too, her pleasure in it had doubled.

She felt a sharp and unexpected pang at the heart of her contentment.

She turned at her mother's call to see that Max was watching her, the expression in his eyes assessing, speculative. She looked away. She didn't want him reading what was in her eyes when she couldn't understand what she felt herself.

"Darling, I want you to meet Clay Taft," Allie was saying, drawing a tall, lean young man forward. He wore old jeans and a T-shirt with a caricature of Edgar Allan Poe on it. His hair was shoulder length, straight and glossy black. His eyes were hazel. "Our brilliant photographer."

Delaine reached out to shake his hand and found hers held a little longer than necessary. "Mrs. Porter," he said with a small bow. He studied her with a gaze that went even deeper than usual male appraisal. Delaine felt unsettled by it for an instant. "Good bones *and* eyes with soul in them," he said. "Well. Hi."

"Hi," Delaine replied, drawing her hand away. "Mom's been raving about you."

He smiled modestly. "I'm pretty good."

"Clay," Allie said, physically pulling Clay toward Max as Fernanda released him. "I'd like you to meet Max Porter, Delaine's husband and a very jealous man."

Clay offered his hand and grinned. "Sorry. It was just professional distraction. Anyway, I've heard that men with beautiful wives only consider it a compliment when other men find them beautiful, too."

Max smiled amiably and shook his hand. "You'll live longer if you don't believe it," he said. "It enrages us. So watch it. I'd hate to have to kill you."

Clay barked a laugh. "I don't think I'd like it either. Help you with the bags?"

Allie, Delaine and Jalisa stood on the lawn as the two men followed a jabbering Fernanda into the house.

"Was that establishment of the male hierarchy?" Jalisa asked.

Allie frowned thoughtfully. "I think so. And definition of territory."

Delaine rolled her eyes. "You make me sound as though I'll be having cubs in the fall."

"I wish you would have cubs," Jalisa said, taking the makeup bag Delaine handed her from the back of the car. "I'd like you to get fat and blotchy and thick around the ankles."

Delaine pulled out her sketchbook and a pile of reading material she'd brought for quiet times and handed those to her mother. "Why?" She laughed.

"I'm tired of you being the pretty one," Jalisa replied candidly. "I'd like the role for a change. But that's not going to happen unless you age suddenly or grow warts."

"Now, there's a delightful image." Allie shook her head at her younger daughter. "Anyway, you're the clever one. Your creative input and your brilliant copy are going to gain everyone's attention."

Jalisa crossed her eyes and stuck her tongue out at Delaine. Then she smiled smugly. "I'm smarter than you. Mom said so."

Delaine laughed softly. "Yeah, but Mom *had* you. I think that makes her judgment suspect. Aah!" She danced aside to miss the toe of her sister's upraised foot.

"Here you go," Allie said, shepherding Delaine into the room where Max had already placed their luggage. He stood in the open closet, hanging up their suit bag. "This room okay? You're not tired of it?"

Delaine met Max's smiling gaze when Allie went to throw open a pair of French windows. Silently they shared the private joke that they'd be forced to room together.

It was a moment curiously without guile, cynicism or suspicion. Delaine smiled back.

Allie glanced at her watch. "Dinner in about an hour, then I'll show you the clothes you'll be wearing." She rubbed her hands together in eager anticipation. "You won't believe how wonderful they are." She smiled at her son-in-law and pinched his cheek with maternal affection. "When we get to work, you're going to have to try to look less military and more romantic."

"Military?" Max asked.

"Yes." She worked his shoulders as though to loosen them up. "And please don't threaten to kill the photographer again. It dims the ambience."

Max grinned. "Sorry. But he has to keep his hands off my lady."

"I'm sure he will now. Shout if you need anything."

When the door closed behind Allie, Max took a stack of underwear out of his open suitcase on the bed and carried it to the dresser near the window. He felt curiously irritable, edgy.

He'd known when he'd seen Taft take Delaine's hand and lose himself in her eyes that these few days weren't going to be a cinch, as he'd insisted they would be.

He didn't want to play this game. He wanted to hold Delaine down and tell her what had really happened with Paulette. He then wanted to explain that though he could murder her for what she'd put him through this past year, he still loved her and wanted her back.

But her mind didn't work that simply. He had to bide his time, choose his moment.

He opened the top dresser drawer and dropped his things inside.

"This is strange, isn't it?" Delaine wandered around the room, rubbing her arms, looking at the furnishings as though she'd never seen them before. She stopped at the window to part the lace curtains and look out. She was caught in a shaft of midafternoon sunlight. It etched the side of her delicate profile and gleamed in her golden hair, caught back loosely in a simple white ribbon that matched her shirt.

An emotion with barbed edges rose and swelled in Max's chest. He looked away.

"I mean," she went on pensively, "this scene is so familiar to me. I spent all my summers here as a child and a teenager, and you and I have been here together half a dozen times."

Something in her voice made him glance her way. She sat on the open windowsill, one leg folded under her. She frowned at the ocean vista. "But it feels different this time."

He pulled his shaving kit out of the suitcase. "How so?" he asked.

She shrugged a slender shoulder. "I don't know." She turned to him, something like pain in her eyes. She looked back at the water again. "I guess all the other times, my life was on the ascension."

The melancholy tone surprised him. He sat on the edge of the bed with his leather kit bag. "Delaine Designs just signed a seven-figure deal with National Greetings. I read about it in the *Boston Globe*. It's hard to think of that as life taking a bad turn."

She smiled a little sadly. It made him feel as though she'd learned some truth he had yet to understand.

"That's just business," she said. Then she got to her feet and came to the other side of the bed where he'd placed her bag. "And I'm not even doing that very well lately." She smiled thinly at him over the top of her case. "I think I'm about to become a has-been at twenty-six."

"That's absurd," he argued reasonably. "Artistic talent needs room to breathe, time to renew itself." Then he suggested quietly, "Maybe this weekend will give you that."

She looked skeptical.

He watched her pull out a stack of silky, softly colored garments and carry them to the dresser. She opened the second drawer and placed them inside. He watched the elegant line of her shoulders in the simple cotton blouse, remembered that he could span that slender waist with his hands, saw the full, rounded contour of her buttocks in the snug jeans and swore he could feel their satin weight in his palms.

She turned and started back to the bed. He lowered his eyes to his case and tried to remember what he was doing.

"Whatever happened to Paulette Bristol?" she asked quietly.

The mood shattered suddenly, violently, and all the old anger erupted in him to burn away any notion that they'd once shared something he now missed. The woman's head was harder than oak.

He took a pile of casual shirts out of the bag and let the lid fall down with a slam.

"No idea. I haven't seen her since that night in the Revere Building when I chased you down the stairs and you hit me with the flower arrangement. Why? Did you think I had her set up in some Beacon Hill mansion and visit her two afternoons a week?"

Delaine felt a curious stab of satisfaction at his open anger. Except for that night in the office building lobby, he'd been calm and controlled throughout the divorce. She'd hated that.

"I guess I expected you to marry her," she said, deliberately goading him. She carried a pair of hiking boots to the closet and dropped them into a corner.

"Goes to show you how wrong you can be," he said, picking up his empty case and sliding it under the bed. He straightened, and his dark eyes met hers across the bed. "I know that's an alien concept—that you could be wrong."

All-too-familiar feelings of hurt and helplessness billowed inside her, and she looked back at him, fists balled at her sides. "I found you *together*!"

He closed his eyes for an instant, as though to summon patience. Then he opened them again and conceded her point with a brief nod. "And reached all the wrong conclusions."

"She told me about Nantucket!"

"And I told you she lied."

"So you did," Delaine said, folding her arms. "And when I called the hotel, they told me you rented only one room for the night."

"Disregarding the fact that you felt you had to check on me," he returned angrily, "you consider that irrefutable proof that I made love to Paulette?"

"Isn't it?"

"Did I make love to *you* last night?" he demanded. "*We* shared a bed."

She opened her mouth to reply, then closed it again, pushing down the doubt that tried to rear its head. When Paulette had come to Delaine with the story about her and Max having discovered they were in love while marooned in the fog in Nantucket, she'd believed her easily. Supposedly they'd gone in response to a call from a panicky client who suspected embezzlement in his hotel chain. Somehow *that* had sounded like the lie.

Her father had left her mother for his secretary. It had been so easy to believe that the same thing had happened to her. Added to that, she and Max hadn't been getting along well for months.

She'd been working day and night to launch her business, and he'd been putting in fourteen-hour days as a new partner in the firm.

She sighed and accepted that it didn't really matter now. She dismissed the issue with a swipe of her hand. "It's all water under the bridge," she said quietly.

"You're a free agent. And you made it clear that night in the Revere that you don't feel you have to explain yourself."

He made a scornful sound and reached for the jacket he'd tossed on the foot of the bed. "A free agent pretending to be a married man so you don't have to explain to your mother that you blew off our marriage. I *tried* to explain myself that night, but you wouldn't listen. All you did was scream and hurl accusations and everything else you could find. I told you then, and I'm telling you again—you want details about that night, you have to ask me like a civilized human being."

She glared at him hotly, remaining stubbornly silent.

He yanked the door open. "I'm out of here," he said. "I'll be back in time for dinner."

Chapter Five

"LOOK AT THIS ONE!" Allie exclaimed in a reverent whisper. "Isn't it the most beautiful thing you ever saw?"

They were gathered in the huge living area. Allie had spread several clean sheets on the floor of the magnificent room. It was the perfect setting for their task, with its fieldstone fireplace and wrought-iron chandelier hanging from the vaulted ceiling.

On the sheets she'd placed the dresses Delaine would be modeling and several of the groom's shirts.

The dress she held up now had a low neckline, a high Empire bodice and layers of ruffle at the bottom of a slim skirt.

Jalisa, sitting on the floor taking notes, gasped at its beauty.

Delaine leaned lightly against Max in a corner of the sofa. He stretched an arm along the back to create the illusion of affection without actually having to touch her.

"It's gorgeous, Mom," she said.

Allie nodded. "And carries a four-figure price tag. So be careful with it tomorrow."

"Is this the dress you want to shoot on top of Puffin Rock?" Clay asked. He sat beside Jalisa, his back propped against the sofa.

Allie smiled as Delaine turned to her in dismay. "On *top* of Puffin Rock? How am I going to get up there?"

Allie deferred to her younger daughter. "Jalisa has that handled."

Jalisa looked up from her notes. "Helicopter," she said. "I've hired an expert crew."

"Coast Guard?" Clay asked.

She shook her head. "No. A private rescue team."

Delaine winced. "Rescue? I don't like the sound of this."

"Trust me." Jalisa winked.

There was something in that wink, Delaine noted. Some message being sent. But her mother was holding up the next dress, a Victorian confection with too much lace and fussy trim, and Delaine turned her attention to it.

SHE LAY IN BED that night, a broad expanse of mattress between her and Max, and stared at the ceiling. The salty, fresh smell of the ocean invaded the house, and the surf rolled and effervesced beyond the window.

She felt lost in time, caught somewhere between all that had been familiar in her childhood and the nebulous future to which she'd given so much thought since the onset of success.

She now had everything she'd thought she wanted, the big house, the thriving business, her name all over the retail world. But when she went home at night, she was alone in the big house and often found herself wondering if that was all the future had to offer—days filled with success, nights filled with loneliness. When she had been a teenager, she'd imagined things very differently.

She wondered for the first time if that was partially responsible for her creative crisis.

"What's the matter?" Max asked quietly in the darkness. "Still get insomnia?"

"Sometimes." She flung a foot out, fidgeting, and connected with his shin. Each of them drew back quickly, as though from danger. "I'm . . . just restless, I guess. Too much coffee tonight."

There was a moment's silence, then she felt him turn toward her. "Roll over," he said. "I'll rub your back."

The suggestion surprised her. All evening he'd been so careful not to touch her. She'd presumed he was still angry over their brief discussion about Paulette.

She should protest. She even wanted to, but the words wouldn't come.

"Come on," he prodded. "It always used to help when you worked too hard or were worried about meeting a deadline."

That was true. Color suddenly flooded her face, and she blessed the darkness. He'd once had some artfully ingenious cures for her sleeplessness. She turned onto her stomach and rested her hot cheek against the pillow.

Propped up on an elbow, Max firmly but gently pinched the base of her skull between his thumb and forefinger and massaged in firm circles down the back of her neck to her shoulders and up again.

His fingers left a warm puddle of relaxation in their wake and he repeated the process several more times.

Then his hand moved over her cotton nightgown from shoulder to shoulder, then once down the middle of her spine.

"That's not going to work," he said, then tugged at the back of her gown. "Brace up on your elbows," he directed, "so I can get between you and the gown."

Delaine complied, thinking in mild panic that it probably wasn't a good idea to let him get between ... But by the time she'd formed the thought, his warm, strong hand was splayed between her shoulder blades, the tips of his fingers making firm circles down and up her spine.

It felt like heaven.

She bit back the moan of delicious approval on the tip of her tongue and lay quietly under his hand, trying to remain as clinical about it as he appeared to be.

The warm puddle of relaxation spread from her neck down her back, then rayed out from her spine, soothing all her muscles, even relaxing the fists into which her hands had curled when he'd dipped his fingers under her nightie.

His hand worked at the back of her waist, then dipped a little lower until he reached the very base of her spine. And everything inside her that had been lulled into quiet comfort came sharply to life.

She lay tensed, waiting. Hoping.

"Better?" he asked softly. She thought his voice sounded a little strained. But she had no voice at all and couldn't reply.

Probably presuming she was asleep, he was still for one long moment, then tugged her nightie down and pulled the blanket up over her.

She expelled a breath of profound disappointment into her pillow.

Max turned onto his back, trying to block out the floral scent of her cologne, the tactile memory of her curves and hollows on his fingertips.

At least *she* was asleep.

So much for the theory that confronting his private agonies would make him better able to deal with them. He was in such a state of frustrated arousal that he probably wouldn't be able to relax sufficiently to close his eyes until October. Late October.

THE ARRIVAL of the helicopter was heralded by a droning sound that grew rapidly louder until the aircraft hovered over the front lawn like a raging insect. Everyone ran out to watch it land, then huddled near the house as the rotors created cyclone-force winds.

Max turned instinctively to shelter Delaine, who was already dressed for the shoot. Her veil caught the wind and wrapped around them.

She found it all so stunningly familiar. Her body against his, her cheek against his chin, his arm around her.

Then the wind stopped and she looked up, expecting to find that teasing look in his eyes that reminded her they were only pretending.

But it wasn't there. His dark eyes were filled with that brooding passion she'd once been so proud to be able to arouse. Then she remembered his hand on her bare flesh the night before.

Something in his eyes told her he knew all her secrets, was on to all her little charades. That he knew she still loved him.

She opened her mouth to tell him . . . she wasn't sure what. But at that moment her mother screamed, "Tony!" Delaine and Max both turned in the direction of the sound.

"Oh, my God," Delaine muttered under her breath as her father leapt lightly from the helicopter. The rotors had stopped, and two jumpsuited, helmeted men disembarked behind her father.

But Delaine ignored them. She concentrated solely on the man in jeans and a blue sweatshirt emblazoned with the name of his construction company, Castles on the Ground. Jalisa ran across the lawn to greet him. He wrapped his arms around her and swept her off her feet.

Delaine suddenly understood the significance of Jalisa's wink the night before. She'd been trying to get their parents back together since the breakup thirteen years ago. Her machinations had become a family joke.

The rescue team she'd hired belonged to Sal Bartola, who'd once worked in construction with their father and who sometimes flew him on short hops to look over sites or meet with clients.

Still in shock, Delaine watched her father walk toward her mother, who reached out stiffly but civilly to shake hands with him.

"What are you doing here, Tony?" she heard her mother ask crisply.

"We needed a father of the bride for this shoot," Jalisa replied. Then she smiled into her mother's look of disapproval. "He'll do it for free. And he hasn't seen Delaine and Max for a couple of years."

Tony turned in their direction as Allie and Jalisa whispered harshly to one another. Delaine went toward him, torn as she always was by warring feelings for him of love and fury. She'd once loved him so much, and he'd made Jalisa's and her lives so happy. Then he and her mother had begun to quarrel constantly, and before she'd understood what had happened, he was gone. She'd overheard her mother telling a friend tearfully that he'd left her for his secretary.

Even now, all these years later, she couldn't stop holding it against him. But he was big and charming, and her heart always tried to push all that aside and simply embrace him.

He crushed her to him, smelling faintly of the expensive cigars he still smoked despite all the surgeon general's admonitions. He framed her face in his hands and kissed her cheek.

"You and Lisa are still the most beautiful structures I've ever put up," he said, standing back to study her at arm's length. "How are you doing? When are we going to have bambinos?"

She'd parried his question a few times over the phone the past year while pretending she and Max were still married. But for some reason, this time her color rose, and she began to stammer.

Her father studied her narrowly.

Max stepped in. "Good to see you, Tony," he said, offering his hand. "She's busy designing other things. No time for babies right now."

"Max." Tony used that hand to pull him into his arm. He gave him one bone-crushing slap on the back, then pulled away. "Well, don't wait too long. I'm not going to last forever, you know."

"Okay." Jalisa moved in to take Delaine by the arm. "We're paying for this bird by the hour. Come on. You, too, Max. Mom, would you put Dad in costume while I explain the scenario to Dee and Max?"

DELAINE WAS LOWERED onto Puffin Rock in a wire basket in which a sheet had been spread to protect the gown. She took comfort in the knowledge that Max and her father had spoken to the helicopter crew beforehand and inspected the basket and its rigging. It was all accomplished far more simply than she'd imagined.

The top of the monolith, a good thirty feet up, had a flat surface about the size of a kitchen table. It was obviously damp and a trifle slick, but she discovered if she moved carefully, it wasn't difficult.

Clay shouted instructions to her, with which she tried to comply. "Look at me. Spread your arms. Turn into the wind. Look up. Look behind you. Look out to sea."

Waist deep in the water in high waders, he took shot after shot.

"Imagine you and your groom have had some kind of squabble," Jalisa had explained before Delaine boarded the helicopter, "and you've put yourself out of his reach until you feel it's resolved to your satisfaction. You love him but you don't want him near you until you understand what motivates him."

Delaine had frowned at her sister. "Good Lord, Lise. I'm not Meryl Streep."

To which Jalisa had patted her shoulder. "No, but you've always been Sarah Bernhardt. You can do this."

And she could, she decided. There was something about standing alone atop a thirty-foot mass of volcanic rock in the Pacific Ocean that gave one an air of icy solitude, a sort of royal command over all who stood below.

The air was cool, the sun filtered by tufty clouds moving across it, then exposing it again, lending even more drama to an already majestic seascape. The air was filled with water droplets from the surf crashing against the rock.

Clay directed Max into the water.

Max had put on the gray, shadow-striped wool pants and the frill-fronted shirt of the Regency period, only the shirt was undone to the middle of his chest, and the sleeves folded back.

Jalisa, also wearing waders, strode into the water to talk to Max, gesturing widely with one hand while pointing to Delaine with the other.

He glanced up at Delaine, his eyes piercing even across the height and distance that separated them.

She waved at him, feeling euphoric, like a powerful sea goddess.

Then Jalisa stepped back, Clay stepped aside and focused on him, and Max strode into the water.

The scenario, as Jalisa had explained it, was that he was coming for her. He would try reason, and if that didn't work, he would resort to force. That was the mind-set of the man of the period.

But she was thirty feet up on a rock.

Delaine joined her hands behind her back and looked down at him with haughty speculation. Clay stepped back to get both of them in the shot.

"Talk it out!" Jalisa shouted. "*Act* it out!"

Max, waist deep in the ocean, hands on his hips, looked up at Delaine with gentle indulgence. "Come down, my love," he said, telling her with a grin that he was willing to do his part for their little drama.

She folded her arms. "No," she shouted down. "Not until you..." She paused, considering some fictional wrongdoing that would lend zest to their pretense. Then it came without conscious thought. "Until you explain the little doxy on your arm last night at the opera."

Something flashed in his eyes that she saw even from her distance way above him. And she was suddenly very grateful that they were separated by thirty feet of rock. The fiction had struck too close to home.

"I explained," he said, expression set, "that she was the sister of a friend. She meant nothing."

Clay came in closer and shot several times. Then he moved behind Max for a longer view of them, still shooting.

She tapped her foot and looked away. "You looked very interested," she accused.

"I'd promised to squire her for the evening," he replied evenly. "You, as I recall, were supposed to be at the country house with your aunt."

She looked down at him. The night she'd found him at his office with Paulette in his lap, she was supposed to have been at a gallery reception for a friend. Paulette had told her about the Nantucket incident and asked her to give Max up. She'd thrown her out, then set up her own plan to catch Max in the act.

When she'd asked him to join her at the reception and he'd begged off, pleading too much work, she'd accepted his decision without argument, then gone to his office instead of the reception and walked in on him and Paulette.

"It was fortunate I had a change of plans," she said, "else I'd have learned too late you never loved me."

Max let his head fall back in exasperation. Clay shot a picture. "You misunderstood what you saw," he said. "I love you."

Delaine dropped her role for a moment, and let herself hear the words as Delaine, not as the spurned Regency bride.

She saw the sincerity in Max's eyes and tried desperately to read whether he, too, had forgotten the little drama they played.

She remembered with odd clarity that at the time she'd divorced Max, she had never even wondered if she could be wrong. Her pride had been too injured for her to think clearly, and all her divorced friends had commiserated. Besides, the same thing *had* happened to her mother.

But she found herself wondering now. She wondered absently if her top-of-the-world perch made her see things differently.

Was it possible that she'd been wrong? Could it be as he'd claimed that night in the Revere's lobby, that Paulette had set her up, that nothing had happened in Nantucket, that nothing had ever happened?

And as she took a step toward the edge to look down at Max, trying to read that possibility in his face, she forgot to be careful and slipped.

She flailed her arms with a little scream. Everyone watching gasped and stepped forward. Her mother screamed.

"You all right?" Max shouted.

She regained her balance, but realized with some surprise that she was not all right. She felt very insecure suddenly, personally and physically. The rock seemed all at once very slippery, very narrow and very high. And Max was so far away.

Her breath came in noisy gulps, and she felt extremely precarious, as though one well-directed little breeze could push her off the rock and into the swirling, shallow water.

"We need to get her down!" She heard her mother's voice, saw her push at the pilot, who'd landed on the beach, awaiting the end of the shoot.

"Dee, sit down!" Max shouted up at her. He pressed down with his hands to illustrate as the wind picked up and blew his voice away from her.

But even in her sudden fear, she remembered the dress's four-figure price tag, the friend from whom her mother had borrowed it and for whom she'd promised to keep it safe.

"The dress!" she said, spreading her hands helplessly.

"Forget the dress!" her mother shouted. "Sit down! The copter's coming for you."

She didn't think she could move anyway. She stood frozen, glancing down, hoping for a glimpse of Max. But he was gone, and her father stood there, smiling up at her. "It's okay," he said. "We'll have you up in a minute."

The trouble was, she didn't want *up*, she wanted *down!* But from this precarious perch, there was no way down, only up. And suddenly the ride in the basket suspended on a cable over the ocean, which had seemed like fun on the way in, was the last thing in the world she wanted to repeat now.

But she didn't want to stay here, either. The wind blew, the water swirled and the clouds seemed to be racing past her, disorienting her, making her body sway.

The desperate sound of her own breathing served to panic her further. She hated that. She'd never been the hysterical type.

Well. There had been that time in the Revere's lobby, but that had been fury, not fear.

"Max!" she said, fretting quietly. "Max, I wish you were up here!"

"I am," he said, hands appearing on the flat surface near her feet. His fingertips found a ridge of rock and tightened on it as he braced his foot against an outcropping. His head and shoulders appeared over the top of the monolith.

"Max!" she gasped, wanting to reach down for him but afraid in her vertiginous state that she would harm rather than help him.

He gained the top of the rock on his knees, then rose smoothly to stand in front of her, a wry smile on his lips.

"I'm here," he said. "You had plans for me?"

She wrapped her arms around him and held. The wind blew a little harder, but for her the world stabilized. There were shouts and applause from down below, and the growing sound of the helicopter as it arched out over the water and turned back toward them.

"I don't know what happened," she said into his ear as the roar grew louder. "I've never been afraid of heights. But I looked down at you and . . ."

He drew his head back to look into her eyes as she hesitated. "What?"

She saw his mouth form the word, though she couldn't hear the sound. The helicopter was now directly overhead. The basket was being lowered toward them.

And she suddenly understood that it hadn't been just fear of her rocky perch that had frozen her. It had been the sight of Max so far beyond her reach. It was as though the physical distance was a metaphor for the unbridgeable personal distance between them that she'd endured for the past fifteen or so months.

Tears pooled in her lower lids, and Max studied them with a frown. But the basket dangled right beside his elbow. He reached out to pull it in and hold it steady for her.

She leaned forward to shout in his ear. "Can't we go up together?"

He shook his head and pushed her gently into it.

Her eyes told him she didn't want to leave him. He let himself believe there was more behind that look than a need for the physical safety he provided.

He locked her into the basket.

"I'll be right behind you," he said into her ear, then kissed it. He looked up to signal the pilot, and she was hauled away.

THE LATE MORNING turned blustery, and they ate lunch in the living room before the fire. Though it was late June, the day had turned dark and gray, and the dancing fire provided warmth and cheer.

Delaine was wrapped in a blanket sipping her coffee, curled up against Max in a corner of the sofa. When she settled there, she hadn't stopped to think if she was doing it to promote their deception or if she was doing it for herself. She only knew it was where she wanted to be.

The Regency gown, miraculously unharmed, hung on a hanger on the guest-closet door, awaiting the afternoon shoot.

Max's shirt unfortunately hadn't fared as well, but Clay insisted the incident had resulted in several great shots.

And Jalisa had a solution to the shirt problem. Sitting cross-legged in the middle of the floor, she munched on potato chips and shook her pen at her mother, who'd expressed concern about the shirt.

"I think the front ruffles are okay," she said. "And the afternoon shoot is the formal family portrait and requires his jacket. That'll cover most of the shirt. So for the photos, we'll make do. We just have to reimburse Mrs. Goodwin."

Allie smiled fondly at her youngest. "You smart little thing."

Jalisa sighed as though the praise was burdensome. "I know. When's my first raise?"

Her mother laughed. "I think we should actually get an edition on the stands first."

"About the session this afternoon," Jalisa said, obviously getting into her role of director. "It's all pretty straightforward. Just family stuff."

Allie frowned at the rain spitting against the window. "But we were going to shoot outside."

Jalisa shrugged. "Not a problem. We'll just do it in here, use the fireplace for a backdrop, move the modern stuff out and replace it with a few period things like Daddy's flintlock, your glass bottles. It'll be fine."

Allie glanced across the room at Delaine, who raised an eyebrow in admiration of her younger sister's command of the situation.

Jalisa added casually, "I have your gown, Mom, and Daddy's things in my closet."

Allie asked flatly, "What?"

"It's a family setup." Jalisa met her dark gaze. "We talked about it, remember? That's why Dad's here."

Allie shook her head stubbornly. "I remember that your father's here. I don't remember that I was going to be part of the shoot."

Jalisa, perusing her notes, didn't look up. "Well, Mrs. Goodwin lent us a gown. And it's in your size."

"Interesting that you didn't mention this before."

Jalisa remained focused on her notes. "You selected the fashions. I thought *you* picked out the clothes for the parents of the bride for a purpose."

"No." Allie stared at the top of her head. "I didn't."

Jalisa looked up at that. Delaine admired the bland composure in her dark eyes. "Want to leave it out? We can. I wouldn't mind resting this afternoon. But it is our first edition of the magazine, and it seems a shame not to do our best because you'd rather not stand next to Daddy and look happy. Dee had herself lowered from a helicopter onto a rock, for God's sake. And it isn't *her* magazine."

Allie turned to her husband, sitting in the recliner near the fire with a glass of wine in his hand. "It might kill me," she said coolly.

Tony raised his glass to her and uttered a light, scornful laugh. "Come on, Allie. You'd have to be at ground zero for a nuclear bomb to even slow you down. It'll be fun."

"It'll be a lie," she said significantly. "And you know how I hate lies."

Delaine leaned into Max and closed her eyes, thinking that this was going to be one hell of a long, long weekend.

Max patted her shoulder consolingly.

THE AFTERNOON SESSION went far better than anyone dared hope. Tony and Max wore dark blue jackets with square-cut lapels and swallowtails. Delaine thought both of them looked heartbreakingly handsome.

Her mother, in a blue Empire gown with an overdress of lace-edged net, sported a satin turban with an ostrich plume and long kid gloves. She looked like a grande dame, Delaine thought, gone to Bath for the waters.

They played their roles. They posed in front of the fireplace, bridal couple between the parents, parents toasting the couple with Allie's antique crystal, mother talking with her daughter, father talking with his daughter, parents talking to the groom.

Then Clay suggested the bridal couple embrace in front of the fireplace.

Delaine was not surprised by how easy it was to slip into Max's arms and look as though she belonged. She was not even surprised when he looked down at her as though he wanted her there. After all, he'd climbed the rock to get her safely off.

Then Clay, who knew nothing about Allie's and Tony's history and apparently presumed the little exchange at lunch had been a joke, suggested putting them in front of the fire in each other's arms.

"You're handsome people," he said to Allie's open-mouthed surprise. "And you want this magazine to be different from all the others. When have you seen the parents of the bride looking as though they remember their own wedding day with tenderness and a little healthy lust? Come on. Give it to me."

Delaine put a hand over her eyes and turned her face into Max's shoulder. Jalisa waited expectantly behind the camera for her parents to comply.

Then, after a moment, Delaine heard the repeated click of the shutter, and Max whispering in her ear, "Dee. Look!"

Delaine turned to find that her father had a firm grip on her mother's neck beneath the back of her turban, the troublesome plume bent double in his other hand. He was studying her with far more lust than Clay's instructions had suggested.

Delaine remembered clearly how they'd been with each other when she was a child. They'd always argued and challenged each other on every issue, but they'd laughed a lot and been openly affectionate. And there'd been a constant glow about her mother and a twinkle in her father's eye that had suddenly, inexplicably disappeared.

But apparently it hadn't died.

And then he kissed her. Even Clay forgot his mission for a moment until Jalisa elbowed him. Then he shot frame after frame.

Delaine felt tears streaming down her face.

Chapter Six

DELAINE AWOKE after midnight, curiously conscious of being alone in the bed, even though the night before she and Max had taken great pains not to touch each other.

After the incident on the rock, she'd been looking for a way to broach the subject of their divorce. But for over a year she had buried it in pride and pretense, and she knew the effort to uncover it would hurt. She was tired of hurting.

The sound of male laughter vibrated from the living room. The men had begun a poker game shortly after dinner, and it was in full swing when she'd gone to bed. She presumed the exuberant good humor meant they were still at it.

Pulling a cotton robe on, she went the back way to the kitchen so as not to intrude upon their male camaraderie. She wanted a cup of tea and the last slice of the poached lemon cheesecake Fernanda had made for dessert.

She stopped on the threshold in surprise. Her mother was walking from the stove to the counter with a steaming kettle. On a plate beside a pottery mug was the slice of cheesecake.

"Couldn't sleep, either?" Allie asked. She wore tailored silk pajamas. Her face had been scrubbed clean, and Delaine thought she looked young and vulnerable without her carefully applied makeup.

Delaine shuffled across the tiled floor in her scuffs to join her. Male laughter rang out again, and she tilted her head in its direction.

"What is it about gambling," she asked as Allie took another cup down, "that bonds men? I mean, instead of feeling competitive and worrying about losing money, they seem to have a great time."

Allie carried their filled cups to the small table. Delaine opened the utensil drawer. She smiled over her shoulder at her mother. "I'll bring two forks. I know you intended to share this with me."

Allie pointed in the direction of the door. "Better make it three."

Delaine turned to find Jalisa standing there, hair mussed, legs tanned and slender under a long purple T-shirt with a drawing of a cat on it.

"How come they're making so much racket?" she asked with a yawn, hooking a thumb toward the poker game. She approached the table and took the fork Delaine handed her. "Thank you."

"To hide their fear, I think," Allie replied, going back to the kettle and brewing another cup of tea.

Jalisa frowned at Delaine. "Fear of what?"

"Us," Allie replied, placing the steaming cup in front of her. "Women."

"Why?"

Allie took a chair at an angle to Jalisa and across from Delaine. "It's a very old story. I guess because they're born and bred to be such fearless loners—and we present the temptation to compromise that independence."

Jalisa studied her mother vaguely under messy bangs. "I thought we represented affection, hot food and the opportunity to have regular sex."

Allie nodded. "That's what tempts them to compromise their loner life-style and take up with us."

"And they don't like that? Or they're afraid of it?"

"It makes them need someone other than themselves." Allie dipped her fork into the corner of the cheesecake closest to her. "They find that difficult."

"Maybe that's why they have so much fun gambling," Delaine speculated, also forking a bite. "It must seem a lot like love to them. Or marriage. When they marry us, they're gambling that their worlds will remain the same, that they can have affection, hot food and regular sex and still remain . . . detached."

Delaine heard the words come out of her mouth and wondered for one tense moment if she'd betrayed the true state of her marriage—or absence of it. But no one seemed to have noticed.

Her mother stared ahead, eyes unfocused.

Jalisa brushed the hair from her face and looked from her mother to her sister. "You guys are awfully philosophical for the middle of the night. And you're going to look like hell for the camera in the morning."

"Oh, it'll just be realistic," Delaine said, feeling suddenly reckless. "Many brides go to their weddings after a wild rehearsal dinner and party."

"You're wearing a sort of Guinevere dress tomorrow," Jalisa said. "I wanted you to look ethereal and virginal."

"Don't tell me." Delaine laughed. "You're going to balance me on a parapet."

Jalisa grinned wickedly. "Actually I was going to use the Pizza Palace's crenellated wall. Then I thought better of it. After we ruined one of Mrs. Goodwin's shirts, it didn't seem fair to send a gown back to her smelling of the four-meat combination. We'll use a woodsy setting instead, and pretend we're on the grounds of a castle." She sobered suddenly. "What happened to you on the rock today? One minute you were fine, and the next you looked . . . paralyzed."

Delaine had thought about that off and on all afternoon and since she'd gone to bed. She couldn't explain it, except that Max had seemed so far away, so out of reach. And after having him back in her life again, even in a fictional sense, that had seemed frightening.

She tried to look as though she'd shrugged it off. "I took a step and slipped, then I guess I suddenly realized how high up I was. It scared me."

"Good thing Max is strong and agile," Jalisa said, her eyes remembering the romance of the moment when he'd cleared the top and taken Delaine into his arms. "I had visions of losing you in the water." Then she looked apologetically delighted. "But I'll bet we got great stuff. Clay kept shooting even after Max reached you."

Delaine remembered how comfortable she'd felt in the shelter of Max's arms. Then she heard his laughter coming from the living room and couldn't help a fractional smile. The sound warmed her as it used to the first few years they were married.

There was the sound of quiet conversation, then her father's laugh boomed and she saw her mother's eyes refocus. Delaine remembered their kiss in front of the fireplace.

She turned to her sister, to find her watching her. Jalisa gave her that wink again. Was her scheme going to work this time? Delaine wondered.

The kitchen door pushed inward suddenly, and Tony walked in, the stub of a cigar clenched between his teeth, his eyes narrowed against the thin spiral of smoke rising from it.

He stopped short at the sight of the women. "Sorry," he said amiably. "We wake you?"

Allie's smile was bland. "It was a little like trying to sleep on a runway. When are you going to show a little respect for your health and stop smoking those things?"

He took the cigar out of his mouth, studied it, then used it to point at the middle of the table. "I see three forks poised over a combination of butter, cream and cheese. Not only high fat, but high cholesterol."

Allie angled her chin and put her fork down. "That's different. Other people can't suffer from secondhand cholesterol."

"No," he said with a significant look at her. "Secondhand stubbornness can be deadly, though." He held up the cup in his other hand. "Mind if I refill my coffee?"

"Go right ahead."

He did and was gone with a parting smile.

Allie sagged wearily against the back of her chair.

"Maybe," Jalisa said quietly, stabbing at the cheesecake, "it's time to forgive him for Maureen, Mom."

Allie studied her youngest defensively. "He never said he regretted it. And if he'd wanted forgiveness, he'd have asked for it a long time ago."

Jalisa dropped her fork and looked at her impatiently. "They were together one short month, and ever since then he's been right there on the fringe of our lives, stepping in every time we need him—that time you ran the red light and ended up in the hospital, then—"

"It changed when I was halfway across," her mother disputed haughtily.

Several eyewitnesses had reported differently, but Jalisa apparently chose not to argue. "Whatever. You spent three weeks in the hospital, and he moved back in to take care of us. Then when you came home and he wanted to stay, you said no just to punish him!"

"Punish him!" Allie shouted. "Of course I wanted to punish him. He ripped my heart out and . . ."

"Oh, stop it," Delaine ordered quietly. She shook her head at her mother. "You have a longer memory than the Mafia, and you turn everything into a production in three acts." Then she turned on Jalisa. "And you think you can take a major emotional problem and fix it with a few clever manipulations. Well, you can't. This never was a perfect family, and it never will be."

When she'd finished, the room rang with silence. Her mother and sister were staring at her. She was not surprised. She had no idea where that superior little speech had come from, either. Unless it was that she'd always wanted her parents reconciled as much as Jalisa did, but she'd been old enough to know it couldn't happen.

She stood abruptly and carried her fork and cup to the sink. "What time are we starting in the morning?" she asked Jalisa.

"Nine," Jalisa replied stiffly.

"All right. See you then. Good night. Good night, Mother."

"Good night, George."

Delaine turned at the door to raise an eyebrow. "George?"

Allie pulled the cheesecake toward her with a bland glance in Delaine's direction. "That was General Patton's first name. I couldn't help noting the resemblance."

Delaine headed back to bed and almost collided with her father, coming out of his room with a fresh cigar. She gave him a condemning look. "Mom's right. You should go easy on those if you expect to see your bambinos." *Particularly*, she thought, *if you have to wait for Jalisa's.*

He leaned a shoulder in his doorway. "That's always been your problem, baby," he said. "You think your mother's right about everything, and she's not."

Delaine folded her arms and felt the words rise up out of the dark corner where she'd kept them for thirteen years. She didn't know why they chose this moment to surface, but didn't question it. She questioned him instead. "Is that why you left her for another woman?"

He stared at her a moment, but betrayed no real surprise. "All right," he said, straightening away from the door and stepping backward into the room. "Let's have that out now. Come in and sit down."

She followed him into the room, but declined his offer to sit. "It shouldn't take too long," she answered, "to explain why you cheated on my mother and ruined my life."

That did surprise him. She could see in his dark eyes that he was deciding which part of her two-pronged attack to deal with.

"I left your mother," he said, pushing the door almost closed, "because...I was a coward."

That was not an admission Delaine had expected from the very male Tony Fanizza Winfield. She dismissed it with a scornful sound. "That must be why you were decorated for bravery in Korea."

He smiled thinly. "Death is relatively easy to face in certain situations," he said. "But looking into the eyes of a woman you love who wants something from you you can't give her is..." He made a subtle sound of pain that raised gooseflesh on Delaine's arms. "It's worse than death."

Delaine felt her anger buckle at the distress she saw in him. But she had no idea what he was talking about.

"What do you mean? You gave her...you gave *us* everything. Financial *and* emotional. Until..."

He caught her chin between his thumb and forefinger and looked grimly into her eyes. "It was all that social stuff, Dee. In the beginning I thought I could deal with it because I loved her so much. But the more involved she got with fund-raising for the arts and for charity, the more I felt out of it." He smiled apologetically. "I was just a kid from the Haight with big ideas, always dirty and sweaty from long days on the site. I didn't belong in the circles she moved in. Then my business went through some tough times, and we had to live on her money and I began to feel inadequate. Unfortunately that happened at the same time she volunteered to chair the fund-raising for the music complex and spent most of the next few months immersed in it and oblivious to me." He pinched her cheek. "You and Lisa she always had time for."

"Daddy..." Delaine took hold of his arm, feeling solid muscle there though he was now in his sixties. "You brought the business back. You now own most of the hot property on..."

He shook his head. "Doesn't matter. In that slump I made my fatal mistake. I turned to Maureen because all she wanted from me was flattery and sex. Those were easy to give. Of course, it didn't take long for me to realize that was stupidity, but then it was too late." He smiled with fatalistic acceptance. "I'd betrayed the princess. And that just isn't done."

Delaine stammered helplessly with this new information. "Dad...I'm sure...I mean, Mom never saw you as inadequate. She adored you!"

He shook his head again and pulled her close to kiss her forehead. "She did once. And that'll always be the killer."

"Does she even know you felt that way?"

His eyes went dark and bleak. "We weren't talking much by then." He focused on her again and smiled gently. "The point is I hurt her. She can't forgive me. Maybe I don't even blame her."

The door shot open suddenly, and Allie stood there in her tailored pajamas, her hair tumbled, her face white. In her arms was an extra pillow.

She handed it absently to Delaine. "I was bringing you another pillow to help you sleep." Then she asked Tony, her tone sharpening, "What do you mean, inadequate?"

As her parents frowned into each other's eyes, Delaine backed out the door and closed it quietly behind her. She wandered dazedly down the hall, a new confusion in her already addled brain. Her father had turned to another woman because he felt inadequate? And her mother hadn't known? For thirteen years?

In the bedroom Delaine kicked off her scuffs without putting on the light and fell onto the bed with a dispirited bounce.

She landed on something hard and angular. She cried in surprise at the same time as she heard a low, breathless "Ooof!"

"Whoa," Max said with a soft laugh as she tried to scramble to her feet. He hooked an arm around her waist and pulled her under the blankets. "What's the matter? You feel like an armful of nitro."

Delaine was torn between frustration, temper and excitement. And for a moment she couldn't decide which emotion should be uppermost. So she struggled against all of them—and Max.

But he held firm, her squirming body pinned securely to his with one of his arms around her waist and the other holding her flailing arms to the front of her. In that position his forearms were locked across her breasts. She prayed he didn't feel their tips beading against his muscle.

"Relax," he said. "Tell me what happened."

She stopped struggling, though there still seemed to be a war going on inside her. "I thought you were playing poker," she said defensively.

"I was," he admitted.

"Then what are you doing *here?*"

"I lost," he explained simply. "And I'm supposed to be playing your loving husband, aren't I?"

She began to calm down. Of course he was. It wasn't his fault that her family was a mess and, in an insidiously innocent way, had turned her into a mess. She wondered absently how parents could be so loving on one hand and so hopelessly confused on the other.

She sighed and stopped fighting him. "Mom and Lisa and I were having tea and cheesecake in the kitchen. It turned into a fight."

He turned their bodies so that he lay on his back and she curled into his shoulder. "That used to happen all the time," he remarked, his quiet voice filled with humor. "And you'd take it in stride."

How many times in their shared past had they lain just like this? she wondered. She couldn't help relaxing against him, looking for that comfortable hollow in his shoulder. But she stopped short of flinging a leg over him as she'd always done to get really comfortable.

"This was about Daddy," she said. She sighed heavily, then told him briefly about confronting her father, about his revelation of feeling inadequate and her mother's sudden appearance.

His tone sobered, and he tightened his grip on her. "Geez. You okay?"

"I guess. My mother acted as though she'd had no idea he felt that way. When I left them, she looked as though she intended to wring every detail out of him." She was quiet a moment, then she asked softly, "I know it's been thirteen years, but do you think there's a time limit on forgiveness?"

He considered that, rubbing her shoulder. "No," he said finally. "I don't think there's a time limit on anything where love is involved. And I think they still love each other."

She felt a pang of guilt and sadness. "I told Jalisa she was wrong to try to force them together. I think I was being mean because deep down I've sort of...lost faith."

"In what? In them? In love?"

She tilted her head back to look up at him. "I think I've lost faith in my ability to...understand what it is. For instance..." She hesitated, wishing she could put a light on so she could look into his eyes, but was grateful that it was dark so that he couldn't look into hers. "Does climbing a thirty-foot rock mean you still care for the woman frozen in fear at the top?" she whispered. "Or is it simply a chivalrous reaction to a dangerous situation?"

There was that treacherous moment of silence, and she braced herself to hear the answer she didn't want to hear.

"Caring," he said, smoothing the hair from her face, "is such an insipid word for what I feel. Do you want me to tell you about it?"

Air clogged in her throat. "Yes," she said softly.

"All right." He used the arm she'd tucked across his waist to pull her up, and the arm he'd held around her to boost her over him until she knelt astride his waist.

She went with a little cry of surprise. "Pay attention," he said.

He reached under her nightie to gather it up and push it over her breasts.

After an instant of continued surprise, Delaine pulled it the rest of the way off, wondering with some functioning part of her mind if she were dreaming this. Could this be happening?

And then even that corner of her mind stopped working when his hands closed over her breasts and stroked them into taut little hills.

Gooseflesh rose along her spine and up into her scalp as his hands moved to the line of her back, then around again to explore the jut of her ribs, the subtle roundness of her stomach.

Warmth followed in the wake of his touch, and she felt his tenderness cover her like a cloak.

Then his hands stroked the length of her thigh to her knee, then up again, shaping the contour of her hip, closing over her to hold her in place as his manhood rose against her femininity.

He laced his fingers with hers to help her balance as she leaned up to accommodate him. She whispered a moan of longing as he pressed against her, then the sound rose in pitch and volume as he thrust upward and filled her with his solid warmth.

Like flame finding oxygen, the heat and passion that just a moment ago had enveloped her burned higher still. It was all so wonderfully familiar yet deliciously new, full of warm memory and strong surprise.

She felt the magic begin to uncurl deep inside her, further even than he had reached, and there was no longer any doubt that she was dreaming. This was real. And every nerve ending in her body pulsed, waiting for it.

Delaine began to move on Max, gently, subtly. *God*, he thought, firming his grip on her hands as she began to sway in a wide circle. It had been such a long time. He wanted her to know what he felt with all the fullness and depth words could not convey. He wanted to do it slowly, completely. But she was sabotaging his efforts.

He tried to free his hands, to catch her hips and slow her down, but she had plans of her own, and they required his cooperation.

She tightened her grip on him, narrowing and quickening the movement of her hips until he was caught in her tightening spiral.

He heard her little cry and felt her body shudder as his own was rocked with pleasure. It broke over and over him, multiplied by her high, broken sounds of fulfillment.

Then she collapsed onto his chest, still enfolding him, and wrapped her arms around his shoulders. Delaine looked up at him. Her tears glistened in the darkness.

"I love you," she whispered. "Though you said it far more brilliantly."

He pulled her up until he could reach her lips. "I love you. I've always loved you. I've loved you all the time we've been apart."

She absorbed the words, let them seep into her pores.

She tightened her arms around his shoulders and sighed deeply, thinking how deliciously contented she felt in mind and body.

Then the sigh hitched somewhere deep inside her as she realized that he'd told her he loved her, but he still hadn't explained what she'd seen in his office.

Certainly he would now. She held him and waited.

Max felt the subtle tension in her and accepted the inevitability of it, just as he'd accepted that he would always love her.

She wanted an explanation of that night in his office, but she was too proud to ask for it. And he didn't intend to explain until she did. So he simply held her close, determined that this marriage was going to be reinstituted, but on his terms.

He hoped he wasn't being too optimistic.

Chapter Seven

CONTINUING RAIN the following day halted Jalisa's plans to shoot the Guinevere gown in her romantic outdoor setting. But with true professionalism, she simply altered her plans to fit the situation.

"We'll shoot the Victorian gown in the gazebo," she said at breakfast, her clipboard in one hand and a coffee cup in the other. She seemed ebullient this morning, Delaine thought.

When Delaine had come down to breakfast, Clay was sitting across from Jalisa, and her sister's cheeks were pink.

She wished *she* felt ebullient. Instead, she felt confused. Max's lovemaking had brought back all the old wonder of their relationship. Even more, it had invested it with a new spark that held a promise she wanted so much to explore. But she couldn't dismiss her disappointment that he'd remained silent about the incident in his office.

And she knew Max was aware of how she felt. She could see it in his eyes across the breakfast table. She read love there, desire and passion blended with all the tenderness he'd shown her the night before.

But she could also see that stubborn resolve in place. If she wanted him to explain, she was going to have to ask. He'd made that clear that night in the Revere Building.

"You'll have to put your hair up, Dee," Jalisa went on. Max, I'm going to put you in a tailcoat."

He sent Delaine an ironic glance as he chewed and swallowed a bite of toast. For the sake of the shoot, he wore an easy manner. "What I do for family."

Jalisa patted his shoulder. "Don't think we don't appreciate it. You took Delaine off our hands."

Delaine frowned teasingly at her sister. "You'll notice no one's taken you off the family's hands."

She nodded matter-of-factly. "Contrary to all the feminist propaganda, many men still prefer beauty to brains."

Clay walked into the kitchen and past her to the coffeepot. "Suggesting that you don't have both?" he asked.

She looked back at him in blank confusion. "Both?"

"Beauty," he clarified. "And brains."

Pink filled her cheeks again. She shifted in embarrassment and tucked her hair behind her ears. She clutched the clipboard to her like armor.

"My mouth is too wide," she protested very quietly, "and I have chipmunk cheeks. My..."

Clay shook his head, and she stopped talking. "I'm going to photograph you when we're finished with the session," he said. "And show you what I see."

Delaine caught Max's eye. He raised an eyebrow in reply.

Clay left the room to prepare his cameras. Jalisa remained where he'd left her, a stunned look on her face.

"Are Mom and Dad in the shots this morning?" Delaine asked.

Jalisa stared into space for another moment, then turned, seeming finally to have assimilated the question. She replied vaguely, "Ah . . . no. They drove off. Early. That's why you have to do your own hair. Makeup should be natural, though, so that'll work."

"Drove off where?"

"Up the coast. Astoria, I think."

"Astoria!" Delaine exclaimed. But Jalisa was already pushing her way out of the kitchen. Delaine turned to Max. "Mom and Dad honeymooned in Astoria. You think they're reminiscing or something?"

He smiled, remembering the way Tony had taken Allie in his arms in yesterday's shots. "Or something. Come on. Miss Ford Coppola is going to want us ready promptly."

She made a face at him over her shoulder as he pulled her chair out. "I don't think Miss Ford Coppola knows her own name at the moment."

THE VICTORIAN wedding dress had more ruffles, bows and draped Belgian lace than Delaine had ever seen anywhere at one time.

"It was a fussy period," Jalisa replied in response to her complaint that the dress was gaudy. "Women were revered and embellished." She stood back and observed, hands on her hips, her clipboard tucked in her elbow. Then she looked up at Delaine with a grudging smile. "The dress does exactly what Mom knew it would do."

"Make me look like a cookie jar?"

"No," Jalisa said as though the result surprised even her. "Somehow all the...the *stuff*...reveals the wearer's simple beauty. You look wonderful."

Max appeared, striding from the house under an umbrella, and Delaine felt a clutch of emotion in her chest. Talk about wonderful...

He looked long and lean in the dark formal trousers and tailcoat with its silk lapels. The stark white of the vest, tab-collared shirt and bow tie exaggerated the darkness of his features, the angles of his chin and jaw lending a kind of danger to his elegant appearance.

"Wow," Jalisa said quietly. "You're gorgeous, Max." She went to give a straightening tug to his tie. Then she looked from her brother-in-law to her sister. "Okay, listen up. It's cold and wet out here—I know you'd like this to go as quickly as possible. So, what I have in mind is a sort of steamy encounter before the wedding. A bride and groom very much in love forced by society to keep their distance from each other before the wedding, coming together to promise themselves a lifetime of passion and devotion.'' She looked from one to the other again. ''Got it?''

Max and Delaine looked at one another. Delaine thought it sounded like trouble, but she had little choice in the matter at this point.

And the look in Max's eyes convinced her she was right. But they nodded simultaneously at Jalisa.

''Okay. First we want to show off the dress. Max, I'd like you a few paces behind her and slightly to the side so we can get all of you. Dee, why don't you concentrate on the roses.''

She tried, but as Clay set up the tripod and took several shots, she became sharply aware of Max's presence behind her. And she couldn't help letting her eyes stray in that direction, though she didn't dare turn her head.

''Good, Delaine,'' Clay said. ''That look is hot stuff.'' After several shots he abandoned the camera on the tripod and moved around them with another camera that he used for close-ups. ''Good. Now tilt your head back toward him as though that's as close as you can hope to get. I need lust from you, Max. Power, determination. That's it. Good. Excellent!''

Jalisa came forward to smile at them as Clay reloaded. ''You two been practicing with Brando on the side or something? That was great. Okay. Now I want your arms around her from behind, Max. Then reverse positions and try it with Delaine behind. Then we'll do one on the bench, gazing into each other's eyes.''

Delaine felt as though she were being tortured. Last night's lovemaking was still alive on her skin, in her mind, in the tender place inside her that remembered every subtlety of Max's touch.

And all that sensitivity was heightened by the mystery that remained between them. The closer Jalisa required that they be, the more distant Delaine felt Max become.

Max wrapped his arms around Delaine, his hands locking just above her waist. His height required that he bend over her. His nostrils were filled with her floral scent, the silky quality of her hair caressed his cheek and her breasts rose and fell against his thumbs.

He almost groaned aloud in frustration. How could she trust her body to him as she had last night, yet still suspect his fidelity? Somehow, despite his present state of sensory overload, it occurred to him that it was probably because he'd never made a great effort to reassure her.

"Lean into him, Dee," Jalisa instructed from behind Clay. "Put your hand to his face."

Delaine complied. Max punished her by turning his lips into her palm and kissing it. Her little expulsion of breath puffed against his ear—punishing him.

Clay grinned and ran his finger inside the neckline of his sweater. "Whew, guys! Okay, Delaine. You behind Max. Let's see just your hands around him, and your eyes over his shoulder. We have to show off the coat. Hands in your pockets, Max."

Delaine placed her arms around Max, her hands flat against his chest. She felt his warmth and his steady heartbeat. She also felt his trim, tight buttocks against her stomach. She dropped her forehead between his shoulder blades, grateful for a moment without the watchful camera lens on her.

Max tried to deal with having Delaine wrapped around him. Her hand rested circumspectly on his chest, but he felt the soft roundness of her breasts against his back, her stomach pressed into his backside—and his body decided to react as though it were last night again. Only long months of well-honed self-discipline prevented him from yanking her in front of him and embarrassing all of them.

"Let's see your eyes over his shoulder, Dee," Jalisa called.

With a sigh of reluctance, Delaine lifted her head.

Max felt her breath against the back of his neck—and all the way down his spine.

"Look at me," Clay directed, moving back and forth, taking several shots. "Now look at him, but Max, don't move." Clay snapped the shutter, backed away and snapped it again.

Delaine knew what was coming and braced herself.

"Good, good," Clay said, coming in closer. "Now look at her, Max."

Max turned his head, and Delaine felt herself melt against him. She didn't want to, tried not to, but in his eyes was everything he'd ever felt for her, all they'd shared the night before.

But wrapped in his gaze, too, was condemnation, and that made her want to bristle away from him. Conscious of the camera, she didn't move. But she knew the need was there in her eyes.

Clay swore and took the picture.

The effect on film, Delaine guessed, was as powerful as it felt in reality. Love and anger, nature's most powerful forces, braided together to bind or to destroy. The significance of this magazine page would be that the reader would speculate over the result of the conflict, without ever learning the answer.

They posed on the wrought-iron bench, then, because the sun had come out, they posed among the roses outside the gazebo. Then they broke for lunch.

Max strode moodily down to the water while Delaine took the opportunity to go inside and stretch out on the bed. Her taut muscles ached as they uncoiled.

Max was angry with her, and she was disappointed in him. Now that she was tired, she'd forgotten why she'd felt that way. All she knew was that they'd made love, but nothing had changed.

Because lovemaking hadn't been the problem in the first place. It had served to remind them how much they needed each other, but in a way it had only served to drive them further apart.

She wished desperately she could just beg off and go home. But this was important to her mother and sister, and she had to follow it through.

A light rap on the door was followed by Max's sudden appearance in the room.

"Up, Sleeping Beauty," he said, his movements quick and edgy as he tossed a dress bag at her. "Sun's out, so Guinevere and Lancelot are on this afternoon, after all. Clay just chased me down."

Delaine groaned and sat up. "I don't want to," she complained halfheartedly.

He cast her a wholeheartedly admonishing glance before pulling his sweater over his head. "But this isn't about you, my lady. This is about your mother and your sister's production. And this time try not to blow in my ear, all right?"

She bolted off the bed and glared at him, nerves stretched tight. "I know very well what this is about and *who* is responsible for our being here, so don't you dare preach to me. And I have *not* blown in your ear."

He sat on the edge of the bed to pull his jeans off. "And don't give me those seductive looks, either." He tossed the jeans aside and stood, magnificent in white cotton briefs. "If you want me, tell me."

For an instant Delaine was speechless. He was next to naked, and she wore nothing under her light cotton wrap. If she concentrated, she could feel their bodies fusing.

But his eyes were spitting fire, and she felt her temper roil inside her like a storm. "Last night didn't resolve anything," she said, ripping the zipper down on the garment bag. It was the first mention either had made of the night before. "What would make you think I want you?"

He studied her a moment, his eyes dark and arrogant, then he pointed his index finger to four livid scratches on the right side of his rib cage.

She remembered the wild last few moments of their lovemaking. She remembered needing to hold him to her for steadiness in her reeling world, for security, for . . . for permanence.

She dropped her eyes and reached into the bag to pull out the dress. "You instigated that," she reminded him quietly.

His manner softened. He lowered his voice. "You were more than willing."

"Yes," she admitted.

There was another rap on the door, and Jalisa's cheerful voice shouted through it. "Hurry! The horse is here!"

Delaine turned to Max, who looked as surprised as she felt. "The horse?" they asked each other simultaneously.

Chapter Eight

BO WAS a pure white gelding seventeen hands high, according to the guide who ran the trail rides a mile down the coast. Jalisa had rented the horse for the shoot.

Bo was five years old, muscular but gentle, and his mane and tail had been woven with flowers for the occasion.

Delaine fell in love instantly.

Max watched her approach him, a hand outstretched with a slice of apple the guide had given her, and felt his heart roll over.

The court-style gown she wore with its fitted dropped waist highlighted her slenderness and reminded him how fragile she felt in his arms.

The horse snuffled at her hand, stole the bite of apple, then snuffled again, looking for more. When he didn't find it, he rubbed his velvety nose into the loose bell sleeve. Delaine's laugh rang on the fragrant breeze.

Jalisa fussed with Delaine's hair, worn long and loose and topped with a coronet of daisies she'd stolen from Allie's coffee-table arrangement.

A long, satiny train stretched out behind her, and Max felt himself slip easily into character. He knew precisely what Lancelot must have felt when he'd first set eyes on Guinevere. And why it hadn't mattered that she belonged to someone else. Theirs was a love too strong for common sense. And he, like the French knight, was terminal with it.

"Make friends with Bo, Max," Jalisa said. "I'd like you on him for a couple of shots, then leading Delaine on him and, if all goes well, the two of you riding double." She grinned at him and patted his chain mail. "You make a very sexy knight."

He looked down at the gray velvet hose, over which he wore cuffed soft leather boots, and the short blue tunic covered with chain mail, then made a face at her. "You're telling me some groom is going to want to show up in church in a getup like this?"

She laughed and shook her head. "No. This shot is specifically to dramatize Delaine's dress. I'm going a little Hollywood with this one."

"No kidding," he teased. "As long as you know I wouldn't wear tights for anybody but you."

Max walked the horse across the quiet road into the wooded foothills Jalisa considered the perfect setting for this scenario. There'd been an old bay mare on his grandparents' farm in upstate New York, where he'd spent many summers as a child. He hadn't been on a horse since then, but Bo seemed gentle and calm enough to convince him that sitting astride him wouldn't be much of a problem.

Max turned to look over his shoulder and had to smile at the eclectic parade behind him—Delaine in the pristine white dress, the train being held up from the damp road by Jalisa, wearing black leggings and a long white sweatshirt. Behind her came Clay with several cameras around his neck and the tripod balanced on his shoulder. The guide followed him in jeans and a denim jacket, carrying Clay's lights.

The woods were like something out of a fairy tale, Delaine thought. As a child she'd found this wonderful place for tree climbing and exploring. Once she'd become a teenager, she'd preferred to lie on the beach in pursuit of the perfect tan.

As a young girl, she'd been too fascinated with the birds and other creatures that lived in the woods to notice the romantic mystery of them. But Jalisa had obviously seen it when scouting locations.

Sunlight filtered through the canopy of leaves and needles to create natural mood lighting. Lush ferns crowded at Bo's feet, and bright green vines of various species moved languidly in the soft afternoon breeze that sighed around them.

Max, who'd walked farther up the trail with Clay to help set up his equipment, emerged from a thicket at the same moment that Delaine looked up.

He appeared for all the world like Lancelot walking out of the misty past and into her time. Her eyes slowly perused his muscled legs in the soft hosiery, his flat stomach under the jeweled belt, the sword dangling at his narrow hip. A slanted bar of sunlight slashed across his chest to light up his chain mail and highlight the breadth of his shoulders. It glossed his closely cut dark hair and traced the frowning line of his brows.

She wondered if the dark expression meant he was thinking of her.

"Okay." Jalisa took charge with sudden briskness. "Let's get Delaine aboard."

Delaine looked down at the relatively narrow proportions of the gown's skirt. "How am I going to do this?" she asked as the guide bent to cup his hands and boost her onto the horse.

"Sidesaddle," Jalisa replied, "only without the saddle. Women weren't riding astride yet."

"Oh. Right." She hitched herself onto Bo's back with more enthusiasm than style. She'd ridden the trail horses often as a child, but never sidesaddle.

"Bend your right knee and face forward," the guide directed. "It'll give you better balance. Sorry. All I had were Western saddles."

She complied with his instructions and found that she felt more secure if not exactly comfortable.

Jalisa looked pleased. "All right, Max. Lead her off into the woods. Maybe you've kidnapped her from her father who doesn't approve of you. Delaine, don't fall off."

Delaine cast her sister a very unqueenly glance, then accepted the reins as the guide handed them to her.

Max stroked Bo's muzzle, then hooked a finger in the bridle and tugged him down the trail.

Clay ran ahead of them and walked backward, snapping the shutter as Bo moved forward at an easy walk.

Max swore he caught the scent of Delaine's floral perfume woven into the fragrance of pine and cedar in the woods. He kept his eyes forward, unwilling to look back at her. The sight of her in that dress, with the flowers in her hair, softened the spine of his resolve and made him want to tell her everything she wanted to know about Paulette, even if she never apologized for mistrusting him and ruining their lives.

So he spoke quietly to Bo and ignored her. He'd just gotten too caught up in the romance of Jalisa's contrivance, he assured himself. He would come back to his senses the moment he got out of these damn woods.

Delaine looked down at the top of Max's head and fought an overpowering impulse to lean down and bury her fingertips in his hair. But he would probably just give her that condemning look. Or she would fall off the horse. Neither alternative was desirable, so she simply held on and tried to look romantically regal.

A little way down the trail they reached a brook and the spot where Clay had set up. Bo snorted when he smelled the water.

Max held firmly to the bridle, turning toward the guide. "Can he drink this?" he asked.

The guide nodded. "Sure. Comes nice and clean right out of the Coast Range."

Jalisa came forward to pat the horse's rump. "Good job, Bo," she praised, then she turned to her other models. "Max, I'd like you to look at Delaine and just pretend you're having a heart-to-heart. Dee, lean down, but don't fall off."

"Would you please stop saying that?" Delaine swung at her sister playfully, then had to struggle for balance.

Max reached up instinctively, clamping his hands on her thighs to steady her. It succeeded—physically at least. Emotionally it undercut her already shaky equilibrium.

"Like I said," Jalisa directed with a dry grin, "No falling, please. Ready, Clay?"

The camera on them again, Max turned to lean an elbow on the horse's sturdy shoulder and braced himself to look up at Delaine. She leaned down, her golden hair falling forward in a glistening, rippling stream. She looked coolly distant.

He felt anything but romantic. "How're you doing up there?" he asked tightly as Clay moved back and forth in front of them, doing his job.

"Okay," she replied tersely. Her eyes ran lightly over him, and he felt the glance as though her fingers had touched him—or burned him.

Then suddenly, without warning, her expression changed. She looked at him with hope rather than suspicion. He didn't know what to make of it.

"Do you feel like a noble knight?" she asked.

He blinked once. "Actually," he said, "I feel like the Tin Man in bike pants." Something in her eyes reached inside him, and he couldn't help but respond. "Why?"

She sighed, and he felt as though a barrier that existed between them had slipped down. "I was wondering if I asked you nicely," she said, keeping her voice down, "if we could talk about . . . Nantucket."

It took all his control not to react to the question. He wanted to resolve the issue, but pride required that she think he didn't care whether she trusted him or not. Everyone around them was busy with their duties, oblivious to their having chosen this moment for a long-overdue discussion.

"All right," he replied. "What do you want to know?"

She measured him with her quiet gaze, as though certain her first question would make him angry.

"Why did you rent just one room in Nantucket?" she blurted out.

"I tried to explain that to you in the lobby of the Revere. But you wouldn't listen," he couldn't help reminding her.

She nodded, then scolded him with a look. "I know. I'm listening now."

He conceded her point with a nod. "Because it was the Friday of Memorial Day weekend," he replied. "There was only one room left. I tried to sleep on the floor."

Her eyes darkened. "Tried?"

"Tried," he repeated with a frown, daring her to question him. "She wouldn't let me."

"So you joined her in bed?" she asked angrily.

What he would have given at that moment for a hungry dragon with a taste for blondes. "Am I telling this or are you?"

"Okay." Jalisa bustled through, patting Bo's neck. "Let's get both of you on Bo and reverse our trip. You might stop at that trail of morning glory just around the bend. That'd be a pretty shot."

For practical purposes Delaine found it helpful to have Max mounted behind her because he gave her something to lean against.

But there was danger, she felt, in being surrounded by his angry strength. His hand around her midriff was like steel, and the cradle of his thighs kept her firmly in place while simultaneously acting as a primitive threat to her physical and emotional stability.

"Lean back against him, Dee," Jalisa directed. "Let's see the embroidery on the neckline."

Delaine leaned her head back onto his shoulder and turned her face into his throat to do just what he'd asked her not to—breathe softly against him. If she had to suffer, so did he.

She felt his knees tighten around Bo to urge him forward. In consequence they tightened around her, too.

Beneath them Bo undulated gently up the trail. Clay walked alongside them, taking pictures, and Jalisa ran through the woods to get ahead. The guide trailed along behind, apparently satisfied with Max's handling of Bo.

Like an automaton, Delaine complied with Jalisa's instructions, barely aware of what she was doing as she tried urgently to find out what had happened in Nantucket. "Paulette said that you admitted you loved her, that you'd loved her from the day the temp service sent her to you. And that you seduced her."

"I told you she lied," he replied simply.

"You just admitted getting into bed with her."

"No, I didn't. That's what you said I did."

"Then why did I find her in your lap in your office?"

"Because she deliberately set you up," he answered, feeling a sense of relief at finally being able to say the words. "She came to the office about eight, saying she had to catch up on something she was doing for Burgess. She saw you coming through the glass partition, came into my office from the connecting door and landed in my lap just in time to convince you I was playing around on you. And you were primed to believe it."

"Guys? Guys!" Jalisa's voice intruded as she reached a hand up to the reins. "Stop. Whoa, Bo! Here's the morning glory."

Absently Delaine took hold of the trailing vine and draped it across her chest and over Max's shoulder. Clay photographed the movement. "That's a pretty sophisticated strategy," she said of Paulette's ploy.

"She had a million of them. She was determined to find a husband—even if he was somebody else's." He snapped a blossom off the end of the vine at his shoulder and tucked it into her coronet. "And you would have made it easy for her if I'd been interested in her in any way."

Delaine looked at him over her shoulder. "You're telling me nothing happened?"

"Yes."

She sat up, forgetting Clay and the camera. "Then where did you sleep the night you shared the room with her?"

The question had apparently been spoken loudly enough for Clay to lower his camera, for Jalisa to look up from her clipboard in shock and for the guide to turn around and walk back the way they'd come.

The anger in Max's eyes ignited. "You'll have to excuse us for a few minutes," he said to Jalisa.

Delaine shifted to prepare to jump off of Bo, thinking Max meant to dismount. But instead, she felt his knees tighten around the horse and felt the steely grip of his hand at her waist as they broke into a gallop up the trail. She shrieked in alarm as they reached the highway, but he pulled Bo to a stop to check that it was clear.

The horse pranced in place, apparently excited by the brief run, then raced off when Max nudged him on.

Delaine couldn't believe this was happening. She was riding pillion in front of a knight on a white horse across Highway 26 in late-twentieth-century Blue Bay Beach.

She *had* lost it.

She held on breathlessly as Bo raced down the driveway of the house, leapt the azaleas and headed for the gentle slope behind the house that led to the beach. Max's grip on her robbed her of breath but kept her firmly in place despite the slightly forward pitch of the ground.

He finally pulled on Bo's reins when they reached the waterline. The horse whinnied and tossed his head, obviously disagreeing with the decision to stop. But Max insisted, and Bo came to an easy halt.

Max braced his hands behind Delaine to propel himself off the horse, then reached up to pull her down.

She fell into his arms and found herself planted firmly in the sand, one soft slipper lost somewhere in the flight from the woods.

Max caught Bo's bridle in one hand and made a broad, exasperated gesture with the other.

"In the coffee shop," he roared at her as though their conversation had not been interrupted by the wild ride. "I slept in the coffee shop!"

She faced him, wanting him to know that just because she'd made love with him, just because she'd forfeited her pride to ask him what had happened, that didn't mean she'd settle for less than the truth.

"The desk clerk," she said, "didn't see you come down."

He studied her for a moment as though he didn't believe his ears, as though she were someone he'd never seen before.

"You asked the desk clerk . . . ?"

Suddenly she realized how that appeared and quickly tried to explain. "You hadn't touched me in months, so when Paulette told me you'd seduced her—well, I'm sorry, but it was believable! I called to find out how many rooms the company had booked for that night, and the desk clerk was a gregarious young man who told me only one room had been booked. Then he mentioned that a distinguished man and a pretty redhead had occupied it. He assured me he'd been on duty all night and he said, and I quote, 'I saw them go up, and I saw them come down in the morning.' "

He was beyond angry now. His face was set in ominously angular lines. "And it never occurred to you to ask *me* what had happened?"

She saw the complete error of it now but was afraid that it was too late, that all was lost. She simply tried to explain.

"I thought I *knew* what had happened. You fell in love with someone else. Just like my father did."

Max closed his eyes and let his head tilt back for a moment. When he looked at her again, she knew for certain that the tenuous possibility for reconciliation that had grown between them was gone.

"All right," he said, his voice quiet and without emotion. "I'll explain why the desk clerk didn't see me leave, and those are the last words I have for you, Delaine. It's absurdly simple. There are back steps that lead to the parking lot. They were closest to our room, so I took them. From there I walked into the outside door of the coffee shop."

The wind ruffled his short dark hair as he raised his face to the cloudy sky. He heaved a sigh, as though suddenly free of a burden. The burden was her, she thought with a pointed jab of regret.

"And you know what?" he went on, focusing on her with chilling detachment. "I don't give a damn if you believe that or not, because I am not your father. I can't wait at the back door of your life until I'm an old man, wondering if you'll come around to realize you love me. It's beginning to dawn on me that a suspicious nature isn't something you can wish away. You'll always believe that I'll do what your father did, though God knows he's tried to make that up to you in a thousand different ways. But because your mother can't put aside what he did, you never will. And you'll always confuse our lives with your parents' because you never really moved out of theirs into ours." He shook his head and added grimly, "If you had, you'd have trusted me. Or at least asked me for an explanation."

She held back a sob through gritted teeth. She couldn't believe that losing him a second time could hurt more than it had the first.

"If *you'd* loved *me*," she insisted, the sob escaping the moment she opened her mouth, "you'd have wanted to explain to me what happened. But you're about as modern as the chain mail you're wearing. You don't think a man ever has to explain himself. What if you'd caught *me* in another man's arms? Wouldn't you have wanted an explanation?"

He folded his arms and the chain mail clinked. "I like to think I wouldn't have filed for divorce before I heard what you had to say."

"You never said anything!"

"I tried. You wouldn't listen. And I wasn't going to chase you around, pleading for the opportunity to explain. Paulette was a stranger to you, and you believed her. And not because of something I did, but because of something your father did. How in the hell do I fight that?" He turned the horse toward the house. "Come on, Bo."

Chapter Nine

DELAINE SLIPPED into the house through the back door, intending to stand for an hour under a hot shower and try to wash away the feeling of loss. She had to put in one more session the following morning for the fifties spread Jalisa had in mind, then she was out of here and back to work.

She felt a sad ambivalence about going home. On the one hand her fingers itched to create again. Her mind was suddenly crowded with new ideas, fresh images. And she knew precisely what was wrong with the design on her drawing table. She could fix it in a moment.

On the other hand it was reignited love for Max that had brought her to this pass. She felt as though these few days with him had stirred everything inside her, turned it over, made it breathe. Creativity had blossomed.

But she'd lost him forever.

She accepted that with the dark despair that occupied a major part of her heart. She would be plagued forever with memories of lying with him in the lace-curtained bedroom, of feeling his arms around her in a gazebo laced with roses, of sitting before him on a white horse and riding through the trees.

It could be argued, she supposed, that most of that had been fiction staged for the sake of a camera. But she knew it hadn't been. The moment they'd touched each other, it had become real. They were the lovers they'd been meant to be before career pressures and the troublesome leftovers of childhood had interfered.

She pressed both hands just under her heart, still feeling Max's hands there.

"Dee!" Jalisa launched herself at her as Delaine tried to tiptoe through the kitchen toward the bedrooms. She studied her cautiously. "You okay? Did the lovebirds have a fight?"

Delaine used all her resources to shake off the overwhelming sense of depression. She was going to finish this project for her mother and her sister. She smiled. "Yes. But don't worry. It's good for every relationship."

Jalisa looked relieved as she waved a white piece of paper in the air. "Good. Because Mom and Dad left a message with Fernanda that we're to meet them at the River Rose Restaurant in Astoria. We're celebrating something."

"What?"

Jalisa's smile glowed. "They didn't say, but I'll bet they're getting back together." She hugged Delaine. "Can you and Max meet us there?" Her smile widened. "I'm riding with Clay."

Delaine doubted Max would want to do anything with her, much less be confined in a car, then pretend to still be her loving husband.

But she nodded. "Sure." She changed quickly and went in search of Max, prepared to ask him if he could push the rubble of their relationship aside so that the celebration would not be ruined.

She found him in stone-colored slacks and a brown jacket, waiting for her by the front door.

"Fernanda told me," he explained briefly. "Let's go."

Because she felt as though she needed desperately to control *some*thing, *any*thing, Delaine slid in behind the steering wheel.

Max headed without complaint to the passenger side.

Delaine noticed grimly as she negotiated the curving road to Astoria that the atmosphere in the car was strangely without tension. She'd expected to be uncomfortable during the drive.

Then it occurred to her that tension resulted from uncertainty, unresolved issues. But there was nothing more to discuss between them. Max didn't want her. Period. He simply sat relaxed in his seat, window rolled down to let in the late afternoon sun.

She wondered how he would react to an abject apology, an admission of guilt and a plea for him to reconsider their relationship. But she dismissed the notion. He'd made it pretty clear on the beach that he'd had it with her.

So all she could do now was hope that her parents had spent the day talking and were now about to announce their own reconciliation.

They completed the trip to Astoria in weary silence. The town of ten thousand was the oldest west of the Rockies. Winding streets lined with Victorian homes lay like lacy seams in the folds of the hills that sloped down to the river.

Delaine was familiar with the River Rose Restaurant because her mother celebrated every summer occasion there. The building had once been a cannery and sat at the end of a broad-planked pier, giving it a splendid view.

Delaine pulled into the parking lot at the other end of the dock right beside Clay's brown Jeep. That edge of the dock was protected from the river that lay ten feet below by a barricade of two-by-fours.

As she looked out at the breathtaking view, the sunny sky above and the sun reflecting off the river melted the pride that stood in the way of her love for Max.

If her parents could put aside thirteen years of mutual anguish, she could expose herself to rejection and plead her case to Max. A year ago she'd been exhausted, alarmed by her success, overwrought and terminally stupid. She would promise to work less and devote more time to their marriage. She was sorry. She'd do anything if he'd be willing to try again.

She leaned forward to turn off the engine at the same moment that she shifted her weight in Max's direction, prepared to bare her soul. "Max, I want to..." she began.

But her foot slipped on the accelerator. There was the sudden, loud revving sound of an engine at the same moment that she saw the barricade around the pier splinter as though in slow motion. The wood tore, flew apart, and she experienced a weird sensation of flight as the rental car became airborne.

She heard Max's shout, saw the sunny sky above and the gray blue water below and knew with sickening certainty that this time she was not going to be dropped delicately atop a rock.

Max pulled her down and stretched out over her as the car hit the water with a sickening jolt. His weight was thrown off her, and she heard a harsh knock, as though he'd collided with something.

Her heart thundering in her ears, a scream of panic escaping her lips, she felt the rocking, sinking motion of the car as water rushed in through the open windows and quickly began to climb up her body. Max was slumped beside her, blood on his forehead.

Some remote store of common sense told her to stop screaming and close her mouth as the water inched up past her chin. In a moment it was over her head.

She had the strangest sensation that she was simply a young girl swimming, and that she would surface beside her little sister and see her parents sitting on the shore with a picnic basket beside them.

Then her eyes refocused on the wooden understructure of the pier, and she fought a resurgence of panic.

The car settled with an eerie tranquility on the river bottom. She forced herself to think, to act.

Open. The windows were open. It would be a simple thing to get out if she just remained calm. But Max was unconscious.

Max! She reached out to shake him, her movements slowed by the weight of the water. His hair fluttered in the water, and a little trickle of blood floated away from his forehead.

The only thing she knew for certain, she thought, was that she wasn't leaving without him. And somehow the resolution empowered her. She loved him, had never stopped loving him. And he might not know it, but she did. And it gave her strength.

But she needed air. Air! The need came on suddenly and desperately, and she wriggled through the open window and shot to the surface like some colorful harbor seal.

She gulped in air, was only minimally aware of a commotion on the pier, then dove down again with all the speed her meager skills allowed. She squirmed through the window, reached for Max and tried to haul him backward through the opening. It was harder than she'd imagined.

Despite the water's assistance, he was heavy for her much smaller frame. She finally braced her feet against the side of the car and pulled. Miraculously his long body began to emerge.

Once she had him free of the car, she hooked her arm under his chin and prayed she didn't strangle him before she got him to the surface.

He was heavy, and she felt her puny store of air diminish. And all the time she wondered frantically if there was air left in his lungs.

Maybe I can't do this, she thought weakly. If she let him go so that she could surface for air, he'd sink to the bottom, and getting him up would be even more difficult.

She could see light when she looked up and guessed they hadn't sunk more than fifteen or twenty feet. But her arms ached, and her legs were growing heavy from the energy expended to get Max out of the car. No, she wouldn't let him go. They would go up or down together. Together at last.

No. Not down. Up! She was going to tell him she was sorry and wanted him back if it was the last thing she did in this world. And he was going to listen to her!

She kicked with renewed determination.

She broke the surface of the water to find her father and Clay bobbing beside her.

"Delaine!" her father cried, boosting her out of the water, holding her up with an arm around her legs as he used to do on those beach picnics so long ago.

The action made her lose her grip on Max. She struggled against her father. "Max!" she cried. "Daddy, Max is unconscious!"

"Got him!" Clay said, an arm looped around him as he swam with confident skill toward the pier where someone waited on the ladder to receive him.

Delaine watched for a moment, felt relief drop inside her like a weight, then everything else within her seemed to sink and she held tightly to her father as she fainted dead away.

MAX WENT TO THE GURNEY as Delaine was brought back into the emergency room from the radiology department. He'd been given a pair of patient's pajamas to wear and a blanket, which he threw off.

He looked down at her slender body on the gurney, her pale face above the blanket and her blue eyes heavy with exhaustion. Fear gripped his heart like a claw. So much had been sacrificed for foolish pride. Sure, his dignity was intact, but what good did that do him now that Delaine looked as though she might expire at any moment?

He caught her hand. She closed hers lightly around it. It was cold and trembling.

The little idiot, he thought. She had saved his life. After the abuse he'd heaped on her that afternoon, she'd risked her life to pull him out of the car. He couldn't decide whether to be proud of her or mad as hell. Then he forgot his dilemma when he remembered that she loved him. She'd proved it without a doubt.

The technician and the doctor conferred, then approached their patient. Tony and Allie, and Jalisa and Clay closed in around Delaine.

The doctor turned to them with a wide smile. "Good news. She came through her tests as well as you did, Max. C-spine clear, and no evidence of bleeding on the CAT scan. She's fine." He turned to the older couple. "These two have someone to keep an eye on them tonight?"

Allie came around the gurney to wrap an arm around her daughter. She held her tightly for a moment. "Yes. They'll be home with us."

"Okay. Then they're free to go."

Jalisa pulled off the long cardigan she wore over her shirt and put it around the hospital gown Delaine wore.

Allie turned to Tony. "There's also a blanket in the trunk of my car."

Delaine rode home in the back of her mother's Mercedes, sitting on Max's lap with the blanket wrapped around her. She felt limp and spent and strangely light-headed.

"You're sure you're okay?" she asked Max softly for the tenth time since they'd left the hospital. "No concussion or anything?"

"No, I'm fine," he replied, tucking the blanket in at her shoulder. "Just a bump. Thanks to you."

She didn't need thanks.

She sighed into his throat. "How are we going to tell the car-rental agency," she asked, her voice raspy, "that I parked their car at the bottom of the Columbia River?"

"I wouldn't worry about that now," Max said.

"It was in your name," she reminded him.

He caressed her cheek with the knuckle of his index finger. "You're all I'm worried about," he said softly.

She raised her head to look into his eyes. Darkness had fallen, but his eyes were bright in the shadows of the car. He looked . . . happy. "I am?"

"Yes." He pulled her back down to his shoulder. "You are. Now, lie quietly until we get you home."

Fernanda greeted them with wide eyes, excited Spanish tumbling from her lips. Allie had called her from the hospital, and she had soup on the stove for Delaine and Max and an impromptu buffet prepared for everyone else. She'd also built a fire.

Max carried Delaine in from the car.

"I'm going to put her in a hot shower," he said to Allie.

"Good idea," she said. "We'll wait for you for dinner."

Holding on to Max's neck as he headed for the bedrooms, Delaine called to her parents over his shoulder. "I'm sorry about dinner at the restaurant. What were you going to tell us?"

Tony blew her a kiss. "It'll wait until you come out."

Delaine stood on the carpet in the bathroom and dropped the blanket. While Max adjusted the shower in the tiled stall, she unbuttoned the cardigan Jalisa had lent her and pulled off the hospital gown.

Tension crackled around her like an electrical storm. She remembered her earlier observation that tension resulted from a sense of uncertainty between two people. She'd noted that there'd been no tension in the car.

The large bathroom, however, was alive with it. Though the doctor had declared her healthy, she could scarcely breathe and she was trembling.

Max turned from the shower, his eyes reacting to the sight of her standing in the puddle of blanket, her arms wrapped around her nakedness.

He lifted her bodily into the stream of warm water, then pulled off his clothes and joined her.

She wrapped her arms around him the moment he closed the door. Despite the tension that lay between them, she was determined to tell him what she'd wanted to say before she'd driven them into the river. God, she thought. Has any other woman in the history of the world made more of a mess of her marriage than she had?

She looked up into his eyes as the stream of water beat against her back. "Max, I'm sorry," she began. "I..."

He lowered his mouth to hers, and she got no further. He kissed her deeply and for a long, long time. When he raised his head, his eyes were troubled.

"What?" she asked fearfully. "Do you feel all right?" She put her fingertips to the livid bruise on his forehead. "Does your head hurt?"

"No," he said quietly, turning them so that his back took the impact of the water. "My heart hurts."

She nodded apologetically, thinking she understood why. "I know. I think our marriage was so good that in the back of my mind, I was sure it was going to be taken away from me, just like my parents'. Then, when it even *looked* the same—a woman from the office—a . . ."

Max covered her mouth lightly with his hand. "I'm not talking about that," he said. His eyes looked deeply into hers as though he were seeing her for the first time. "You saved my *life*," he said, "by risking yours."

She wondered why he insisted on talking about that when all she wanted to discuss was the possibility of their reconciliation.

She dismissed what she'd done with a shake of her wet head. "You covered me with your body to protect me from the impact. That's why you were knocked unconscious. And there was nothing heroic about what I did, Max," she said. "It was just . . . love."

He nodded, his eyes still dark with that wonder. "I know. That's what amazes me. You *do* love me. After I was so hard on you this afternoon."

She shrugged a shoulder. "You were right about all of it. I was fascinated by success and spent too much time working. I think that's why I was so sure you were fooling around with Paulette—because I'd been so neglectful. I'm sorry." She looked into his eyes and smiled wryly. "That's what I was going to tell you when I drove us into the river."

The turbulence left his eyes, and he smiled suddenly.

She drew a breath and went on with the rest of what she had to say. "I was also going to ask you if you thought we could go home...give all this some time...and maybe start over?"

He frowned and shook his head.

She felt the world shatter and dissolve, hope drowning in the rush of despair.

He took her face in his hands and studied her with an all-consuming concentration. Then he smiled gently. "I have no intention of waiting that long," he said, holding her closer and reaching for the soap. "We're going for blood tests tomorrow. And a license after that."

Joy burst inside her as her world was restored. She raised her lips to his.

"WE WERE GOING to announce our plans to remarry," Allie said.

Everyone sat in a circle before the fire in the middle of the living room floor. Allie and Tony sat back to back, Jalisa and Clay sat cross-legged, side by side. Max leaned against the sofa, and Delaine rested with her back against him, an arm wrapped around his neck. They sipped from the same cup of soup.

Jalisa squealed at the news and hugged Clay. Delaine cheered, and Max put their cup down and applauded.

"So we thought it would be perfect," Tony said, "if you all stayed a few more days for the wedding."

Delaine winked at Max. Now, she thought smugly, the problem of pretense was over. She felt a curl of relief inside her. They'd pulled off the ruse that they were still married, and no one need ever know about the deception that had brought them here.

"We can do that, can't we?" she asked Max.

He nodded. "Wouldn't miss it."

Allie and Tony exchanged a knowing glance, then focused on Max and Delaine.

Delaine felt pinned, as she had as an errant child when they'd turned those parental looks on her. She leaned a little harder into Max, suspecting trouble.

"When were you going to tell us about the divorce?" Allie asked. She fixed her daughter, then her son-in-law, with her judicious, maternal stare.

"Uh-oh," Max breathed.

Delaine sighed and admitted candidly, "Never, if I could help it. I didn't want to admit that I'd failed."

Tony frowned. "Like we wouldn't understand that?"

Delaine made a helpless gesture with her hands. "I was so sure I'd handle my marriage better than you had handled yours." She smiled apologetically. "I'm sorry, but that's true. How'd you find out?"

Tony pointed to Allie. "Your mother just told me."

Delaine blinked at her. "How did *you* find out?"

"Clarie Goodwin came back to San Francisco last September for her mother's ninetieth birthday. She told me she was sorry to hear about the two of you splitting up. She'd read the notice in the *Globe*."

"She lives in New York! What's she doing subscribing to the *Globe?*"

"Her husband has business in Boston."

Delaine groaned, then realized what her mother had said. "You've known since...last September?"

"Yes."

"Why didn't you *say* something?"

"Why didn't *you?*" There was no answer to that, of course, so Allie simply went on. "So, when I decided to start *Bygone Bride* and Jalisa told me we'd never be able to afford models, a plan was hatched."

Delaine's eyes widened on her sister. "*You* knew?"

Jalisa gave her a sly look. "Of course. Mom told me."

"I can't believe you didn't try to *fix* it."

Jalisa studied her fingernails with a superior air. "Who do you think was the brains behind the plot?"

Allie narrowed her gaze on Max and Delaine. "You are getting back together, aren't you?" She pointed to Max. "He got knocked unconscious trying to protect you from the impact, and you practically drowned trying to get him to the surface. If that isn't love, I don't know what is."

"Good thing," Tony said, his expression grave, "we had a window seat at the River Rose. I was watching you pull up and saw you go in the drink."

Delaine turned to Max, thrilled to see love glowing in his smiling eyes.

"She's right," he said. "Our position is indefensible." He wrapped both arms around her and squeezed, then grinned at his mother-in-law. "I'll be eternally grateful to you, Allie."

Jalisa cleared her throat. "I wouldn't be too smug, Mother," she said, smiling brightly. "You might remember *who* brought Daddy here as her yearly effort to get the two of you back together. Now we're probably going to have a double wedding, and it's thanks in large part to me."

Allie frowned at her youngest with reluctant acceptance. "I always said you were the clever one."

Clay hooked an arm around Jalisa's shoulders and pulled her sideways to kiss her temple. "I wouldn't be too smug either, Miss Ford Coppola. That's what we all call you now, you know."

She gave him a playful moue of disapproval. "No, I didn't know. And why should I not be smug?"

He gave Jalisa a look that made Delaine catch Max's eye, then her mother's.

"Because, guess who saw you looking over clothes in Goodwin's back room all those weeks ago, overheard that you were looking for a photographer, and pleaded with your mother for the job so he could get to know you?"

"You're kidding," she breathed, dark eyes wide.

"I'm not."

Fernanda walked in as though on cue with a tray of snifters, and passed around the brandies.

Tony held his glass aloft. "To love," he said.

Delaine turned to kiss Max before adding, "And marriage!"

Weddings by DeWilde

Since the turn of the century, the elegant and fashionable DeWilde stores have helped brides around the world turn the fantasy of their "Special Day" into reality. But now the store and three generations of family are torn apart by the separation of Grace and Jeffrey DeWilde. Family members face new challenges and loves in this fast-paced, glamorous, internationally set series. For weddings and romance, glamour and fun-filled entertainment, enter the world of DeWilde...

Watch for The RELUCTANT BRIDE by Janis Flores Coming to you in May

Rita Shannon has just been hired as Grace DeWilde's executive assistant. Helping to create the new San Francisco store was a dream come true...until Rita was forced to rely on deal-maker Erik Mulholland, a man whose past betrayal still wounded her to the depths of her soul.

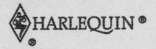

HARLEQUIN ®
®

WBD1

MILLION DOLLAR SWEEPSTAKES

No purchase necessary. To enter, follow the directions published. For eligibility, entries must be received no later than March 31, 1998. No liability is assumed for printing errors, lost, late, nondelivered or misdirected entries. Odds of winning are determined by the number of eligible entries distributed and received.

Sweepstakes open to residents of the U.S. (except Puerto Rico), Canada and Europe who are 18 years of age or older. All applicable laws and regulations apply. Sweepstakes offer void wherever prohibited by law. This sweepstakes is presented by Torstar Corp., its subsidiaries and affiliates, in conjunction with book, merchandise and/or product offerings. For a copy of the Official Rules (WA residents need not affix return postage), send a self-addressed, stamped envelope to: Million Dollar Sweepstakes Rules, P.O. Box 4469, Blair, NE 68009-4469.

SWP-M96

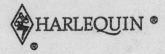

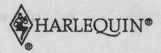

BRIDE'S BAY RESORT

UNLOCK THE DOOR TO GREAT ROMANCE AT BRIDE'S BAY RESORT

Join Harlequin's new across-the-lines series, set in an exclusive hotel on an island off the coast of South Carolina.

Seven of your favorite authors will bring you exciting stories about fascinating heroes and heroines discovering love at Bride's Bay Resort.

Look for these fabulous stories coming to a store near you beginning in January 1996.

Harlequin American Romance #613 in January
Matchmaking Baby by Cathy Gillen Thacker

Harlequin Presents #1794 in February
Indiscretions by Robyn Donald

Harlequin Intrigue #362 in March
Love and Lies by Dawn Stewardson

Harlequin Romance #3404 in April
Make Believe Engagement by Day Leclaire

Harlequin Temptation #588 in May
Stranger in the Night by Roseanne Williams

Harlequin Superromance #695 in June
Married to a Stranger by Connie Bennett

Harlequin Historicals #324 in July
Dulcie's Gift by Ruth Langan

Visit Bride's Bay Resort each month wherever Harlequin books are sold.

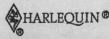

HARLEQUIN ®

BBAYG

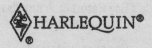